AVENGING EDEN

AVENGING EDEN

FIFTH NOVEL IN THE EDEN SERIES

LEXI POST

Avenging Eden

The Eden Series, Book 5

By Lexi Post

Sometimes the price of revenge is too high.

When Mya discovers a badly wounded Edenist in the jungle, she hopes by saving him, he will help her enter the city of Naralina. She takes him to the safety of her home, only to find another Edenist is already there…and he's looking for her.

Keeva's mind is more than intrigued about the invisible woman who came to his rescue since there's no such thing as a female Edenist, not that his body cares. When he learns of her history, his protective instincts flare to life, bringing with them a need to avenge her.

Bent on revenge, Haldone seeks Mya's help to punish those who harmed his brother, at least that's what he tells himself, but his feelings for her go far deeper than the "friend" she dubs him. Unfortunately, he's not the best at communicating his feelings…or anything else for that matter.

The men's thirst for vengeance on those who took her parents gives Mya hope and a new sense of family. It isn't long before she develops a growing attraction, the first in her life. But surprises in the enemy camp and dangers to them all mount until she realizes they each must decide what is more important, revenge or each other.

Acknowledgments

For Bob Fabich, my own perfectionist, who accepts me for just the way I am.

Thank you to Paige Wood whose insights and suggestions were invaluable.

Thank you to Marie Patrick for holding my feet to the fire and for her belief that I could get it done.

I also want to thank Lisa Fishback, Eileen McCall, KC Crocker, and Pamela Todd for coming to my rescue at the last minute. You ladies are awesome!

The Families of Eden

Naralina:

Toni Reid – Former stuntwoman – Akasha and Sandale's Beloved

Akasha – Kindred of Light (Controls color spectrum) – Ruling Circle

Sandale – Kindred of Heart (Calms people) – Ruling Circle

Erin Danielson – Former IT expert – Beloved of Wareson and Nassic

Wareson – Kindred of Air (Pushes air) – Ruling Circle

Nassic – Kindred of Mind (Forces people to tell the truth) – Ruling Circle

Loraleaf:

Serena Upton – Former explosives expert for movies – Beloved of Jahl and Khaos

Jahl – Kindred of Eden (Controls all nature that is not alive)

Khaos – Kindred Unknown (Foresees the future in parts)

Jaelene Upton (Serena's younger sister) – Former interior decorator and an animal lover – Beloved of Theron, Konala and Rekah

Theron – Kindred of Light (Creates reflections)

Konala – Kindred of Eden (Communicates with animals)

Rekah – Kindred of Heart (Senses others' emotions)

Author's Note

Avenging Eden was inspired by Emily Dickinson's poem, *Time's Lesson* which was first published in 1891.

This poem is a simple one about revenge. It basically states that while anxious for revenge a person is driven, but once revenge is accomplished it leaves one empty. Therefore, action should be taken quickly because to prolong it, one becomes fat with anger. Yet upon completion, there is nothing, instead of satisfied, one is empty. Essentially, revenge is not only, not sweet, but not fulfilling.

So, what if a man was bent on vengeance but fell in love while working toward his goal? Can there be room for love with so much anger inside him? Would he put that love at risk? And what if both the woman he loves, and the friend he makes, join him in his goal? Will they still have a connection or will it dissolve when the vengeance has been wrought?

Time's Lesson

Mine enemy is growing old, —
    I have at last revenge.
The palate of the hate departs;
    If any would avenge, —

Let him be quick, the viand flits,
    It is a faded meat.
Anger as soon as fed is dead;
    'T is starving makes it fat.

For free books, updates, sneak peeks, and special prizes, it's easy
to sign up to receive the latest news from Lexi at

http://bit.ly/LexiUpdate

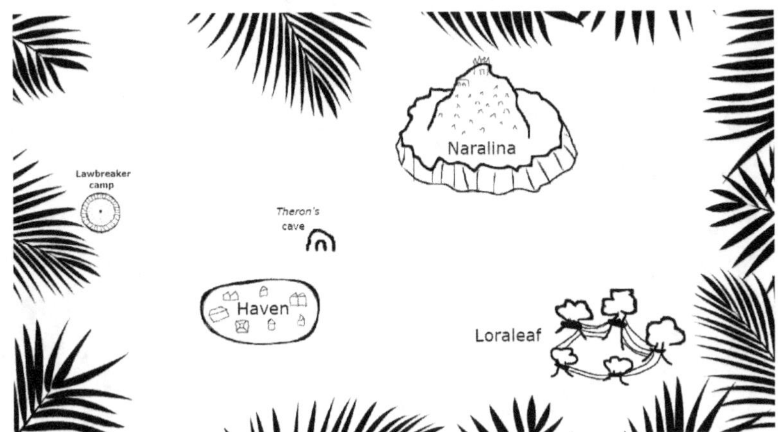

Lawbreaker camp
Theron's cave
Naralina
Haven
Loraleaf

CHAPTER ONE

Mya stared at the unconscious man lying beneath the salis bush, the trail of blood the only thing that had alerted her to his presence. The bush's light but solid canopy kept him hidden from anyone walking by.

She held the leaves to the side, flicking her long hair over her shoulder, not sure what she should do. She wasn't afraid since he couldn't see her. She was invisible to everyone except Edenists with the ability to produce blue light, but this man didn't have a Kindred of Light birthmark.

His was Kindred of Eden. The mark, two parallel lines with concave lines on either end, was plainly visible on his biceps, which meant he had a special ability that had to do with the planet's flora or fauna.

If he'd been Kindred of Mind, she would have run as soon as she'd found him. Though she was invisible, her mind could be sensed, and she could be heard or even smelled. The man before her posed no threat…at the moment.

She'd grown up assuming every man she met in the jungle was a lawbreaker, but in the past year, she'd discovered there were others from the white and gold city of Naralina, who also lived in the jungle. If this Edenist was not a lawbreaker, he might be able to help her get into the city.

If he lived.

Even from where she stood, she could see the towering walls of Naralina, the city carved into a mountain and where her fathers had been born. The only way in was through a portal, but only those deemed worthy were granted the Crius chips that allowed two people to open one.

She'd traveled through one of those to get to Naralina from her cave, but the men who opened the portal had landed outside the walls. She'd been too taken with the city to catch them as they portaled inside.

She'd walked around the city for days, but there was no entrance at ground level. That's when she'd heard the noises that had brought her here. She waited until they had stopped before investigating. She'd lost her parents to lawbreakers and didn't plan on getting caught by them again.

Her mom had always said the salis bush was like a stubby version of a weeping willow tree on Earth but that it hid things better. Kneeling down beneath the bush, she could see the blood had stopped flowing. Did that mean he was dead? She followed the trail which led to a gouge under his right arm. The flesh there was torn as if by an animal. But there was similar damage beneath his other arm.

For a moment she was puzzled then she froze. The lawbreakers! Her words remained inside her head as fear tightened her throat. Beneath the arm is where the Crius chips were inserted. The lawbreakers must have been after them so they could get inside the city.

Compassion filled her, and she lowered her ear to the man's chest. The slow thumping noise was a welcome sound. She had to help him.

He needed to be bandaged and watched. If a direlot discovered his scent, she would have a hard time keeping the two-headed, two-tailed canine away. Unfortunately, they had an excellent sense of smell.

She glanced through the trees toward the walled city. Finding her family would have to wait. Maybe the Edenists who had portaled to just outside the walls would do so again, and she could ask them for help.

She untied her bag from her waist and set it next to her. Her mother had used a hesta, one of their see-through blankets, whenever one of her fathers was hurt. Pulling out the one she'd brought, she carefully used her knife to tear two long strips. She didn't want to use too much of the blanket because if it rained, she might need it. A salis bush would keep off a light rain, but a downpour would go right through.

Mya pushed back the leaves and scanned the immediate area, but with the continued sound of the blue caball birds' songs, she felt safe. She dropped the leaves and quickly cut a slit in each end of the material. She would have to get the bandage around the man's large chest, and there was nothing to leverage him on.

She studied him as if his appearance could give her any ideas. He didn't look much older than her, maybe twenty-nine. He had thick, short black hair and a kind face while asleep. His eyes, nose, and mouth were perfectly set on his face, making her fingers itch to paint him. His eyebrows were as black as his hair and his jaw had the lightest of stubble starting.

That had to mean he hadn't been in the jungle long. The Wild Man, as her family had dubbed him, had a ratty gray beard, which made them think he had to be one of the longest surviving lawbreakers in the jungle. Lawbreakers usually preyed on each other, so the fact the Wild Man existed was an oddity in itself. Then again, her parents had been sure he'd gone mad years ago.

She shook her head to dislodge her thoughts. She needed to stay on task, and that was to bandage the man. For now, she'd think of him as Hope since he was her hope for entering Naralina and finding her extended family. Crawling to his head, she knelt with her knees to the side. She'd have to push him up and get herself under him to hold him in a semi-sitting position.

She'd never touched a male Edenist before. The only males she'd ever had contact with had been her fathers. Actually, she hadn't touched another person in fourteen years.

Uncertainty made her hesitate. What if he woke and attacked her? She scanned his whole body. On planet Eden all people lived naked, so she'd seen a few. This one was well proportioned like his face. The problem was, he was all male with a muscular chest, arms and legs. Even his stomach had undulating bumps like the stream near the west exit of her cave.

She could leave him. Avoid this whole experience. *Every new experience is a chance to learn. And to learn is to grow.* Her Air father's words echoed in her head.

She had to do this. It was the human thing to do as her mother, who was from Earth, had always touted. She took a deep breath and pretending the man before her was no different than a dead feroon taken down by a pack of direlots, she pulled his shoulders up and sat them on her thighs. Unfortunately, his skin was smooth and warm and not even remotely similar to the short course hair of a feroon. And his hair was soft against her breast, making her body flush.

Hope's head lolled to the side, but he didn't wake. She paused as his weight, and her fear, caused her heart to race. When her breathing had calmed, she pushed his shoulders higher and scooted farther beneath him. His back was harder than she expected as it settled on her lap.

The scent of blood as it started to flow again took her mind off everything else. Quickly, she grabbed up the piece of hesta and wrapped it around him beneath his arms. After tying the ends together, she lifted the second bandage.

Hope moaned, and she froze.

She watched his face, barely breathing, hoping his eyelids wouldn't rise, yet curious as to the color of his eyes. When no other sounds issued from him, she gently wrapped the second bandage around him, covering the lower part of the wounds. The raw savagery of the attack angered her, but she forced her fingers to be careful as she tied the final bandage.

Now that the wounds were covered, she needed to remove the excess blood. If only she could simply move him somewhere else, but he was far too heavy for her to carry. By touching him, she made him invisible to others, but that wouldn't mask the scent of blood.

Carefully, she moved out from beneath him, holding his head in her hands so it wouldn't drop to the ground and cause him further injury. His hair was silky, and she couldn't help letting it glide between her fingers. It was so much like hers but thicker.

Hope's lip quirked.

She pulled her hands away and scooted backwards. He couldn't see her if she didn't touch him. Her invisibility was a product of her being Kindred of Light and was a result of refracting light, which made her disappear for those using their sight, but not for those using other senses.

Unfortunately, her parents died before they could teach her how to control it. The second she touched something, it appeared invisible. On the other hand, whatever she touched could also see her, at least that was what she'd discovered when she'd touched a tigran and a welchet. They could see her and continued to rub against her.

The smell of the fresh blood caught her attention. She had such a hard time staying on one activity path. Probably from living alone for so long. Scanning the ground immediately around Hope, she found most of the blood pooling on last season's fallen salis leaves.

On her hands and knees, she crawled around him, but her hair fell to the ground. Quickly, she pulled it away, not wanting blood in it. Kneeling again, she tied her knee-length hair into a knot until it hung no lower than her shoulder blades.

Leaning over, she began to methodically push the blood-stained leaves away from Hope's body. When she had the pile shoved out from beneath the salis bush canopy, she crawled to the other side and did the same. On that side, some of the blood had soaked into the dirt, so she would need to dig it out.

When she was satisfied that she had the leaves away, she lifted the salis branches and crawled out into the jungle. A quick search yielded a large, thick piece of bark from a long dead magee tree. She scooped both piles of leaves onto the bark and walked away from the bush. Looking back, she noted a racide bush not far away, its poisonous orange flowers a bright identifying mark. Then she turned and walked deeper into the jungle, away from the walled city of Naralina.

Would Hope be able to help her get into the city? He had no Crius chip to open a portal, but he should know other Naralinians who were living in the jungle. She could take him to the settlement she'd discovered, and he could get others to help them.

Pleased with her plan, she searched for a place to dump the leaves. A dead animal or a stream would work best. She didn't want to go too far. If Hope needed her, she should be there. Then he'd be grateful and help her, but if he woke and left without her…

She halted. She didn't want that. He was her chance. She didn't dare approach a settlement of able bodied men who couldn't see her. Hope was hurt, giving her the chance to help him and in turn he might feel he had to do the same for her.

Looking back the way she'd come, she couldn't see the great wall that protected Naralina anymore. Scanning the area, she listened. The calls of the multi-colored elseire birds assured her she was alone, but beneath them she heard gurgling. Quickly, she ran farther to the north, pausing a couple times before she found the stream. Crouching down before it, she dumped the leaves into it.

She washed her hands in the cold water before picking up the bark and turning to leave. Her heart stopped at the bloody sign on a tree not three steps away. It was a circle drawn in blood with a large X over it.

Lawbreakers.

Immediately, she dropped back into a crouch and scanned the jungle, but the birds continued their happy sounds. Not in a hurry to run into the band of lawbreakers that marked the trees in such a way, she ran back into the undergrowth, making a straight line for the salis bush and Hope.

It didn't take her long to find him once again. She just needed to dig out some of the dirt beside him and then she would feel safer…from animals. Kneeling down, she pulled back the salis leaves and froze.

Light brown eyes focused on where her hand held two strands of leaves back. "Come in with me? Please."

She didn't move. His voice was soothing and his eyes were beautiful. She'd never seen that color before. They were a warm brown that reminded her of the siri caterpillari fur.

"I know you are out there. Did you help me? Bandage me?"

She had three choices. To run away was her immediate response, but she squelched it. That wouldn't help her enter the city. That left two, either touch him so he could see her and nod, or try to speak. A little afraid of him, she swallowed hard. "Yef."

His lips turned up into a gentle smile. "Thank you. My name is Keeva. What is yours?"

He spoke as if he could see her, but his gaze was directed at the salis leaves. He probably thought she was outside and afraid to come in. He was half right. Not confidant in her voice, she reached down and with her finger wrote her name in the dirt.

His eyes widened as the ground appeared to move on its own to him, then he frowned. "Ahw?"

How stupid could she be? Brushing the ground with her hand she wrote the letters upside down.

"Aym?"

This was too hard. She brushed the dirt aside. She couldn't

even tell him her name. How would she be able to ask him to take her to Naralina?

As if he could sense her frustration, he frowned. "I can figure this out. "Wha? Mya?"

"Yef!" She clapped her hand over her mouth, dropping the salis leaves.

"Wait! Do not go." His voice sounded more disappointed than scared.

She moved the leaves back again.

"You do not have to be afraid of me. As you know, I am not in a very healthy state right now. I have never been outside the city of Naralina. I have spent days trying to find a way back in and then I was attacked." He scowled, making his young face look a lot older than she thought him.

He moved his right arm and laid his hand on his chest, his eyes squinting at the pain the movement caused him. "I promise I will not harm you. Could you come under here with me? I'd like to see you."

Her heart started to race at the idea of showing herself to him. Maybe if they were in a clearing in the jungle or by the wall where there was more room. "Nu."

"No? Why not?"

That was far too hard a question to answer verbally or otherwise. "Nu." He probably thought she moved the dirt with air and that she was a Kindred of Air, but she wasn't, and no matter what she had done for him, he could overpower her.

He appeared to ponder her reluctance. "I am guessing you have lived out here for a long time. But if you are a lawbreaker, why—"

"Nu!" The word flew from her mouth with such force that the caball birds in the nearby trees stopped chirping. Damn, now she wouldn't be able to tell if lawbreakers were coming.

Hope's, or rather Keeva's, eyes widened before his lips split into a grin. "This may be a bit of an assumption on my part, but I am guessing you do not like lawbreakers any more than I do."

Her heart fluttered at his smile and her body relaxed. He looked so nice when he did that. She tried to keep herself on alert, but no one had smiled at her since her parents were alive. Not that he was looking directly at her, but it still made her feel good.

"I am glad you are not a lawbreaker. Could it be that you, like me, were falsely accused and exiled from the city?"

She didn't understand what he meant by exiled. That wasn't a word she'd learned, so she didn't say anything. The chirp of a cabal bird made it easier to relax, especially when its mate answered back. At least they were still alone and hidden.

"You do not talk much do you?"

She frowned. She'd like to, but it had been so many years since she'd used her voice for talking. The words in her head were perfect, but her mouth didn't make them well. "Nu."

"I guess I can talk enough for both of us. Actually, talking was what landed me here." He scowled as if he remembered something that made him angry.

She didn't like it when he did that. It reminded her that he could be dangerous. She started to let the leaves down.

"No wait. Do not go. I am not upset with you. Please stay. At least overnight. I think it would be better if we each took a turn watching for lawbreakers. You could sleep for a while then I could. We'd be much safer that way."

She'd never done that before. To sleep while he was awake would be dangerous.

"I have an even better idea. If you could find some food, I think with a little nourishment I could at least lift us up into the trees, so we are not so likely to be found."

The trees? She looked up through the salis bush leaves to the tops of the majestic magee trees. He could lift them up there? She brought her gaze back to him and studied his birthmark again. He was Kindred of Eden. Maybe he *could* get them into the trees.

She was good at finding food, but first he would need water. She dropped the salis bush leaves.

"Wait!"

Ignoring him, she searched in her bag for her water container, then moved the leaves again. She set it within his reach and quickly pulled her hand away. "Yef."

She didn't wait to see if he drank. Quickly, she turned and headed out into the jungle to hunt for their mid-day meal.

Keeva stared at the wooden cylinder that had dropped onto the ground next to him. Carefully, he lifted it so he could pull the lid off with his other hand. The movement hurt, but the bandaging his helper had done, kept any new blood from releasing.

The moment he'd woken, he'd noticed the leaves pulled away on either side of him. The Edenist, Mya, he called himself, obviously knew something of the jungle to have moved the scent of blood from where he lay.

Mya was an odd name. Definitely not one he'd heard before in Naralina. Could the man be from another city? Actually, from the tone of voice, he sounded more like a boy in the middle of his transition.

Lifting the strange container to his face, he sniffed. There was the faint scent of a flower, but it seemed to come from the outside. Tentatively, he lifted it to his lips and took a sip. Water. It wasn't cold, but he hadn't had any in over a day. Greedily, he gulped it down.

When it was half gone, he forced himself to close the cylinder and put it aside. He wouldn't repay Mya by taking all his water.

If he hadn't been so weak in the first place, he could have kept the lawbreakers at bay, but when the windstorm hit him full on, he'd been knocked unconscious. He gripped the container at the memory of when he woke to the lawbreakers cutting into him.

Forcing his anger away, he stared at a single salis leaf to calm himself and move into more productive thoughts. The first thing he needed to do was repay the young man who helped him by keeping them safe.

He had no doubt Mya was Kindred of Mind. They were the only ones he knew of who had the ability to move objects without the use of their hands. He would ask as soon as Mya came back.

Curious, a common problem of his, he moved his hand to sweep aside some of the salis branches. Not far away he could see a crudely made bag of some sort. Reassured that Mya would be back, he dropped the branches. He felt blood seeping into the pieces of hesta wrapped around him and forced himself to stop moving.

He needed to save his strength. If Mya found them enough food then after eating and a short sleep, he should have the strength to make the live infragile vines lift him into the upper branches. First, they would need to find a tree with the vine. He hoped there was one nearby. The more energy he used to discover one, the less he had to lift himself up.

He had complete faith in his new companion's ability to find food. He'd obviously been in the jungle for a long time. The man's shyness was an oddity. Keeva had no doubt if he wasn't wounded, he probably would have never made Mya's acquaintance.

His curiosity burned with solving the mystery of Mya. Until he'd been falsely accused and exiled, he'd thought only lawbreakers lived in the jungle that covered planet Eden. And that those who followed the Criuson and Dickinson laws lived within the walled cities, traveling to each other when absolutely necessary through portals. That there was an Edenist, not a lawbreaker, living in the jungle for years was even more interesting than building a portal that could transport a dozen people at a time.

He gritted his teeth. He had to get back inside Naralina and warn the Ruling Circle about what Grandall planned to do with that giant portal.

No, he couldn't do that. That was what landed him in the jungle in the first place. He'd told Yiting, one of the younger members of the Ruling Circle, that Grandall, a Ruling Circle member himself, planned to transport eleven women from Earth to Eden at once. Next thing he knew, he was in a holding cell in the Ruling Circle Complex with a healer standing by to remove his Crius chip.

Grandall hadn't even give him the chance to speak at his own hearing, knowing full well he'd tell everyone in attendance what their leaders' plans were. So, when he found a way into Naralina, who could he tell? The Triad?

Yes. No. They didn't get involved in such mundane issues as breaking the law. But if Grandall brought women to the planet by the elevens, not only would it upset the balance of power between the cities, but it would also cause Earth to notice something was amiss.

Their history had already warned of such mass transports. Between Roanoke and the Bermuda Triangle, Earth already had some suspicion that not all was as it should be.

He shook his head. He'd been blinded by the challenge to create a large portal, never questioning its use. The Ruling Circle said it was for other city leadership to visit, but he should have known better. As a Discoverist, he had the obligation to learn what purpose his discoveries would be used for.

A soft swish of leaves beyond his hiding spot had him listening. If it was a feroon, he was safe as those large docile creatures only became aggressive during mating season. From the sounds, it was definitely not a person. Unfortunately, in his few days beyond the walls of the city, he hadn't run into any other creatures and his knowledge of the jungle was based on what he'd read in books and what animals he'd seen at the Discoverist Oasis.

A tiny black nose pushed beneath the salis bush leaves touching the ground, and he held his breath. As the snout pushed farther inside, he recognized the two small tusks extending from the bottom of the jaw into the ground as the animal grubbed for beetles. It was a welchet!

He held very still, wanting more than anything to see a real one. The nose came off the ground and sniffed the air. As if satisfied nothing unusual was in his way, the welchet stepped inside.

Keeva hypothesized that his natural wood scent helped disguise him from the animal. The welchet walked along the side of his body, its long needle-looking fur brushing his thigh, its softness causing him to smile.

As if the animal sensed his reaction, it picked its head up and stared right at him.

He tried not to laugh at the sudden alarm in the animal's dark little eyes, but when it spun around and scurried out on its six stubby legs faster than an elseire bird could fly, he finally gave in.

It felt good to laugh, though he quickly muffled the sound. He hadn't laughed much at home lately. Naralina had changed since Nassic and Wareson had been exiled. There was a strange apathy holding it enthralled. He laid the blame at—

Footsteps derailed his thoughts. If it was a lawbreaker, the large branch above him was the only weapon at his disposal. The steps stopped just outside his bush and something dropped to the ground. Could it be Mya back so soon?

The leaves of the bush were pulled aside. "Hinni."

He relaxed. "You caught a henny bird?"

The ground to his side started to move. He watched as four lines formed in the dirt. Holy Bendis! "You caught four henny birds?"

"Yef."

Now didn't he feel like an ithio. He'd been surviving on berries and leaves, unable to catch anything to eat, and this young man, in less time than it takes to use a rainbox and wash himself clean, comes back with four birds, a veritable feast. Mya was someone he definitely needed for a friend out here.

"That is impressive. I cannot tell you how hungry I am just thinking about eating those, even if they are raw."

"Nu!"

He grinned in relief. "I am glad to hear you say that. I have never had henny raw, but I do not think it would taste very good."

Mya dropped the branches and moved around outside his

shelter. He should just lay where he was and let the man cook up the food for them, but his insatiable curiosity wouldn't allow for that.

Slowly, so as not to alarm his newfound friend, he moved his hand under the branches and lifted the leaves just far enough for him to see. But there was nothing to see.

He stared as dead wood appeared in a shallow hole in the ground as if by a portal. Then the crude bag of supplies disappeared only to reappear and in a matter of seconds, the twigs on top of the wood suddenly burst into flame.

He looked up into the trees. Was Mya perched up there? He brought his gaze to ground level and peered through the bush. He could find no one anywhere. Yet, the hennys disappeared and reappeared skinned and speared on four separate sharp sticks as if they undressed themselves and put themselves there.

Next, two rocks rolled to either side of the pit. One was higher than another, so it rolled away and the ground hollowed itself out before the rock seemingly rolled back by itself. The four sticked hennys disappeared one at a time before appearing balanced across the rocks as the fire lapped at the meat.

Despite the grumbling of his stomach, his curiosity burned to be satisfied. "What Kindred are you?"

The bag that had disappeared into thin air suddenly dropped on the ground from nowhere on the other side of the fire pit.

Ithio. Now he'd startled the man. He was either very young, or the jungle had him on permanent vigilance. "I had not meant to surprise you."

Nothing moved except the flames licking at the meat. There was something wild and untamed about Mya that was far different than any Naralinian. He couldn't even speak English, which all Naralinians used as that was the most common language of the Earth women they brought to Eden.

Mya *had* to be from another city, which just made him even more anxious to learn all he could. "I am Kindred of Eden. I can make live plants do my bidding. Are you Kindred of Mind?"

"Nu!" The word, so close to where he lay made him jump.

He chuckled. He'd deserved that. "I take it you are not Kindred of Mind, and you do not particularly like that Kindred."

The man didn't say anything.

"Then what Kindred are you?"

The ground, not far from where his hand held aside the salis leaves, started to move. First, two parallel lines appeared and then on each side of them a line was drawn with the lower part closer to the two center ones and the upper part farther out. Above the lines, but even with the spaces between them, three dots appeared.

"You are Kindred of Light? But how can you make things move? Do you move them with light?"

He wasn't sure, but it sounded like Mya sighed. Frustration? Impatience? He couldn't tell. It was hard when he couldn't even see the man. It was as if was invisi— "By the Crius! Do you deflect light so it appears as if you aren't here?" The implications of such an ability had his brain spinning.

"Yef."

The answer had come from the other side of the fire pit, and now, one at a time, the sticks disappeared then reappeared having been turned so the meat didn't cook only on one side.

Keeva dropped the salis leaves and relaxed. An invisible Edenist. It made sense. He just had never met anyone with that particular ability. Kindred of Light usually emitted a particular colored light, or created reflections or darkness, or even pictures they could see in their minds, but invisibility? It was an amazing ability and was probably what had allowed the man to survive in a jungle rife with lawbreakers.

The salis leaves were pulled aside again, and he could smell the cooked henny but couldn't see it. "Does everything you touch become invisible too?"

"Yef."

Ah, he started to understand. Reaching his hand out, he found the stick. Mya must have let go because as the weight transferred to him, the stick and bird appeared. He wanted to grab the man and force him to tell him everything, but he wasn't the ithio he called himself. He was far too weak and needed his strength to get them above the ground by darkness. Eden only had twenty-two-hour days, and he had no doubt it was well past the peak of Helios.

Grinning, he raised the stick toward Mya. "I am grateful." He wouldn't let the man know exactly how grateful he was. Instead, he bit into the breast of the bird. His eyes widened at the flavor. This was no basic flavor. The man had added something to it that he didn't recognize, but it was excellent. It had a savory flavor with a touch of citrus.

The leaves fell as Mya left, and he let down his guard, eating far faster than he should. After finishing half the meat, he lifted the container and drank again. He had no concerns that Mya could easily refill the container now. The man obviously knew how to survive in the jungle.

Keeva had just finished licking the last piece of meat from the bird when the salis leaves lifted again and the scent of a second bird filled the space. Once again, he resisted grabbing the man. He just couldn't afford to make an enemy of Mya right now…or ever for that matter. His fellow Discoverists would be fascinated by such an unusual ability. Already, he planned to have Mya accompany him home.

Having filled his shrunken stomach with the first henny, he took his time with the second one. Mya continued to hold the salis leaves aside. It sounded like he was chewing, but Keeva could see no henny. "So, everything you touch turns invisible?"

There was a pause, probably because the man chewed his food. "Yef."

"But you can see it, right?"

"Yef." This time the answer came immediately. "Hinni."

The stern tone made it clear that he was to eat his food and stop talking. He gave in, studying the leaves held to the side. It was only the branch that Mya touched that was invisible, which meant he wasn't that far away.

He couldn't resist judging where the man might be. If Mya could see what he touched then that meant a man touching him could see what he looked like. It didn't matter, but his curiosity wanted to know.

He took another bite and savored the henny. It was super. The idea of adding a fruit of some kind was genius. He took another bite and focused on the tang. He knew that flavor. What was it? He took a smaller bite and concentrated on the outside glaze. Tangy, yet sweet.

Holy Bendis! It was kerasi fruit! That was only used to help people sleep. He stared hard at the spot where Mya had to be. Why did the man want him to sleep? Suddenly, all the kindness Mya had shown him took on ulterior overtones. He would have never thought so before, but after realizing the depth of deception in Naralina, he was better aware of what a fellow Edenist could do to another, never mind someone from a different city.

Without warning, he grabbed for the man, determined to see his face when he asked him why he'd given him kerasi fruit. His luck held as his hand clamped over a very narrow wrist.

He stared in shock.

He was a she! And an incredibly beautiful one at that. Black hair fell around her in waves, touching the ground, covering part of her smooth bronzed skin and violet eyes stared at him in fear. Holy Bendis, what was she?

"You are a female? Impossible!"

CHAPTER TWO

Haldone stalked from Theron's house. The man's constant refusal to allow him to leave because he hadn't learned enough about the jungle yet made him in need of a calming drink. As a favor to his younger brother, Sandale, who had moved on with his new life in Naralina, he forced himself to remain polite, but Rekah, another of Theron's filoz, was well aware of how he felt. That giant of man could tell anyone's emotions, and his frustration was bubbling at the surface.

He slammed the lever forward and the lift rose through the trees, higher and higher until it came to a stop on the third level of tree bridges that made up the settlement of Loraleaf. Stepping onto the wooden walkway, he paused to allow two men to go by before striding for Libations, the only drinking establishment in the jungle.

His walk slowed. No, there was one other at the settlement of Haven. Konala, the third man in Theron's filoz had told him of the walled settlement the current leaders of Naralina had set up when they'd been exiled. That was the closet civilization to the place he secretly planned to make his home while he stalked the lawbreakers. And where he would seek out the woman who filled his dreams.

He walked into the wood building wrapped around one of the huge trees and stepped up to the counter. "Bilzer, give me a Skyblue Seer."

The liquidator behind the counter raised his eyebrows. "Another tough session with Theron?" Luckily, the man spoke while blending the calming drink.

"Is there any other kind?"

Bilzer poured the shaken drink into a clear cup and topped it with a white mist that floated over it until it was placed down in front of him.

At the movement, the mist spun around on top before infusing itself into the blue liquid beneath, turning it from the dark blue of the Latzeran Sea to the brilliant light blue of the sky with tiny silver lights spread through it. Just looking at the drink reminded him of his brother and his much-missed calming abilities.

He raised the glass in salute to Bilzer, then took a hearty swallow. The liquid flowed across his tongue, its sweetness edged with a mellow spice before it glided down his throat, causing tiny tingles of icy coldness. "Perfect as usual."

Bilzer nodded in acceptance of the compliment before turning to help another Edenist.

Haldone left the counter and sought out a table in the back corner. The visual walls played the scene of a tiered jungle waterfall into a dark pond. He liked that scene the best since it showed him what he could run into while on his quest for lawbreakers.

His brother may be able to move on, but he couldn't. The

lawbreakers needed to pay for what they did to Sandale. Yes, he had his brother back, now one of the new members of the Ruling Circle of Naralina, but the man Sandale was now, was very different from the one he was before the lawbreakers inserted a mind of one of their own into Sandale's consciousness.

He took another swallow of the Skyblue Seer, waiting for it to calm his psyche. The mindwipe his brother went through afterwards had been performed by Saphr, whom Haldone met the very first day he arrived in Loraleaf.

Saphr was Kindred of Mind, but his ability was to erase the mind. He tried to erase only the evil presence, but it had tangled itself so much with Sandale's personality that the choice was to leave his brother caged forever or wipe his mind clean.

Whoever had performed such a complicated and evil procedure on his brother deserved to die, which is why he'd returned with Jahl and Khaos to Loraleaf to start his journey of retribution. Unfortunately, Sandale had asked Jahl to look after him as if he was no more than a babe.

The Loraleaf leader, after turning him over to Theron, had declared he couldn't leave until he learned all he needed to know from Theron's filoz.

What he wanted to know was how to find the cave Theron had lived in for a while because that was where Mya, the beautiful invisible woman was last seen, but he couldn't just ask or they'd all know he planned to go there. Only he and his brother's filoz knew she existed, and he planned to keep it that way.

Now he'd been in Loraleaf over a week and he was tired of learning. He was ready to act.

The door of Libations opened and a very tall man strode in

that Haldone recognized only from what Theron had told him. Cordtz was his name. According to Theron, the man wasn't stable, having claimed to have seen a dirgon, which everyone knew was a mythical creature. Rekah said the man was perfectly sane and was just furious that no one would believe him. For some reason, Konala seemed to agree.

He watched as Cordtz received the same drink he had. When the man turned around, he saluted him with his own glass.

As if surprised by his gesture, Cordtz came to his table and pulling out a chair, joined him. "I am Cordtz."

He nodded. "I know. I am Haldone, Sandale's brother."

Cordtz raised his brow. "I did not know you had joined us."

He shrugged. "Just for a short while."

The other man lifted his glass and chugged half his drink.

He chuckled, pleased to see he wasn't the only one frustrated. "What has you angry?"

"Why do you think that?"

He pointed to the half-full glass. "Since I ordered this drink because I was frustrated with Theron, I am guessing you ordered your drink for a similar reason."

Cordtz studied him, his very light blue eyes intense. Then as if making up his mind, he nodded. "Yes, I am frustrated. I wish to leave and track an animal. My filoz partner is willing to go with me, but I am being told I can only use portals because it is too dangerous with the lawbreakers having come so close. Tracking by portal would take forever."

Despite the calming drink, Haldone's body tensed with excitement. "There are lawbreakers nearby?"

"There were." Cordtz shook his head. "But that was past two

turns of Selene and there have been no more sightings of their mark since then."

Though disappointed, he didn't completely give up. "Is that because they have moved on? Which direction did they go? Have any of the recent patrols spotted them?"

His companion pushed his drink toward him. "I am thinking you need another sip."

He chuckled. "Yes, I probably do." He took swallow and waited for the ice cold to dissipate. "I have come here to hunt down the lawbreaker who harmed my brother. Unfortunately, Jahl will not allow me to leave until Theron says I have learned enough about the jungle, but most of what he has told me is nothing different than what I learned in school. My fear is while I stay here, the lawbreakers are travelling farther away."

"You could be right." Cordtz ran his thumb along the rim of his glass as if contemplating what to say next. Finally, he stopped and pierced him with his eyes. "I, myself, am after a dirgon."

Haldone didn't even blink. "I know. I think Konala and Khaos believe you." He understood what it was not to be believed and what a relief it was when someone finally did.

When he'd gone to get his Crius chip, they didn't believe it was his choice not to be part of a filoz, two to five male friends, and denied him the first time. His mother had told him to explain to them that he was a "perfectionist" as she put it. He'd tried to argue with her that he was far from perfect, but she'd laughed at him and explained it had to do with tasks and projects. Luckily, after he explained it to the Triad, they had agreed to give him a chip so he could portal with friends and family even if he never had a filoz.

Cordtz regarded him with skepticism. "They do? How do you know? Did they say something? They have never said anything to me."

He pushed Cordtz's drink toward him. "I am thinking now you need a sip."

The man moved the drink aside. "Tell me what you know."

He rarely reacted well to demands, but this time he kept his anger under control, his instinct telling him he might have an ally. "It is not what they said so much as what they haven't said. Whenever your sighting of the dirgon comes up in conversation, neither of them say a word about it, and if they are in the same room, they always glance at each other as if they know something."

Cordtz's hand came down on the table. "I knew it. They will not let me track it because they know something."

Haldone sat back and shrugged before picking up his drink and taking a sip.

His companion ignored his own drink, his pale eyes shifting with his internal thoughts.

Haldone scratched his beard as he scanned the man's upper body but didn't see a Kindred birthmark. Obviously, he was not Kindred of Mind. "I have a proposition."

Cordtz's gaze whipped back to him as if he'd forgotten he was there. "What kind of proposition?"

It was only a guess that Konala and Khaos knew something more about the dirgon, but if that was all he had to bargain with, he'd jump on it. As a man with no filoz, his ability to portal was restricted by the lack of another man to use his Crius chip since it took two men to open one. "I want to get to the settlement of

Haven and you want to hunt the dirgon. I will find out if they know something about this creature if you help me open a portal to get to Haven."

The man across from him sat back in his chair and held his gaze as if trying to decipher whether he told the truth or not.

He didn't look away. He was as determined to get to Haven and start his quest for Mya and the lawbreakers as Cordtz was to track the mythical creature called a dirgon. He didn't believe what Cordtz had seen was a dirgon, but that didn't matter. If Konala and Khaos knew something about what Cordtz had seen, he planned to find out what it was.

Finally, Cordtz gave him a quick nod and lifted his glass. "To our journeys."

He grinned as he lifted his own. "To our quests." They both touched their glasses to their foreheads then drank.

Haldone set his glass down, but Cordtz finished his off and stood.

"I live on the second tier at the opposite end of the ground entrance. When you know something, find me."

He nodded, and the man strode out of Libations.

Despite the calming drink, his insides revved up. Finally, he had an opportunity to leave. All he had to do was discover what it was Khaos and Konala were hiding. Between the two, Konala was his best chance. Khaos could see the future, so he would sense why the information was so important. Haldone didn't want to risk being found out before he even left.

It still amazed him that Khaos had such an ability. He hadn't seen his birthmark, but he'd heard from Serena, the man's beloved, that it was unlike any other birthmark ever seen in Naralina.

No, he'd stay clear of Khaos. He'd ask Konala. The man's ability to communicate with animals made him the better choice. Not only would he not sense the real reason for the information, but if there was some kind of animal out there, maybe a descendant of a dirgon, he would not only know, but be the most interested in it.

Haldone lifted his drink and finished the last of his Skyblue Seer. As the final icy tingles spread through his throat, he was thankful for it. Now he could stay calm while finding out exactly what he needed to know.

Rising, he lifted his empty cup and brought it to the counter. "Thanks."

Bilzer waved at him as he exited the establishment. Once outside, he checked the position of Helios. It was just after midday and if he wasn't mistaken, Konala should be in the sitki with the animals.

Turning in that direction, he strode down the wooden walkway. Near the end, he found a jump-off ledge with a dead infragile vine and swung down to the first level. Jahl's ability to control dead flora and fauna had built the multi-level settlement in the trees.

At first, he'd been fascinated by the reflection wall that made it seem invisible to anyone outside it, as well as been interested in how the homes were built around the large trees, but that was over five days ago. Now he was consumed with leaving.

He had a theory about Mya, who they found in the tunnels behind Theron's old cave. If he was right, she could help him with the lawbreakers, and he could hopefully shake the obsession his subconscious had with her. But first he had to find her and to do that he needed to leave Loraleaf.

Entering the sitki filled with domesticated animals, he found Konala was not alone. Jaelene and her tigran, Princess, were also there. "I will come back."

Jaelene spun around, her naked form revealing a rounded belly. "Oh no, please. I was just leaving." She glanced back at Konala. "The baby has just started kicking, so I thought daddy would like to feel." She faced him again. "Would you?"

Konala, who was the most easy-going Edenist he'd ever met, scowled.

He wasn't sure he imagined he heard a growl or the man really did. "No. I will wait until the day I have a beloved for things like that."

Jaelene pointed her finger at him. "I'm thinking a filoz might be a good first step."

"Of course." He'd stopped countering her arguments for a filoz the first day he'd arrived. He'd discovered long ago that while Naralinians thought single men odd, they let them be, but their beloved from Earth were constantly trying to match him with others.

He just wasn't made to be part of a filoz. As a young man, he'd felt the pressure to join friends, but he had no real invitations. At first, he'd thought something was wrong with him, but eventually, he accepted that he was what his mother called "a loner."

Jaelene sighed. "I give up. Come on Princess, let's go find daddy Theron."

"No." Konala's quick response to that as he exited a pen with a pair of logar surprised both of them.

Jaelene immediately spun on him. "Why not?"

He put his arm around her growing waist. "Because I do not

want you anywhere near eyllen and that is what he is working with today."

Her hand immediately covered her stomach. "Is that dangerous to the baby?"

"We do not know, but it is dangerous anyway. It is pure energy. So wait until Theron is done at the lab."

She leaned in and kissed him on the cheek. "Okay, I will."

Konala let her walk out of his hold.

Haldone tensed as the big cat joined her. He still wasn't used to tigrans.

Jaelene smiled at him. "If you've come to see the baby henny chicks, you're in for a treat." She walked by him and out the door, Princess following her, obviously well trained since the huge feline didn't attempt to eat any of the other animals.

He released a breath. Tigran had teeth as long as his forearm and though he'd read they liked Edenists to stroke their fur and didn't generally eat them, it had been a shock to find an Earth woman with one for a pet.

"How is your training with Theron going?" Konala moved to a small wash station and cleaned the hand that hadn't held his agapayto.

"It is fine though most of what he has taught, I already know."

Konala chuckled. "Yes, Theron can be over thorough, but that can be good if you have the patience."

He wanted to say he didn't, but he kept his thought to himself, not wanting to reveal that he was anxious to leave. Instead, he leaned against the pen of the logar, the large four-legged animal resembled an Earth horse except for the spiral horn that protruded from its head. They had been used to help build Naralina from what he'd learned in history lessons, but that was so long ago that except for the small Discoverist Oasis on the eighth level of the city, these were the first he'd seen. He had to admit, it was a little distracting.

Konala wiped his hand. "I am guessing you did not come to see the henny chicks." The man's mouth twitched with humor.

He shook his head and offered a grin of his own. "No, I did not, but I have to admit seeing a tigran and a logar and those chicks in one space without any of them becoming a meal is surprising. I imagine when you first entered the jungle, you were excited to see these animals in the wild."

Konala smiled. "To be honest, at first I was intimidated. Communicating with domesticated animals is a completely different experience. The thoughts of the animals out here are sharper, faster, and sometimes I cannot get their attention."

He nodded. That was his general impression of the jungle, and he itched to be beyond the confines of Loraleaf, which was like a stepping stone to the truly wild. "Have you encountered animals you have never seen before, I mean those not even housed at Naralina's Discoverist Oasis?"

Konala dropped the towel and set his foot on a large box. "I haven't yet, but Jaelene and Theron have. Theron was attacked by a boarox."

Now that he hadn't expected, and he widened his eyes. "A boarox?"

Konala's blue eyes gleamed. "Yes. I wish I could have seen it."

"But I thought those were a myth."

The man shook his head, his brows lowering. "No, they exist, but they usually stay far away from the heat of the equator. That a boarox was seen this far south is concerning."

Haldone watched Konala carefully. "So, does the dirgon also exist?"

Konala's gaze snapped to him. "Why do you ask that?"

The man did not immediately deny the creature's existence which told him a lot. "I didn't think the boarox existed and it does, so I figured that must mean the dirgon exists."

Konala took his foot off the box and opened it. He scooped up some fine meal with bugs crawling through it and walked toward the far pen where hennys started to peep at his approach. "I have not seen one."

That Konala didn't deny the existence meant he must have some evidence to the contrary. He wasn't sure how far he could push him. "Have you ever seen anything that might make you think they could be about in the jungle?"

Konala threw the food to the birds and returned to drop the scoop in the box. Finally, he looked at him. "I have come across tracks that I didn't recognize."

"You mean the tracks of a dirgon?" He hadn't expected to hear that.

Konala shook his head. "I would not know what a dirgon's tracks looked like since no one knows if they ever really existed. I simply found tracks that I did not recognize, which means there is a beast of great size out there." He pointed toward the jungle. "Why are you so curious about a dirgon?"

He shrugged. "I am learning all I can about the jungle so I am better prepared to survive in it. Unlike you, I have no filoz, so transporting out of a dangerous situation is not an option."

Konala leaned back against the wall and crossed his arms. "Then I would suggest that you prepare for everything. Loraleaf may be seven years old, but we have not explored that much except what is between Naralina, here, and Haven. There is a lot we don't know." He looked away as if he had more than one concern, but then he pushed away from the wall and grinned as he walked toward him. "I am hoping you will come back and share with us whatever you discover."

He understood his time for asking questions was over. "Thank you for the advice. I'll definitely come back and report." He grimaced. "I do not think Jahl would accept anything less."

Konala walked him out. "I believe I will see you tomorrow for the evening meal. Jaelene said her sister is having us over to celebrate us being five months pregnant."

He chuckled, more determined than ever to be gone by then. Women and babies were never one of his interests. Yes, he went to the Pleasure Temples and learned what he needed to and used them when he felt like it, but overall, talking to women was not one of his strengths, his mother being the exception.

As he strode away from the sitki, he grinned. However, there was a woman he'd make an effort to speak to, if he could find her, and now it looked as if his opportunity would come sooner rather than later.

~~*~~

Damn. Mya tried to twist away, but Keeva's grip had the strength of a fithee snake hanging onto the mountainside. "Leh go."

"Please, I just wanted to see you. What are you?" His light brown eyes appeared lighter as he gazed at her face, his excitement obvious now that his shock had worn off.

"Leh go." She tried to twist away again.

"If I let you go, will you answer some questions?"

She stilled. Anything to be free. She nodded.

As if it pained him to release her, he sighed and loosened his grip. Immediately, she scooted back away from him. She rubbed her wrist, well aware it was her own struggle that had caused the red marks on it.

"Are you still here?" His voice made it sound like he was more nervous than angry. "I did not mean to frighten you. I was only surprised. There is no such thing as a female Edenist. There has never been one in the history of Eden, or at least Naralina anyway. So, I am guessing you are from somewhere else."

There had never been a female Edenist? Her mind raced as she tried to remember everything her parents had taught her. She couldn't remember anything about the gender of Edenists. Her mom was from Earth and her dads from Eden. That she knew.

All the lawbreakers she'd seen except one had been males, but she thought that meant that less women than men ignored the Criuson and Dickinson Laws. What did it mean that she might be the only female Edenist in Naralina?

Keeva's eyes widened and he scanned the area, obviously trying to determine if she was still there. "Are you Crius?"

She smiled at that and let out a garbled chuckle. "Nu." How could he think that when she was obviously an Edenist? Hadn't she just told him she was Kindred of Light and that her ability to be invisible was from that Kindred? Maybe the kerasi, instead of making him sleepy, made him forgetful.

His brow furrowed as if he tried to figure something out and he couldn't. If she could just talk aloud like she heard it in her head, she could tell him things, things he needed to know about the jungle and that she wanted to go to Naralina. She wrapped her hair around her hand worrying it between her fingers.

"Can I see you again?" Keeva looked past her.

She didn't want him to look at her right now. She wanted him to gain his strength so he could be in the tree branches by nightfall. There was no way she could get him up there, and there were more dangers from nocturnal animals than daylight animals. It was the lawbreakers that were about more in the day. "Nu. Seep."

He frowned. "You said if I let you go, you'd answer my questions. Do you break your promises?"

No, but she wouldn't be manipulated either. "Seep forst."

His brows lowered farther, making him look mean. "That is why you gave me the kerasi fruit. To make me sleep. Why?"

"Bedder." She shut her mouth hard. Nothing sounded right.

His brow finally relaxed. "You want me to sleep so I can get better?"

She nodded.

"Mya?"

Damn, she'd forgotten he couldn't see her. "Yef."

He gave a sheepish grin toward a branch near her. "I am sorry. I thought you gave it to me for another reason. I have been betrayed by people I trusted, so I am seeing an enemy everywhere. I apologize."

He paused as if trying to decide what to say next then shook his head. "I think the kerasi has already made my brain tired. I will sleep." He closed his eyes. "If something threatens us, wake me."

She shook her head. What would he do? He'd lost so much blood, she wasn't sure, even with a full stomach and sleep, that he'd be able to get himself into the tree.

If anyone came near, she'd distract them. Her Mind dad always said if she could avoid confrontation in the jungle, she should, but if she needed to solve a problem with someone in her family then she shouldn't shy away from it.

But with no family left…she looked toward the great wall. Missing the portal was probably a good thing. If she'd been inside Naralina, no one would have known she was there, and she would have had difficulties making herself known and communicating. Now with Keeva, she might have a chance to find her family.

Pleased by her prospects, she lifted the branches of salis leaves and ducked out from under the bush. She listened intently for unusual sounds, hearing nothing but the caball bird and the rustle of leaves at the top of the trees, she set to looking for straight branches. While Keeva slept, she'd set a few traps and whittle some more cooking sticks.

As she broke off a straight branch from a jansen tree, a noise beyond it caught her attention. Without a sharp stick or her rope noose, she had little chance of catching dinner yet, but she still crept quietly toward the noise. As she peaked around the dark leaves of a pander bush, she grinned.

A feroon munched upon the grasses of a small clearing. The large dark brown animal's back was at least as high as her head and its lack of horns on its white head declared it a female. Her brown leathery skin was smooth, but she was on the fat side.

She only killed feroon when she needed to stock her cabinet with meat, and since she wasn't home, there was no place to store it, not that she had her hunting weapon with her. She was about to walk out to visit with the animal, when the feroon turned her head to look behind her and out of the bush came a baby.

Mya halted her forward motion and froze. A mother feroon was as dangerous as male feroons during mating season. Suddenly, the animal became a danger. Quietly, she backed away, stopping when the feroon turned her head forward again and sniffed the air.

Her own scent, what her mother called lilac, wasn't common on Eden, but it was a floral smell that should keep the feroon from charging. She held her breath until the feroon lowered her head to feed, and the baby feroon nuzzled its nose beneath the mother's stomach for its own meal.

Once she'd gathered her branches, she returned to where she'd made the midday meal and sat to work on her cooking sticks. She also fashioned a spade, as her mother called it, from an old piece of magee tree. She could dig up a jansen root and cook it with their evening meal. She usually used the leaves of the tree for a warm drink, but the root added a nice bite to food.

As she worked, she kept thinking about what Keeva had said. Was it true she was the only female Edenist from Naralina? Was that good or bad? Was she a freak or special? Her heart softened. Her dads always said she was special, but they had doted on her, something she didn't realize until they were gone.

She rose and set her traps. The sadness in her heart was like an old friend in a new environment. It had been so many years since her parents had been captured that she'd accepted their deaths. If they could have come home, they would have. The ache of their loss was now almost a comfort.

Returning to her fire pit, she sat. She never went a day without thinking about her parents, whether it was something they taught her, something they said, or some silly thing they did, her dads being the experts in silly. They were her—movement on the ground caught her attention.

She studied the dirt. Nothing moved. She waited. There! She stared at a small vine that moved across the ground like a fithee then stopped. It started again, moving in no particular pattern. Understanding dawned, and she grinned.

The vine slithered toward the fire hole she'd covered to keep the coals warm and backed away as if it could feel the heat. Instead, it went around it then stopped. She waited, barely breathing. Finally, it started to move again, and when it was within reach, she grabbed it, barely keeping from giving a triumphant shout.

It immediately went limp. She frowned and shook it, but it just lay there across her hand. That was no fun. She dropped it on the ground and watched to see if it would move again. It didn't. Was she wrong?

An itch on her head had her reaching up only to grasp another vine in her hair. "Ack." She jumped to her feet and pulled the vine from her.

Keeva. Quietly, she approached the salis bush then whipped back the branches.

Keeva's eyes went wide at the movement. "Mya?"

She'd planned to make it known she wasn't happy with his game, but realized it wasn't a game. He had no idea what'd he found outside his shelter. "Yef."

His whole body relaxed, the tight muscles of his stomach, arms and legs releasing, smoothing out the skin over them. "I was not sure if I'd found you, an animal, or a lawbreaker."

She wanted to ask how much the plants could tell him, but the words would be too hard to form.

"Now that I am rested, I want to learn so much about you. I am a Discoverist, which means I am very curious."

She tensed. How was she supposed to tell him anything? Once again, she found herself grasping her hair in her hands, wishing she could talk like him.

Keeva's eyes grew lighter again. "Were you born on Eden? Have you lived your whole life in the jungle or are you from another city? How many fathers did you have?"

She couldn't answer all his questions at once. She couldn't even have a conversation with him. Her mom and dads always talked. She wanted to, but—

A squeal outside the salis bush gave her a more important task. "What was that?"

She heard Keeva's question as she ran out but ignored it. She didn't want to risk missing the havling pig she was sure she'd caught in one of her traps. Grabbing up a heavy rock she'd found earlier, she raced to the spot of her second trap, and quickly knocked the pig out.

She dragged the animal, trap and all, back to her fire pit. Pulling her knife from the small sheath tied around her waist, she slit the throat and started to skin it.

The salis bush branches moved to show Keeva had rolled onto his injured side to see what was happening. "You caught a wild pig?" His voice held surprise and his gaze looked on her with admiration, or rather where the skin she'd tossed lay.

It had been so long since someone had been proud of her efforts that she found it hard to swallow. She didn't respond, as it was obvious what had occurred, but she didn't like the wince she noticed when she looked up from her task. "Doon."

His gaze came closer to where she crouched at the sound of her voice. "Doon? I don't understand."

She took a deep breath, forcing her frustration away to focus on her need to communicate. "Lee doon."

His brow furrowed then relaxed as he grinned. "Lay down?"

She liked him a lot when he did that. It reminded her of her dads. "Yef."

"I will, but promise after you get that cooking, you will come in here and talk with me."

Didn't he realize she couldn't talk right? Shaking her head, she sighed loudly, hoping her frustration would communicate itself. "Yef."

His grin widened. "Good." He rolled away, dropping the salis bush branches, but she still heard him moan at the movement. She found herself shaking her head like her mother used to do when one of her dads did something stupid.

When she had the pig ready to cook, she uncovered her hot coals and blew on them, adding small twigs to make the fire live again. Then she staked two larger branches into the ground before setting the pig across them on another.

Lastly, she took the magee tree bark she'd used earlier and dug a hole as deep as her arm and threw in the pig's head, feet and other inedibles. She scraped the dirt with blood on it into the hole then covered it with a few sherry flowers from the patch of them near her trap. Their scent was strong and might have been what had kept any direlots from finding Keeva while he lay bleeding. Finally, she filled in the rest of the hole with clean dirt.

She'd have to come out and turn the pig, but there was nothing else she could do to avoid keeping her promise. Actually, she was surprised Keeva had kept silent so long. Maybe he was asleep. Hopeful, she pulled back the salis bush leaves quietly, but found his eyes wide.

"I was beginning to wonder if you were avoiding me."

She felt her cheeks flush with embarrassment, happy he couldn't actually see her.

Keeva linked his hands and rested them on his rippled stomach. "My first question is how many fathers do you have?"

She relaxed at that because she could draw in the dirt. Carefully, she drew two lines.

"Two. That's the minimum, which just proves further that you are not a lawbreaker. Do you live in another city?"

"Nu." She shook her head though he couldn't see her.

He frowned a bit at that. "Do you live in the jungle?"

"Yef." That couldn't be so odd since she knew there were others from Naralina who lived here, too. There was the new teal walled circle only a half day's run from her cave's south entrance.

But his frown didn't lessen. "Do your family live by themselves?"

They did, but he didn't have to know she was completely alone. "Yef."

"That is odd. Why did they choose to live out here? Were they from Naralina originally? What were their names?"

She grasped her hair, twisting it between her fingers. She wanted to answer him, but she couldn't. "Pee." She ducked back outside the bush and walked to the pig, which was turning a nice brown on one side. She rotated the animal on the spit, making sure it was secure, then looked at the bush.

Keeva asked too many questions. Her parents had said they lived in the jungle because they didn't like how crowded Naralina was. She'd always wondered why they didn't visit her grandparents there instead of meeting them at the home of her Earth grandparents. Her parents didn't even go to the city for provisions, preferring to bring savinstone to obtain items on Earth.

She loved her grandparents, but it was so hard to remember them. She had photos of them she had left in the cave and she'd painted them on one of the walls. She'd love to see them again, but without a Crius chip, or rather two, that would never happen.

"Mya?" Keeva's voice had changed. He wasn't nervous that she was gone or anxious that she remained outside. Something had softened.

Concerned he could be in pain, she made herself go back to the bush and lift the leaves.

"Mya, I think I have figured out why you keep running away from me."

He did? She folded her arms, curious as to what he thought he'd figured out.

"I have narrowed it down to two possibilities. Will you answer yes or no to each? And I mean honestly."

That she could do. "Yef."

"Excellent. My first theory is that I smell pretty bad having been out here for days with no rainbox and only a stream around to wash with. So maybe you only stay so long with me because you cannot stand how I smell."

She grinned as she shook her head. She had smelled a lot worse. She actually liked his smell, it was like a wood they used on Earth to store clothes in. Her grandmother there had what she called a cedar chest lined with it. "Nu."

"I am glad to hear that. I am not sure I could get myself over to the closest stream quite yet."

She shook her head even though he couldn't see her. Maybe she could use more strips from the hesta to soak and bring for him to wash.

"Then the only other theory I have is that you have a difficult time speaking."

She stared at him in shock. How could he know that? He'd said he was a Discoverist. She'd heard that term before. Her mother told her Discoverists had figured out that eyllen could power everything on Eden centuries ago, and that's why they had to keep their eyllen cave a secret. From the way her parents spoke, she understood Discoverists were smarter than anyone else.

"Mya, do you keep leaving because you do not want to talk because you find it difficult?"

"Yef." That he had figured that out not only relieved her but made her more self-conscious. Without waiting to see what he thought of that, she ducked back outside to tend to the pig. Maybe he'd think better of her after she fed him.

Chapter Three

Keeva lay back, satisfied with his new puzzle. It was so hard not to grasp onto Mya and gaze at her beauty again, but like a wild animal one wished to tame, his instinct told him progressing slowly and with kindness was his best course of action.

Every discovery started with curiosity, but bringing understanding to fruition meant patience, persistence, and careful testing. He'd already erred by grabbing onto her and asking far too many questions. But in his defense, she was an Edenist! The words "she" and "Edenist" had never been used in the same sentence since Naralina was settled.

This was a major discovery! He scowled. It was also a delicate one. Mya wasn't a mineral or animal. She was an Edenist, which meant she had to want him to bring her to Naralina, assuming he figured out how to get into the city without a Crius chip.

His excitement dimmed at that thought. Here he was, lying on his back, wounded and totally dependent on a woman to survive and he was dreaming of accolades from his peers. He grimaced.

He'd completely forgotten the whole reason he was in the

jungle in the first place was because of Grandall and his giant portal to bring women to Eden to sell to the highest bidder in other cities. By now, the man probably already had. The machine was almost ready before he'd been exiled.

The scent of cooked pig started to permeate the area under his bush and his stomach tightened as hunger once again made itself known. The hennys had been excellent and more food than he'd had in all his days outside the city, but now that his body had feasted, it wanted more.

Mya's ability to survive in the jungle gave him hope for the first time that he may live beyond a turn of Selene. He planned to keep that in mind and hold back his curiosity somewhat to focus on the basic necessities. Of which, he currently had one.

With no help for it, he rolled onto his side, the pain spreading from beneath his arm to his entire chest and back. Lifting the salis bush leaves on the opposite side from where Mya cooked their meal, he relieved himself.

He used his ability to make a pander bush branch sweep the dead leaves and sticks on the ground over it to cover his scent. He had no idea if this is what he should do in the jungle, but it was something he saw a young tigran do just before it caught sight of him and ran off.

It appeared there was more than one subject he needed to learn from Mya. He lay back, grimacing at the pain. Taking shallow breaths, he finally found the comfort he needed. Mya would be, by far, the most beautiful teacher he'd ever had. It might be hard to concentrate. He couldn't wait to see her again.

In the few seconds he'd had to look upon her, he'd been struck not only by her beauty but her fitness. Her slender arm as she tried to pull away had contracted with strength and her thighs, in her crouch position had shown her muscles clearly.

But before he could see her, he had to win her trust. He hoped she had the ability to speak beyond single words. She appeared to understand everything he'd said, which made him guess that she was very intelligent even beyond her jungle survival skills. So, if her family lived in the jungle, could they speak? Were her parents mute?

He rejected the idea. There was no disease or deformities on Eden…but there was no such thing as a female Edenist either and yet here was one. Had she been an experiment that didn't come out just right?

Even at the thought, he fisted his hands. That would be barbaric. He hoped—

The salis leaves moved, and he breathed in the delicious smell of roasted pig. It had a smoky smell with something sweet yet spicy. Suddenly, a piece of bark with pieces of meat sat next to him. Despite his growling stomach, he waited a moment as he was reminded that anything Mya touched was also affected by her ability to reflect light, and only when she stopped touching it, did it appear. "This smells and looks perfect."

The leaves moved a little but weren't dropped which meant she was still with him.

"Eat."

"Gladly." He smiled toward the sound of her voice. Now that he knew she was a female, he wondered how he could have thought her low, silky voice was a male's. He'd taken his first bite before he realized she'd pronounced the word eat correctly. He closed his eyes as the full flavor of the pig combined with the tang and spice of whatever she'd cooked it with. Chewing slowly so as to enjoy every nuance, he finally opened his eyes. "This is better than anything I have ever had inside Naralina."

"Nu." The salis leaves rustled but weren't dropped.

"Oh yes. I wonder if we have advanced so far in everything else that we have not explored the flavors our own city can afford us." He took another mouthful, which was just as good as the first.

"Eat. Nide soom."

As he chewed, he contemplated her sounds. Ah, night soon. "Yes, and I need to get us up there." He pointed upward with his food covered hand.

"Yef." As she said the word, the leaves dropped.

Disappointed she'd left so soon, he was still pleased that he was starting to understand her vocalizations. He grew more confident that she had a full vocabulary just waiting to come out. And he'd help her make that happen!

It was the least he could do for her helping him. Pleased with his plan, he continued to eat his evening meal. Not only would he teach her to speak, but he would keep her safe in the trees above.

As he finished, he heard her moving around out beyond his bush. He wasn't sure of all the sounds, but he imagined she cleaned up the place where she cooked so there was no evidence they were there. Even he, in his limited knowledge of the jungle, had done so in his nights alone.

The leaves to his bush moved aside again. "Naw."

He searched his brain for what her word might mean.

"Naw. Dirk."

The urgency of her tone conveyed the meaning even more than her words. It was getting dark, and he needed to get them in the tree now. "Yes. Help me out of here."

At first there was no movement, then all the branches on her side were gone. Of course, by her lifting them away they became invisible. With nothing to impede him, he scooted his ass over and then his torso, careful not to turn onto his side. When he'd cleared the bush, he lay looking up at the trees around their camp, the sky a muted gray.

The tallest trees were what he wanted, their large branches near the top perfect for a night's rest, but he needed infragile vines to get himself up there. He'd discovered four were enough to lift him in his first nights in the jungle, but now he couldn't hold on well and Mya would be additional weight.

Studying the trees, he pointed to one nearby on the Naralina side of where he lay. "That will work. It has enough vines to lift me. I will get you up there then join you."

"Nu."

"What do you mean, no. We need to get into the trees. I thought we'd agreed on that."

"Keeva, op."

It wasn't hard to figure out she meant for him to go up. Every protective instinct in his body woke at that. "I'll be a logar's ass before I leave you down here. You are going up there or we are both staying here."

A heavy sigh issued from the air. "Nu. Keeva, frost. Mya, nest."

Nest? He frowned. Her wording was grammatically wrong, but more the sound was wrong. Nest must mean next. Understanding dawned. "You want me to go up first and then you next?"

"Yef." The relief in her voice was telling. She obviously found her own limitations with her speaking frustrating, another sign that her vocabulary could just as easily be better than his if she could learn to say the words. Though pleased he understood her, he still didn't like that she wanted him to ascend first. On Eden, women always came first in pleasure and safety.

He shook his head. "I do not like that idea."

"Keeva, weep."

"No, I am not going to cry about it."

Her surprising growl had him rethinking what she said. Weep must mean wheat or week or, oh weak! She believed him weak. He was an ithio. She was right, he *was* weak.

"I do not like it, but I understand what you mean. Since I am weak, you think I should ascend first. But what if I cannot bring you up after I am there? How will you get to safety?"

"Kimb."

Climb. He studied the tree he planned to sleep in. There were no branches low enough for her to climb on. He'd just have to find the strength to bring her up, but she was right, it would take more of his strength to get himself up so he should do that first. "We will do this as you suggest." He paused at what sounded like a grunt of satisfaction.

He frowned in the direction the sound came from. "After I get up there, I will send the vines back down for you."

From the silence, he assumed she agreed. He hoped so because he wasn't sure he had the strength to lift her if she fought him. "Come over here," he patted the ground next to him. "It will be easier for me to move the vines."

Small twigs on the ground near him disappeared, assuring him that she'd done as he asked, her touch making them appear to vanish, but they were still there beneath her feet.

Hoping he'd gained enough strength to command the vines,

he lifted his hand. The vines quickly obeyed, wrapping around his upper arms and thighs. He ordered a fifth vine to go beneath him and wrap around his hips. That was the easy part.

If he was full strength, he had the ability to force an upper branch to the ground for him to step on, but he was far too weak for that. Edenists didn't need physical strength to use their abilities, but they did need to be healthy.

He looked over to where he thought Mya stood. "I am not sure if this will work on the first try. Stay right there."

She didn't respond, so he had to assume she understood.

Taking a deep breath, he raised his hand slightly and the five vines began to lift him. He wasn't more than his own height above the ground when it became apparent he didn't have the control to keep the vines equal as his head dipped below his waist sending the blood rushing to his wounds.

The pain was bearable, so instead of correcting the issue, he focused on getting his body through a break in the branches. His foot bumped against one and his shoulder was scratched by another, but he finally lifted himself onto a large branch with his back up against the trunk. He wiped the sweat from his forehead as he regained his normal breathing.

Not in a hurry to fall from his perch, he made the branches on either side of him interlock with the one he was on. He released the vines from his body, already exhausted from his efforts but as a final precaution, he tied himself at the hips to the trunk. Luckily, once he set the tree limbs, they would remain for at least eight hours.

Satisfied, he let his head fall back against the tree and rested for a few moments.

"Letter." At Mya's voice, he looked down, but there was nothing to see. There wasn't even any evidence that they'd been there.

"Letter?" Why would she want that?

"Letter. Kimb."

He wished he could see her, maybe then he could figure out—

"Ladder. You want a ladder to climb."

"Yef."

The woman was brilliant! It would take a lot less effort on his part. Quickly, he moved the vines into forming a ladder. "You can come up now."

He watched as each vine step bent under her weight. The ladder swung when she moved, so he anchored the vines to the ground.

She wasted no time, reaching the top rung and stepping off as if she didn't trust it.

He didn't blame her. He'd had to depend on a fellow Discoverist once to move eyllen, which when exposed to air exploded. Carrying the box made of solid air but absent of any air had been concerning. "Are you off the ladder?"

"Yef." Her voice so close, surprised him.

"I am moving the vines now." He unraveled the vines and let most of them go back to their natural state. "I'd like to wrap one around you like I have to make sure you do not fall when you sleep.

Her silence was so long, he had a feeling she wouldn't let him do it. When the vine vanished, he let it go. He had no doubt she was tying herself to the tree.

Though disappointed, he was too tired to argue. Lifting himself off the ground had taken a lot. He just hoped he had enough strength to go down again when he needed to.

"Seep." Mya's soft voice was still commanding.

He grinned. "First, let me teach you. The word is sleep. S-leep."

"Sleep."

Her perfect enunciation gave him more hope than he had since he'd been exiled from Naralina. "Excellent. Now I will go to sleep, but when I wake, I want to teach you how to say every word that I know is in your head."

"Yef. Teach."

"The word is yes. Yessss."

"Yes."

If he wasn't so tired, he'd keep at it, but he couldn't stay awake any longer. "Good sleep."

~~*~~

Haldone added the last item into his bag and threw it over his shoulder. Scanning the living area of the visitor's tree house one more time, he made sure he didn't forget anything.

The new table he'd created as a parting gift stood in the meal room. It had been the only thing that had kept him from yelling at everyone he'd met. By his second day at Loraleaf he'd been ready to take down a few well-meaning settlers. Instead, he'd put his frustrated energy to work and created the table of hard air then filled it with dead bark one of the patrols brought him. Placing each piece in just the right position had taken days, but it was exactly what he needed to keep himself calm. He studied it one more time just to make sure it looked as he wished. Content with it, he strode to the door.

He'd been lucky. The home had belonged to one of the filoz who had returned to Naralina after Grandall had been exiled.

Wareson and Nassic had invited men from Loraleaf and Haven to return to the city and a few had. If not for that, he would have been sleeping on the longseat at Khaos and Jahl's home because they had a woman staying in Toni's old room.

That woman, Star, as he discovered, was a particular problem of Konala's and Rekah's. Not only had they messed up on Earth while watching her to see if she could be a potential chosen one, before they had met Jaelene, but she'd also been caught in Grandall's giant portal and refused to return to Earth. He counted himself lucky in that as well. Without a filoz, he didn't have to study potential mates on Earth. Besides, his mind was already fascinated by a female here on Eden.

Closing the door, he left the home and quietly headed for Cordtz and Paxon's. His body itched with the need to start his quest for vengeance and his heart pounded at the thought of seeing Mya again. In just a few short moments, he'd be on his way. Cordtz's reaction to the information Konala had divulged had been extreme, but he had the feeling that man did not function on any other level. He hadn't met Paxon, but he hoped that man was calmer. It reminded him a little of his and Sandale's relationship, if it was the case.

Not wanting to alert any early risers, he skipped the lift and strode to the first jump off ledge, but there were no infragile vines available. Raising his hand, he solidified the air into a slide to the next lower level and jumped on.

Too late, he discovered he wasn't the only one up before Helios. He raised his hand again and was able to move the end of the slide slightly to the left, but he also picked up speed and landed on the wooden walkway with a thud, barely missing the Earth woman walking along the wood bridge.

She spun around in surprise. "Oh, I'm so sorry. Did I do that? I'm sorry, I didn't see you."

He rose to a standing position and flicked his wrist to disintegrate his slide. "It wasn't your fault. I wasn't paying attention." Just his luck, it was Star, the woman staying with Jahl and Khaos. He didn't want her saying anything to the Loraleaf leaders before he left. "You are up early." The words came out a bit too accusatory.

She stepped backed and frowned. Her red hair was pulled back and she wore tight fitting clothes. He didn't understand why she bothered with the clothes. Earth women confused him. Being naked was natural, yet all but Jaelene in Loraleaf continued to wear clothes.

"I was just out for my morning power walk." She drew her brows together. "I'm just trying to stay in shape."

Scrat, now he felt like a logar's ass. "Please continue. I was just on my way to meet some friends for the morning meal."

She studied him. "You don't live here, do you?"

He shook his head. "Just visiting."

"I won't keep you then. Have a nice day." With that, she turned and started walking very quickly along the walkway again.

He barely kept himself from growling as he strode toward Cordtz's place. When he arrived, he knocked quietly and was bid enter.

He'd never been in this tree house and was impressed with how high the roof was. Then again, Cordtz was one of the tallest Edenists he'd met. The man came from his meal room. "Good, you are early."

Another man followed. He was just as tall or taller than Cordtz, if that were possible. "I am Paxon."

He nodded to acknowledge the introduction. "I am Haldone."

Cordtz gestured to the room behind him. "I have left a note that will be delivered later today as I do not want to alarm Jahl and have him sending out men to search."

"Did you mention me?"

"Yes." Cordtz nodded. "I wrote that you are at Haven."

That was acceptable to him since he didn't plan to be at Haven very long. He nodded to let Cordtz know he approved.

Cordtz pulled his arms through a bag of supplies. "I am ready. Let us leave." He stood two shoulder-widths apart from Paxon and pushed the Crius chip beneath his arm. Paxon did the same and a doorway opened just inside the walls of Haven.

Haldone grinned as he stepped through followed by his companions. They closed the portal quickly. "This is where we leave you."

He looked around the sleeping settlement, curious that no alarm had been given. "Good luck finding the dirgon."

Paxon shook his head. "We will not need luck. Cordtz is an excellent tracker."

Cordtz snorted. "A useless skill in Naralina, but out here…" He lifted his arm to encompass their surroundings and beyond. "It is very useful." He stepped to the side of Paxon once again and opened the portal, this time the scene was nothing but jungle. Paxon stepped through first, then Cordtz turned to him. "We wish you success."

He nodded and then the portal closed and the men were gone.

He scanned the area directly within the walled enclosure. There were a few wooden buildings, but no activity, so he walked to where there appeared to be a wide-open space with wooden buildings on either side the full length of the settlement. Had it been abandoned after Nassic and Wareson returned to Naralina?

Though he could simply walk out the small door in the teal cyndistone wall that protected all that was within, he had no idea where Mya's cave was in relation to Haven. He had to find someone who had been to what they considered Theron's cave.

He continued down the wide path listening and looking for signs of life. Last he knew, when Nassic and Wareson had left Haven to move back to Naralina, since they were part of the new Ruling Circle, only a few of their followers had gone with them. So where was everyone?

A muffled noise caught his attention as he came to the bath house. Quietly, he opened the door and stepped inside.

His first impression was that the bath house in Haven rivalled any in Naralina. His second impression was not as favorable. There were Edenists lying everywhere along with a few Earth women. Some piles of flesh were so entwined, he couldn't tell which limb belonged to who.

In the bath itself, four men, obviously having imbibed far too much ale, surrounded a woman. Two of the men leaned against the wall of the bath for support. The woman with her back to them holding on to their arms stood as another man's hand gave her pleasure beneath the water. The last man was busy sucking on one of her nipples.

If the group was a filoz with their beloved, he shouldn't interrupt, but from the looks of the bath, it appeared to be part of a night long orgy, an activity frowned upon by Naralinians because women could find themselves bonded to men not in the same filoz.

The woman looked up as her pleasure increased and spotted him. Instead of alerting one of her men, she smiled. "Aren't you a handsome hunth? J-join us?" Her slurred speech proved she'd participated in the overindulgence of ale as well.

One of the men leaning against the bath wall, moved his head enough to focus on him and frowned. "Who are you?"

Not about to give away his purpose, he frowned back at the man. "Where are your leaders?"

The man next to that one waved him off. "Only two-level house in Haven." He sniggered. "And the one level house across from the store room."

"You mean the incarceration cell." The first man added.

Disgusted by their behavior and lack of care, he turned on his heel and strode out.

Nassic and Wareson would be furious if they saw this. They had worked hard to create this settlement after they were falsely accused by Grandall. They had slipped out of Naralina in the dark of night with their portal chips intact before they could be exiled. When they discovered more innocent Edenists in the jungle, trying to survive and keep away from lawbreakers, they had gathered them together to create this safe Haven.

He tried to remember who they had put in charge when they returned to Naralina but couldn't. He'd been far too focused on getting to the jungle to pay much attention. As one of the few single men with no filoz, traveling by portal had been his main concern.

The two-level home the bathers had mentioned was the closest, so he started there. After knocking loudly, he finally tried the door and found it open. He walked in and found himself in the living area. With cool efficiency, he moved through the entire downstairs, finding no one, but also no sleeping rooms.

Heading up the stairs, his mood turned blacker as he found a lone man sitting in a chair facing the open deck.

He walked past the messed bed, pleased to see no empty ale jugs littered the room. But when he stood in front of the man in the chair, a shiver went up his spine. He'd seen that look a few times, and it wasn't good. His initial irritation waned.

"I am Haldone from Naralina. Are you one of the leaders of Haven?"

The man's gaze lifted to meet his, and he swallowed. There was no life in it. The man shook his head. "No longer."

Though he agreed with the man that he was not leader material, he still kept his impatience in check. The only men he'd seen look like that had lost their beloved. Though he had no idea what that felt like, he had seen the result of that on men he'd admired. "Do you know anyone who would know the way to M—Theron's cave?"

The man didn't even try to look at him again, just stared off as if living was far too much trouble.

Haldone moved to the small cold box in the sleeping room and opened it. It was empty. How long had it been that way? He looked over at the man in the chair. A quick scan of his body showed a few of his ribs were showing and the growth of beard made Haldone question how long the man had sat there.

Unwilling to bother him anymore, but also concerned the man wouldn't survive in his current state, he proceeded downstairs, determined to find someone else and express his concerns.

Hopefully, the other leader would be in better shape, though his hope was minimal. As he headed toward the small log home across from the stone storage building, he glanced at it. Did it actually house a lawbreaker?

His whole body came alive at the prospect of speaking to one. He might be able to find out all he needed to know right here. Detouring toward the storage building, he halted as a man came out of it, a basket of dirty dishes on his arm.

The man stopped when he spotted him. "Who are you?" Neither his voice nor his attitude was confrontational or inebriated. He had short dark hair and a round face, and the soft-edged heart birthmark nestled between the mounds of his chest declared him Kindred of Heart.

His brother, Sandale, was Kindred of Heart. "I am Haldone, from Naralina. Who are you?"

The man looked past him as if hoping others joined him. "I am Jerumbala, Haven's healer. Is your whole filoz here?"

He squashed his irritation at the common question. "No, I am not part of a filoz. I came here to ask directions to Theron's cave."

Jerumbala's shoulders sagged, but he smiled a welcome at the same time. "I wish I had more hospitality to offer you, but Haven is not what it once was."

Not particularly curious about what happened, he thought about dismissing the obvious opening, but that he might learn about the lawbreaker had him finding unusual amounts of patience. "What happened?"

Jerumbala opened his hand, gesturing to another small home not far from them. "Come, I will tell you. It will be good to rest and talk."

He glanced behind Jerumbala wishing he could simply walk

in and talk to the lawbreaker. He probably could, but this was the jungle and if there was one thing he'd learned since he'd first traveled from Naralina, it was that he needed to proceed with caution.

Allowing Jerumbala to precede him, he glanced back at the storage building, determined to go inside once he learned everything he needed to know.

Jerumbala's home was typical of a healer. He had additional sleeping rooms for men he needed to tend and the home was colored with soft pastels. Cushions were on every seat and shelf and the scent of bonabus flowers filled the air, giving the place a calm feeling.

He didn't like it. "Where is the rest of your filoz?"

The man deposited the basket on the counter and moved to the cold box. "Would you like ambrosia or water? I do not keep ale in my house."

After what he'd seen, he didn't blame the healer. Not knowing when he'd next taste ambrosia, he opted for that.

Jerumbala set down a cup of the drink on the table and Haldone sat, already itching to be on his way. "What has happened here? I thought Nassic and Wareson had named two leaders?"

The healer nodded. "They did. Lennix and Mykl. Unfortunately, just after Nase, Ware and Erin left, Lennix and Mykl's beloved was killed."

"How?"

Jerumbala shook his head. "Lawbreakers. They were showing her the savinstone monolith because she wanted to see it when the lawbreakers found them. Before they could protect her, a twister knocked them unconscious." Jerumbala frowned. "That's what they said, but since they all ended up in different places, I think there may have been other abilities that came into play."

He rolled his shoulders which had suddenly stiffened. "These lawbreakers need to be punished."

"What? We can't punish them. Living in the jungle is their punishment."

"Not when they prey on the innocent. They are only committing more atrocities and need to be accountable." He gritted his teeth to keep from yelling.

Jerumbala studied him. "This is personal for you."

He nodded. "Yes. They captured my brother, Sandale, and inserted an evil mind into his. It was so tangled that the only way to free him from it was to wipe all his memories. When he came back to us, he did not know us. He did not even know his beloved or his filoz."

"I was with Jahl when we went to save your brother. I am thankful that he lived. Yet it does not relieve us of our responsibility. We exiled the lawbreakers to the jungle to survive or die as they might. If we choose to live here as well, then that is a choice we make. We cannot punish them further for being who they are."

He stared at the healer in shock. This was the second time he'd heard such reasoning. He should have known that a Kindred of Heart would not understand. "Is the man you have in your storage building also a lawbreaker?"

The healer shrugged. "We are not sure yet. Even Nase, who is a truth-reader could not get the man to make sense. He is old and I think not a little insane from surviving in the jungle too long. There have been so many Naralinians exiled under false pretenses that it is hard to determine who is a lawbreaker and who is not."

His interest in speaking to the man who was being held waned. He didn't need to listen to the ravings of an addled mind. Mya was still his best hope for finding the lawbreakers who had taken Sandale and the one man responsible for causing his brother so much mental anguish. But that was something he would keep to himself.

"Did Lennix or Mykl see what these men looked like?"

Jerumbala shook his head. "No. In fact, they were unconscious when Sarach and I arrived and we were not that far behind." The healer looked away.

His gut tensed. "Did they still have their Crius chips?"

"Yes. Except for a few bruises and a broken wrist, they were fine, but all that was left of their beloved was her ripped clothing."

Despite not expecting to ever know what it was like to bond with a woman, he found his hands curling into fists at the evil that would harm a woman. With no women born on Eden, every one was sacred and cherished. It was time someone held this particular band of lawbreakers accountable.

"I am sorry for all that has happened here. Is the devastation of your leaders the reason for the inebriation and orgies?"

"Sadly, yes. The men have been sex starved for so long that Lennix and Mykl had some women from the Pleasure Temples come for a few weeks. I am hoping when the ales runs out or the women return to Naralina that everyone will go back to their work to make Haven a good place to live again."

"What about Lennix and Mykl?" I think I saw one of them in the two-level house. He does not look like he has eaten in weeks."

Jerumbala nodded. "I check on him every day, but all I can do is get him to drink water. It is the same with Mykl. They both blame themselves, but verbally blame each other. Can you go back to Naralina and get us help? I do not dare leave with them doing so poorly and with no one to feed the old man." He smiled ruefully. "Besides, I need another to open a portal. Like you, I have no filoz. I have asked the men here, but my request falls on drunken ears."

He couldn't go to Naralina or his family would try to keep him there. He couldn't take the man to Loraleaf or Jahl would tie him up with dead infragile vine, and he'd never be freed. But he couldn't leave Jerumbala in this situation without helping. "Is there someone in Naralina you could talk to through a portal who could get you help?"

Hope shone in the man's eyes, his tired frame straightening for the first time. "Yes, there is. If I tell my brother, he will rally men to aid me."

"Good. I cannot go to Naralina as I must make contact with someone in Theron's Cave, but I can help you open a portal so you can speak to your brother."

Jerumbala rose, his wide smile changing his whole face. "Please. I would be forever grateful."

He didn't immediately rise. "Do you know how to get to Theron's cave?"

The healer's smile faltered. "I have not been there, but I can tell you what Mykl said about getting there, if that would help."

He didn't think he would receive anything more detailed than that from the drunken men living at Haven. "That would help." He rose. "Let us contact your brother, then you can tell me everything about traveling to Theron's cave."

Jerumbala nodded, his excitement shining in his eyes. "I will."

CHAPTER FOUR

At the sound of voices, Mya reached over and touched Keeva, who still slept. Sleep was good for him. His complexion had already improved since yesterday, but it would do him no good if he was seen.

He must not have been about to wake because he stirred and seemed to relax again before his eyelids rose. As soon as he opened his eyes, she dragged her thumb across her chest then pointed below. She sincerely hoped that the motion for being quiet that her dads taught her was the same for Keeva's family.

He stared at her a moment as if not quite fully awake yet, then his eyes widened and he nodded before moving his gaze below.

She studied the jungle as well, her caution around lawbreakers heightened by having another in her care.

Keeva moved his arm, pointing.

She peered through the leaves and saw the movement he noticed. There were at least three men moving toward Naralina. One appeared small and from the rustling of the branches, his movements were quick. Another's head was clearly visible, his height much taller than his companion. Another moved with more caution as if constantly looking for something. It looked like they might have an animal with them, maybe a tigran? She couldn't tell.

As they drew closer to Naralina's walls, she caught actual words like exile, watch, and ithio. She grinned. She'd never come across multiple lawbreakers without one of them being the brunt of the hostility of the others. Then again, some of the Naralinians who had inhabited the end of her cave didn't necessarily get along either.

The men continued toward Naralina and out of sight, but not out of hearing. Actually, it was becoming easier to hear them. She sat up straighter, careful to keep her hand on Keeva's arm.

His attention was on those below as well. His jaw in profile seemed stronger than she'd first thought, or it could be that he held it tight with tension. It was hard to know since she'd only observed him less than a full day.

"There is bound to be more out here." The voice was not far now.

Another responded. "Not necessarily. They only exile men once a week."

"Just keep looking."

The men finally came into view through a break in the leaves, and she tensed, gripping Keeva's arm. He glanced back at her, but she didn't take her eyes off the three men. She'd seen them before and one of them was Kindred of Mind.

They continued along the edge of the jungle. She'd just relaxed her grip but held to Keeva when one of them spoke again.

"Wait. I sense someone."

Damn, that's what she was afraid of.

Keeva took that moment to raise his hand. A loud noise far to the east of where they were reverberated through the jungle.

"Geetic, go!" The command came from another man.

The sound of a whirlwind headed off toward the area of the noise followed by the pounding steps of two men.

She was about to release Keeva's arm when he lifted his hand again and another noise even farther away sounded.

He looked back at her with a grimace.

He'd made those noises with the plants, but because they were far away, it wearied him.

She leaned closer and kept her voice to a whisper. "Leaf. Dirk."

He turned his face toward her, so close she could see the flecks of gold in his eyes. She pulled back.

He turned his head more and spoke to her ear. "You want to leave at dark, but I think we should go now."

His breath at her ear tickled and she pulled her shoulder up. With her hand, she turned his face away and spoke into his ear. "Nu." She paused, not sure how to tell him that the lawbreakers wandered the jungle more while Helios was up.

She sat back and pointed to the sky with her free hand, then walked two fingers across his forearm, the dark hair there felt strange, but she was most concerned with communicating. Then she pointed up again and brought her finger down to the horizon. She put her two fingers on his arm only this time straight down.

He grinned before he turned her face away and spoke into her ear again, but not as close. "When it is dark, the lawbreakers go to sleep?"

Thrilled, she faced him and nodded, but his face was so close, she stopped. A strange tingle spread over her body. She pulled away, releasing his arm at the same time.

His smile disappeared.

She liked it better when he smiled. She touched him again and it returned. She pointed at him and closed her eyes, then opened them.

"You want me to sleep again."

She nodded, pleased to see he not only understood, but kept his voice quiet. She held up her arm and flexed her biceps then pointed at him.

"You want me to get stronger."

She nodded again. She started to move her hand but he caught it in his.

"I understand. I will need my strength to move tonight."

A stronger tingle moved from where he held her hand all the way to her chest before she pulled her hand away to lay it on his hand. She nodded quickly, then let him go.

This time he didn't frown. Instead, he leaned his head back against the trunk and closed his eyes.

She was pleased with him, despite the odd feelings he caused in her. Her dads never obeyed her mother so quickly. It may be that Keeva was hurt and he understood that he had to listen to her directions to get well. She hoped it was more than that.

Despite her reticence toward men, she found she liked having someone to communicate with. Besides, if he could help her speak, she might be able to find her grandparents once inside Naralina. Being invisible and not being able to speak would have made that impossible. Once again, she was thankful she'd missed the portal opening into Naralina.

She peered out through the high branches, listening intently for any movement, but the only sounds were the calls of the elseire and caball birds.

Excited by both the prospect of talking and being seen, she settled herself in for a long day of being on alert.

Keeva woke for the third time that day to find the sun well set. He looked toward the area Mya should be. "Are you here?"

"Yes." Her movement on the tree limb told him she was repositioning. "Food."

The second she touched his arm, he could see her as well as the cold pig ribs she held out to him, but it was her violet eyes catching the ambient light that held him spellbound.

"Eat."

"Right. Thank you." He moved his gaze from her and took the food. It had been the same the other two times he'd woken. She wanted him to regain his strength and he could definitely feel it returning. Biting into the first rib, he savored the cold meat like it had just come off the fire. He couldn't believe how sleeping could cause him such an appetite.

"Keeva, Mya, go soon."

He nodded, Mya's vocabulary was already improving with just the few talks they had when he was awake. The only problem he could foresee was how to get into Naralina. He'd walked around the whole city and hadn't found a way back in.

He swallowed the last of the first rib and wiped his mouth on the piece of hesta she handed him. That she allowed him to see her more now told him a lot about her trust in him. A trust he'd never betray. "I have checked Naralina. There is no way to return to the city without a portal."

"Go Mya huum." She made the statement like a command, as usual.

Her home. Of course, where else would they go? She would have others who could help him get back into the city. He needed to start thinking like a Discoverist instead of a Naralinian. "Home. We'll go to your home."

"Yes, Mya home."

"If it is your home, you would say—"

"Eat. Now."

"Right." Obviously now was not the time to be a teacher either. He started in on the second rib. Mya's life growing up in the jungle had her thinking very differently than himself. Did that mean her social structure was small, maybe one or two families?

His curiosity gathered steam again at the thought of seeing where she lived, meeting her family, discovering how they survived outside the walled cities of Eden.

He ate his meal quickly and washed it down with the last of the water in the container Mya had refilled before they moved to the tree top. After finishing, he held out the bones wrapped in the hesta piece. "Do you want to put those in your bag?"

When there was no answer, he looked down to the darkening ground, his heart stopping at the thought Mya might have fallen. As he peered through the branches, a vine appeared next to him. She'd already climbed down.

That she was safe relieved him, but it was quickly followed by irritation. The least she could have done is let him know she was climbing down. Not happy at her rudeness, he dropped the bones to the ground, so he wouldn't have to worry about them.

"Ack. No it." Mya's voice from below immediately squashed his upset.

Now he really was an ithio. "I apologize. I did not see you."

The grunt from below told him she didn't like his answer.

He needed to focus on what was important like she did. Quickly, he undid the vine that held him to the tree, then he called the four other vines and wrapped them around his limbs.

Taking a deep breath, he directed the vines to lower him to the ground. This time he had the energy to come down in a standing position. He released all the vines except one, holding onto it as he readjusted to standing again. "Is your home far?"

Mya touched him and nodded.

For the first time he could see the full length of her. She was no more than a hand's length shorter than him, and her silky black hair fell to her knees. Her legs were very long and muscular, her arms also long but toned and feminine. Her breasts, which he'd not seen before because of her hair, were now revealed to be a perfect handful with small areolas. Beneath them was a stomach rippled with muscle but delicate as her waist pulled in to curve back out at her hips.

She was breathtaking.

When his gaze moved to her face again, her brow furrowed. "Keeva walk?"

Her question was like a cold box to a hot meal. "I think I can. I just needed to get my balance." He let go of the vine and took a step. His legs were stiff, but Mya must have found him in time to keep him from losing too much muscle.

Nodding, she turned, letting go of him.

"Wait. I cannot see to follow you if you are not touching me." He waited.

Finally, she touched his arm, and relief washed through him. In his condition, he probably wouldn't last many days without her.

She rolled her eyes.

He wasn't sure if she thought it silly that he had to touch her or if she meant she was an ithio for forgetting. It didn't matter as long as she was with him now. He moved her hand down to his. "Take my hand. It will be easier to walk together this way."

She looked down at where their hands were joined as if she'd never held anyone's hand. But when she looked up, her sadness was so startling that he swallowed hard. He was about to ask what made her so, but she turned her face and began to walk, forcing him to focus on putting one foot in front of the other.

Mya's movements reminded him of a tigran he'd seen in the Discoverist Oasis in Naralina. There were many types of animals living there for citizens to view, but her movements were most like the large camouflaged cat. That she'd grown up in the jungle was apparent by the way she travelled so quietly, avoiding bushes like the poisonous racide and stepping over logs that he almost missed seeing.

The night grew darker and darker causing Mya to stop and frown. He had no directions to give her, so he kept quiet, conserving his energy for as long as possible. After a few hours, she stopped next to a very large salis bush. "Stay."

Before he could question her, she slipped her hand from his and disappeared. Not happy she'd learned the word "stay" from their earlier conversations and had used it to leave him, he sat on the ground to rest and worry.

It was odd depending on a woman. He and his filoz had started following a couple of women on Earth five years ago. Though they were all anxious to have a beloved of their own, they were going about it the traditional way of watching for a long time, though watching more than one at a time was a modern twist. Many new filoz were doing it.

In one way, it was good in that by choosing one woman over another because she was better suited meant less chance of rejection. Women who rejected their filoz chose to reside in a Pleasure Temple. If that happened that left the filoz with a second choice. Luckily, from what he'd heard, most women were happy to have two or more men for their agapaytos. But on the other hand, if there were less women going into the Temples, it meant less men would have their sexual urges taken care of and that could cause problems later.

One thing remained the same. Women were to be protected and cared for by men. Having Mya lead him, take care of him, hunt for him, had his male instincts chaffing, but he was intelligent enough to understand it was a temporary situation. Even though she wasn't one of his chosen ones, he would protect her like he would any other woman.

So, where was she? The fact that she was unseeable did not help his psyche. He stared hard at the undergrowth, watching to see if a stick on the ground moved or a bush leaf fluttered, but it had become so dark, even with his excellent eyesight, he could barely see the bush two steps away.

He listened but the only sound in the jungle was the idonee, one of the few nocturnally active birds on Eden. He didn't doubt the ferocious direlots and shy rhybats were about, too. Even grendals could be about, the tusked boars that trampled anything in their path. He wasn't anxious to see a grendal in its natural habitat. Those animals were twice as big as havling pigs and were more the hunter than the prey.

It had never occurred to him before, but Grandall of the Ruling Circle had a name very close to a grendal. Was it prophetic his parents named him so. He certainly trampled anyone in his way.

A swish of a leaf next to him caught his attention. In the next moment, Mya appeared standing before him, her hand on his shoulder.

His whole body relaxed to see she was safe.

She lowered herself to the ground, moving her hand down his arm, which with any other woman would be a caress, but it was obvious she only did it so he could see her. "Dark. Wade fer Bennis."

He mouthed her words as his mind sifted through possible meanings. That it was darker than the depths of the Latzeran Sea was obvious and since she sat, he interpreted "wade" to mean "wait," especially as she often confused the "d" and "t" sounds. Bennis had to mean Bendis, Eden's second moon which only shone a few nights a month, but the word "fer" had him frowning. Did she mean fur? Dark. Wait fer Bendis.

He stared at her in surprise. She'd used a connecting word for the first time. "Wait for Bendis. We need to wait here until the second moon rises?"

She nodded, pleased he understood.

Not half as pleased as he was that she was moving so quickly in her language. "I have lost count of my days. Is Bendis to rise tonight?"

Again, she nodded, not ready to talk more than she had to, from what he could tell. And as much as he wanted to, he understood the need for quiet. So, he sat silent next to her, fascinated by her absolute stillness.

Though her eyes moved as she scanned their environment, he could tell she was listening far harder. In the darkness they found themselves in, he wasn't surprised. Again, he found himself wishing he could learn all about how she grew up, what she might have been taught, who her family was, how she could even exist.

Mya's head turned away from him moments before he heard the noise as well. It was a scratching noise. Her hand in his tightened as she listened intently, still not moving. The sound came closer. There was two or three short scratches and a pause. Other than that, only the idonee interrupted the night.

If it was a grendal, he could lift them into a tree, but it would be best if he did it before the animal saw, or rather, smelled them.

Her hand relaxed at she turned her face toward him with a soft smile. "Wechet."

His heart slowed as his hand, already lifted to move them, lowered to the ground. Welchets were of no threat. Not that they were domesticated or pets, but they were harmless to Edenists. He'd already had the pleasure of meeting one wild welchet.

Their fur looked spikey, but wasn't, and their small tusks that grew from their bottom jaws were for digging the dirt to find bugs. They were somewhat skittish from what he'd already experienced and ran faster than almost all the mammals on Eden.

The scratching came closer and his excitement grew. At the Discoverist Oasis in Naralina, there was a welchet area, but the animals always hid from viewers, coming out at night when the Oasis was closed. Now he could see one from a sitting position and just maybe it wouldn't hurry away.

Mya raised her hand and pointed.

He peered at the large salis bush, his breathing shallow as

he waited to see the little animal. The scratching grew louder and finally the leaves of the bush moved. At the sight of the welchet he grinned.

It was much bigger than the one who had visited him while he lay on the ground. If he stood, its back would come almost to his knees and the tusks it was using to scratch the ground looked more intimidating. Its fur didn't appear soft but from the little one, he knew it was. The appearance was a defense mechanism for animals which relied on sight.

His hand remained in Mya's as the welchet, so focused on the ground, headed toward her thigh.

She laid her hand on the ground, palm up.

The welchet's black nose pulled out of examining a hole it had dug with its tusks, stepped forward and stopped as it sniffed Mya's hand. When it had determined she wasn't a threat, it pushed its face against her palm.

She smiled as she rubbed the animal's head, but Keeva was too fascinated by her lips to pay much attention. When Mya smiled, her usual serious visage transformed. If he was a painter or sculptor, he'd try to recreate it so he'd always have it.

Refocusing his attention, she moved his hand in hers toward the welchet and let the animal sniff.

Its cold nose was soft, and when it rubbed against his hand, Mya let go and he stroked the welchet like she had. The fur was just as soft as the smaller one who pushed against him beneath the salis bush. Sharing this experience with Mya made it more special than the first one.

When the welchet was done with them, it simply moved away, continuing its search for food.

"Thank you for that." He squeezed Mya's hand. Though he could see her, he found he liked holding her hand.

She shrugged. "Jist a wechet."

He leaned in, but not too close to tickle her ear, but enough to inhale her flowery scent and have it permeate his brain. "Just a welchet."

"Just a welchet." Her gaze was steady as she concentrated on forming the words.

He smiled. "Good."

She looked away as if embarrassed, but he didn't think that was why. He scanned the darkness but didn't see anything to catch her attention. At least she didn't take her hand from his. He hoped she would get used to the feeling of touching him since it was the only way to see her.

Or was it? He opened his mouth, but quickly shut it. Now was not the time to ask. They were deep in the jungle and at any moment they might have to flee to the trees. He kept his silence, making up a list of questions in his head that he planned to ask her once they made it to her home.

Though he felt vulnerable sitting still for so long, it was allowing him to rest…and allowed him to touch her. He would have to be dead not to want to touch her. Her skin was darker than the Earth women his filoz had decided upon, and he loved its texture. Even the women in the Pleasure Temples didn't have skin so smooth.

Suddenly, she slipped her hand from his, but he could hear the soft fabric of the bag she tied around her waist. In Naralina, men used a different type of bag and secured it to their backs to keep it out of their way. She touched his thigh with one hand and held out a long, skinny ondile. "Eat. Good for Keeva."

He squelched the excitement that raced to his groin and took the white vegetable from her. It had been washed after being pulled from the ground. She'd been busy the first day they'd met. He'd only found one of these in all the days he'd been walking through the jungle around Naralina looking for a way in.

Biting into it, he savored the raw flavor. Absently, he wondered how Mya would cook it up if she had the chance. She must have a mother who excelled in spices. He continued to eat the ondile, happy for the distraction and the nourishment. He had no idea how far they'd come, but he had a feeling they still had decods to go.

He'd just finished the last of the hard vegetable when Mya took his hand again and rose. He quickly followed suit, ready to continue their journey.

She pointed. "Bendis."

At first, he didn't see anything, but then he noticed a faint pink glow on the leaves to their left and peered through the undergrowth. They stood still as the light slowly grew brighter and finally the top edge of the pink moon broke the horizon, lighting up the jungle with a dappled rose hue.

Mya's demeanor changed from uncertain to excited. "Come." She didn't wait for an answer, but immediately turned in the opposite direction and dove straight into the jungle.

Evidently, she'd needed the moon to find her way home. He kept pace with her, not wanting to delay them getting to safety, but his larger body didn't fit between the branches of the bushes as easily as hers, and he was thankful more than once for the hesta strips she'd tied around his wounds. He could telepath his wish to pass to the vegetation and have it move aside, but in his weakened condition and not knowing how far they still had to go, he refrained from using his ability.

Mya didn't run, but she didn't walk either. Her pace was quick and after a few more hours, his wounds seemed to pound with every step. Their shadows, which had been in front of them, were now gone completely as Bendis had risen, which made finding his way between the bushes a bit easier.

She stopped suddenly and brushed her thumb across her chest. He didn't say a word, listening for what it was she'd heard. He waited, the pink of the moon causing the jungle to look like the inside of a Naralina bath house, only those didn't have quite as many plants.

A moan broke the silence, and he tensed.

An answering moan was followed by a snort, which had the hair on the back of his neck rising.

Mya pointed to the right then turned left and started walking again. It wasn't long before a thud sounded behind them. He tugged on her hand and mouthed the words "What is it?"

She answered in a whisper. "Firoone. Fide." She turned as if that was all there was to say and continued.

He held her hand, careful not to slow her down. It had something to do with a Feroon. That much he understood. The large animals were pretty harmless unless it was mating seas—oh, that's what it was, a *fight* between two males. He hadn't realized they fought at night as well as in the day. Then again, he was no expert on the jungle, though many of his friends thought he was.

He'd studied it more than most Naralinians because of his Kindred. The only plants in Naralina were the ones that were cultivated. Controlling wild ones had a different feel to it. It made him feel strong as if just being around so much plant life could feed his soul.

Their walk, however, did not. When they'd travelled for another couple of hours after hearing the feroons, he finally gave Mya a tug. She stopped, looked at him and scowled. "Sit." She pointed at the ground.

He must look pretty bad, so he did as he was told.

She crouched down in front of him, her foot touching his knee. Untying her bag, she pulled out another sack and opened it. When her hand came out, a baka bun was in her palm.

He stared in amazement. How did she get a baka bun? The round pastry filled with a citrusy gel was a favorite of his. Besides the flavor, the added benefit to baka buns was they were known to give energy, much like ambrosia, though most people ate them simply because they tasted so good.

She took his hand and placed the bun on his palm. "Eat."

He stared, still in shock that she had one. Taking a bite, he closed his eyes as the tart, thick gel filled his mouth. Opening his eyes, he found Mya watching him. "Thank you. Did you make this?"

She nodded quickly before peering into the jungle around them.

Her quick dismissal of him didn't sit well though he had no idea what he expected. Just because she helped him, didn't mean she felt anything for him. It didn't matter anyway since he had two chosen ones with his filoz. He must be more tired than he thought.

He took another bite and chewed quickly. If he was correct, they didn't have much more night left. Their shadows were now behind them. He swallowed. As was Naralina. He hoped Mya and a member of her family could open a portal for him so he could get back into the city. He needed to find someone he could tell about Grandall's plan, which had no doubt been put into effect by now.

Popping the rest of the baka bun into his mouth, he tugged on Mya's hand to get her attention.

She looked at him and the corner of her mouth quirked up. She reached out with her finger and wiped something from the corner of his lip then licked it off.

His cock jumped as his entire abdomen tightened.

Oblivious, she rose, tugging him to stand.

By the Crius, he shouldn't be attracted to Mya. The sooner they arrived at her home, the better. He rose, but she didn't notice his sexual interest, her violet gaze finding his.

"No for." She turned away and resumed their walk.

No for had to mean not far. Good. The sooner he was among her family members and community, the better…for both of them.

It was another hour before Mya stopped again, once again running her thumb over her chest above her breasts.

He swallowed hard as his gaze dipped lower and noticed her nipples had become hard as the air had cooled.

A grunt and a short squeal pierced the air. Grendals.

Mya didn't even look at him, but he could tell by the way she squeezed his hand that she was afraid. Instead, she moved off to the side, walking slowly and quietly. He tried to do the same, but he wasn't as good at it.

Another grunt sounded closer, like the pack of grendals may have picked up their sent. Bushes being swept aside sounded behind them.

Mya tugged his hand and started to run. He wanted to tell

her he could lift them up, but he was so weak now, he doubted he could do so for both of them.

Suddenly, she stopped and pulled him down to the ground. Before he could ask what she was doing, she set his hand on her ankle and crawled between the fragile branches of a sherry flower bush.

Two things hit him at the same time, that Mya's birthmark was on her very smooth rounded ass and he wanted to sneeze even as his stomach recoiled at the overpowering scent of the sherry flower.

Mya continued forward, the sloping ground proving they were burrowing into Eden like a rhybat, though he'd never seen a hole this large anywhere.

Roots he sensed above him calmed his initial nervousness at crawling into such a black hole, but if he was there with Mya, it would be a pleasure. He scowled in the darkness at himself for even thinking that.

They hadn't gone far when Mya reached back, grabbed his hand in hers again and rose. "Sten."

He did as she requested and stood, surprised that he could. He still couldn't see her, so when she let go of his hand, he didn't feel as nervous as he usually did, sensing they were safe. He couldn't even hear the grendals anymore.

A light flared as if floating in mid-air and he stared at his surroundings. He definitely wasn't anywhere near Naralina.

Haldone stood before the large boulders that appeared to be a solid wall at the edge of the small clearing. Wind had wiped away any trace that less than a turn of Selene ago, more than a dozen

Edenists had left this very spot to topple an unethical ruler and overthrow the entire Ruling Circle of Naralina.

Then again, there'd been nothing left at the savinstone monolith either where Jerumbala had said the lawbreakers attacked. He'd hoped to find a trail, but there was nothing, just like this clearing.

Besides a few tigran paw prints on the ground, there was also nothing to suggest that anyone lived behind what looked to be solid rock. Of course, that was all an illusion created by Theron's reflection ability and some eyllen. The energy rock when combined with an Edenist's ability could make anything last forever.

Last time he was in the cave, he had reinforced the outside walls and window with his own ability to create hard air and combined that with eyllen, making it a much safer place to inhabit.

He strode toward the giant boulders and ducking, in case he missed the correct spot, he reached his hand out in front of him. Just as he touched the door, he broke through the reflection to see the entrance. Lifting the latch, he stepped into the living area of what others referred to as Theron's Cave.

But Theron lived in Loraleaf now and while he'd made a living space of this area many turns of Selene ago, Haldone planned only to use it as a base for his quest. His primary goal in that was to find Mya, who he hoped could point him in the direction of the lawbreakers. If she was Crius, as he suspected, she may have powers far surpassing the lawbreakers, and what better ally to have at his side?

He'd come to the conclusion she was Crius after being stunned by her beauty the first time he'd gazed at her in Akasha's blue light. She couldn't be Edenist because no women were born on Eden, so she must be Crius, the alien race that seeded Eden with humans from Earth.

It made sense. No one knew what the Crius looked like, but since no one had ever seen them and Mya was invisible, it made sense that she could be Crius. Plus, he believed, since seeing Mya, that the Crius knew the planet would not be conducive to female births, but it didn't matter because they were all female. For all the Naralinians knew, the Crius had been procreating with Edenists in the jungle for centuries, or maybe they inhabited an undiscovered city. Mya could even possibly be a lawbreaker in Crius culture.

Latching the door behind him with dead infragile vine, which no living Edenist could break except Jahl, he pulled his bag from his back, and dropped it on the longseat. The cold box sat on the floor against the side wall, so he crouched down and opened it to find plenty of ambrosia and ales, but no food, which was just as well. A quick inventory of the cabinet above showed a few items he could use, but that wasn't his first priority.

He quickly untied his pack and transferred the food Jerumbala had given him to the cold box. Though there was a sleeping room with a bathroom off it and a storage room, he chose the middle door on the back wall and opened it. Even with only the diffused light of the front window, the green table and chairs he'd made filled with Akasha's green light still glowed.

This was where they had made plans to take the city back from Grandall. Though not everything had gone as smoothly as they had hoped, he and Sandale had freed their fathers and helped to set up a new Ruling Circle.

He was happy for his brother that he'd formed a filoz, but he had become a completely different man than the one he'd grown up with. That the lawbreakers had caused so much angst and heartache for Sandale and their whole family was why he'd come to the cave. He did not care what anyone else said, the lawbreaker who caused that pain needed to be punished.

And the key to that was finding Mya. It might also be the only key to getting her out of his mind.

Scanning the room, he was happy to find a shiner still hung from the ceiling. Quickly, he grabbed it from its hook and opened the side cover a fraction. Light filled the room, causing the table to shimmer brightly as the green light danced within the hard outlines of air he'd created.

Pride rose within him. It was exactly the type of table where greatness began. He would use it to strategize his attack on the lawbreakers. But first he needed to find them and to do that, he needed Mya. Walking to the end of the narrow room, he opened the door in the wall he'd created last time he was there and stepped into the tunnel of the cave.

The light dimmed as it was absorbed by the pitch blackness of the space. Farther along there would be small eyllen deposits in the walls that would look like tiny orange stars, but he wasn't there yet.

His quandary was how to find Mya when she was invisible. Last time, they'd discovered her because as he'd chipped away at the eyllen, she'd hit him over the head with a large rock. He rubbed the back of his head where a small scar still reminded him of the head pains he'd suffered for days afterward. He hadn't had time to seek a healer as it had taken a while to convince his mother and fathers that he needed to leave with the men from Loraleaf and that he would be safe.

So here he was, his plans to get to her successful, but now he had to find an invisible woman. It wasn't as if he could produce blue light. If he hadn't had the head pains, he probably would have asked Akasha for a shiner made from blue light, if that were possible. Since that was how they discovered Mya in the first place, it would have been convenient right now.

He still remembered every detail of the invisible female. Waves of dark hair down to knees, long toned limbs, pert breasts, a graceful neck upon which was the most beautiful face he'd ever seen. Even in the blue light cast upon her, he could see her eyes had the same color as Sandale's, only a more vibrant purple. Her nose was straight and rounded at the end, her cheek bones high, her lips full. She appeared delicate, helpless, except for the large rock she'd held in her soft looking hand.

He shook his head. He had to find her. There had been no birthmark anywhere to blemish her skin, plus there was no such thing as a female Edenist, which meant she had to be from another planet. He couldn't imagine her to be anything but Crius.

Maybe if he chipped away at more eyllen, she might come to him, but if she knocked him out before he spoke to her, that would not help. Besides, he was in no hurry to suffer head pains again for days. Once he found her, he could box her in with him until she told him where the lawbreakers were, but his air boxes wouldn't help him find her…or would they?

As the idea formed, he grinned. He would start from where he was and make a narrow box. Then he could move through it, to see if he touched anything he couldn't see. If he kept the box narrow enough, he could do a slice of the cave at a time, starting the next box at the end of the last.

Pleased with his plan he began with an air box from the outside wall of Theron's living area to just arm's length. Once formed, he walked through it. When he felt nothing, he let himself out of it and kept the outside wall up. It would take a while, but he was determined.

He set down the shiner and prepared to make a new box when another thought occurred. Would Mya come if he called her? "Mya, I need your help. Will you help me?" He waited almost breathless, hoping to feel a touch on his arm and not a rock in his back. He tried to be patient, not a strength of his, but after a while, it was clear she wouldn't be coming to his aid.

Fine. He wasn't going to give up. He never gave up on something he'd set his mind to and he wouldn't start now. Not only was he determined to punish the lawbreakers, he was also determined to make contact with a being like Mya once again.

Creating another box, he swept through it, but it was clearly empty. Stepping outside it, he created another. He continued to sweep the space, letting all the former boxes dissipate as they would while he worked on new ones.

"Scrat." He'd completely forgotten that there'd been an intersection of tunnels. Last time, he'd taken the one to the left and had found eyllen. He'd also found Mya down there. With no other recourse, he used a small bit of the eyllen within the shiner to make his air wall on the tunnel to Theron's cave solid. He could always undo it to get back there.

Opening the shiner a little wider to get a similar amount of light, he set up another solid air wall at the entrance to the new tunnel, before starting the process over again. Slowly, he worked his way through it. The purple striations in the slick black rock told him he was coming closer to the spot where he'd harvested the eyllen to use for the furniture he'd made.

Eyllen was the only way to make something created with an Edenist ability last beyond a certain length of time. For him, anything he created wouldn't last more than a couple hours unless energized by eyllen. Sandale's ability to calm or on more recent uses, cause unconsciousness could last for over a day if he wanted it to, but he was a far more patient man.

Soon teal veins ran beside the purple ones in the black walls until the first chips of orange eyllen could be seen. It wasn't long before he arrived at the place where he'd been hit on the head. He called out to Mya once again, but there was no response of any kind.

Haldone continued, noticing that the eyllen pieces grew larger as he moved deeper into the cave, yet it felt cooler as the floor's decline grew to be more than just gradual. When the tunnel opened up into yet another domed area, he paused, his frustration disintegrating at the beauty of the cave.

It was filled with large glowing eyllen rocks, which made the teal shimmer and the purple glow. Actually, the eyllen itself appeared to pulse, causing the floor beneath his feet to vibrate in sync with it. He'd never seen so much eyllen in one place. The ground was littered with it beneath the surface, but except for the last time he'd been in Theron's cave, he'd never seen it showing through and yet not exploding.

Now, he was pleased that he hadn't found Mya because the domed area was not a safe place. One brush against the orange rock could cause air to reach the eyllen in that one piece which would set off an explosion that would have a ripple effect among the rest of the rocks. He counted five tunnels branching off from the vibrating dome and hoped Mya didn't live down one of those. If she did, he'd be back.

Quickly, he turned, releasing his air walls until he reached the intersection he'd come from. Then he used the eyllen from the shiner to create a permanent wall so Mya or anyone couldn't venture down that tunnel.

There were three more tunnels off the intersection he was at, which he silently dubbed the safe intersection. As much as he wanted to find Mya, his hungry stomach was telling him he needed to get back to the living quarters. He'd arrived after midday and it felt like it might be nightfall.

Turning to retrace his steps, he opened his permanent wall then sealed it again. He would continue through the tunnels after a good night's sleep. Though he was delayed, he was far closer to his goal than he had been two weeks ago, or even yesterday. Tomorrow, he would find Mya, one way or another.

CHAPTER FIVE

Mya stepped past a pile of feroon skins and strode around the corner of the tunnel. There she pulled a hesta off one of the pegs she'd driven into the cave wall and turned back to find Keeva only a step away. She stumbled back to keep from running into him.

"Ack." Losing her balance, she started to fall backward when Keeva's hand grasped the elbow of her arm holding the shiner.

He pulled her and she fell against him. Air whooshed from his mouth as her body made contact with his.

Immediately, the warmth of his skin heated hers and the tingles she'd felt earlier started, only much stronger now. Her breasts felt on fire yet she held the shiner in her hand.

"Are you unharmed?" His voice, so much deeper than her own, soothed her and excited her at the same time.

Quickly, she stepped back, but let him continue to hold her arm. Just having that space between them helped her regain her mental balance. "Yes." She crouched down and held up the hesta she'd dropped. "Keeva, sleep."

He looked past her into the darkness of the tunnel. "Are we in your home?" His lowered brow showed he was either confused or unsure. Sometimes it was hard to tell.

She pointed into the darkness. "Hors wulking more." She gestured toward the pile of siris webbing behind him. "Sleep now."

He continued to look past her, then moved to the opposite wall. "Is this a picture?

She stepped next to him, the shiner illuminating her painting of the first feroon she'd ever killed. She wasn't as good at hunting or painting back then, but she had cried even as she cut up the meat and hauled it down into her caves. "Yes."

Keeva touched the dried paint reverently. "It is very real looking. Was it here when you came here?"

She preened at his unintended compliment. "No. Mya paint."

He turned and not finding her, reached out his hand, brushing her nipple before moving his hand to her shoulder. The tingles sped like fire to her belly and she gasped.

"I cannot believe you did this?"

He stared into her eyes, his warm ones taking the sting from his words.

"I do." She tightened her mouth willing him to believe her.

"You did. You are not only beautiful, but you also create beautiful art."

Her nipples started to tingle even though he and she weren't touching and it confused her. She frowned at him. "Nuff quesdons. Sleep now."

He finally nodded. "You are right. Enough questions. I need more rest before I continue. Are we safe in here?"

She nodded. "Yes. Come." She didn't wait for him to agree but brought him over to the large pile of webbing that was produced by the siri caterpillari and was used to fill head puffs. She'd collected a lot this year but planned to gather more before moving it into her home, at least that had been the plan before she decided to go to Naralina and find her family.

"You want me to sleep on this? Where will you sleep?"

She pointed back to the pile of feroon skins from those she'd killed for meat. On hooks above it were two more hestas. She kept them there for when she came in this way in case she was wet from rain.

"No, you should sleep here. I'll sleep there." He pointed to the feroon skins.

She sighed as she shook her head. This reminded her of an argument her mother had with one of her fathers when he'd broken his arm. "No. Keeva herd. Mya no."

He opened his mouth, but she pushed the hesta against his chest. "Sleep." It was her home, and he needed to do what she said. She pulled her arm from his grasp and walked with the shiner back to the feroon skins. Though she'd prefer her bed, they'd walked through the night and he needed to rest. It was still a couple hours underground to get home.

She pulled another hesta down and rolled it into a hard head puff. Spreading the skins out a little more, she bent over and laid the rolled blanket at one end. When she straightened to get the last hesta, she caught Keeva staring in her direction, standing motionless, his hesta clasped to his chest. She scowled and pointed to the siris webbing. "Sleep."

As if waking from a trance, he blinked and spun around.

She shook her head at his stubborn behavior and pulled the hesta off its peg and spread it on the skins. Untying her bag, she set it next to the pile before shutting the shiner and lying down. Covering herself, she closed her eyes, happy to rest. Her body relaxed into the skins, but her mind wouldn't go to sleep.

Keeva was nice, like the other Edenists who had come to her tunnels. She trusted him more than any other. He was the only one she'd spoken to since her parents had been taken and killed by the lawbreakers. He also had already taught her how to say many of the words in her head so they sounded the same when she spoke. She wanted to learn how to say them all.

What would he think of her home? Would he stay with her? Help her get back to Naralina when he was well? Edenists healed very quickly.

Her mother said that on Earth there were diseases and something called infections and cancers that could harm humans, but on Eden there were no such things. Keeva would probably be completely healed in a few more days.

She could tell him about the settlement with teal walls and take him there. Then they could portal into Naralina and find her grandparents. Men came and went from the settlement all the time. She was constantly having to avoid them as they walked the area for miles around.

She'd often thought about going there herself, but she wasn't sure if they were nice like Keeva. Plus, she didn't know for sure until Keeva had touched her that anyone would be able to see her, or rather anyone without a blue light ability.

She rolled over, readjusting her position on the leather pile. She'd hoped that those in the settlement would scare away the lawbreakers who followed Strong Mind, as she called him. He scared her. Luckily, when he wasn't hunting for food or Edenists near Naralina, he stayed in one area far away from her cave. Before Theron had made the south cave entrance look like rock, Strong Mind had sent two men into her cave.

They quickly got lost in the darkness, and she scared them back out by snorting like a pack of grendals. That was one reason she'd left Theron alone. By building his living area at that entrance, he actually made her tunnels safer.

Around the corner, Keeva's breathing fell into a steady rhythm. She grinned. He was so curious about her life and everything having to do with the jungle. She could teach him and he could teach her.

Maybe he could explain why she felt tingles when they touched in any way besides their hands and arms. Maybe it was a reaction between all Kindred of Eden and Kindred of Light people. Her mom was from Earth, but her dads were Kindred of Air and Kindred of Mind. She didn't remember their names. They were just mom, Air dad and Mind dad.

She rolled over and stared at her bag in the darkness. The picture of her parents taken on Earth shortly before they'd been captured was safely inside. It was her most prized possession. Closing her eyes, she thought of a happy time when they were all together, relaxing finally as sleep overtook her.

~~*~~

Mya grasped Keeva's hand as they made their way through her tunnels. Now that they were safe, she found she had a lot more patience with him.

"How long have you lived beneath the surface of Eden?" His fifth question in less than a hundred steps had her smiling.

"Aw my live."

"All your life."

"Yes, all my life." She didn't mind answering him since he was teaching her to speak the words in her head correctly.

Keeva stopped for the third time in the last hour. "This one is stunning." He stared at a painting she'd done after her Air father had found a logar. As a child, she'd been mesmerized by the animal, but it was far too skittish to allow her close, yet her Air father had been able to touch it. That made him amazing to her.

She was only eight-years-old at the time, but had painted it a couple years ago when she remembered that day after seeing a herd of logars crossing a river. She pointed to herself on top of the the logar. "No true. Rite hordy on Erdth."

"You did not ride the logar, just a horse on Earth?"

She nodded. "Not ride logar, horse on Earth."

"So you imagined yourself on a logar. That would be quite a feat."

She nodded again, then pulled him forward. He didn't resist, but she was sure he'd stop again before they arrived at her home.

"How did your parents come to live in these tunnels? Were they escaping lawbreakers? Part of a group who left Naralina generations ago? Were they born in the jungle, too?"

She shook her head. "No. My grenprints in Naralina." She looked at him for clarification on how to say the word correctly. She liked watching him since his face was handsome.

He rubbed the stubble on his jaw as if he was unused to having it. "Your grandparents?"

"Yes. Grandparents." Her mouth and tongue were forming the words easier.

"So, who else lives here?"

She shook her head again. "Nowin. Jist me."

She found her arm tugged as she continued to walk but he'd halted.

"Did you say no one. Just you?" Even in the light of the shiner she held, she could tell he wasn't happy.

"Yes. No one. Just me."

He pulled her a little closer. "What happened to your parents?"

It was too much to tell and at the idea of saying it out loud, her heart squeezed. She frowned. "Not want talk about."

He used his free hand to cup her cheek, starting the tingling again. "Was it the lawbreakers?"

She stared into his warm brown eyes, sensing a compassion she hadn't had from another Edenist since her parents. Water started to blur her sight at his caring, and her throat wouldn't let her say the word though she wanted to answer him. She nodded instead.

Keeva stroked her cheek with his thumb. "My heart cries for you. How long ago did you lose them?"

She swallowed hard, wanting to tell him. Her voice came out scratchy. "Thirdeen yers."

His eyes widened. "Thirteen years ago?"

She shook her head. "Thirteen years ode."

Keeva's mouth opened but no sound came out. Instead, he pulled her against him, dropping her hand and enfolding her in his embrace. A forgotten memory surfaced of her mother holding her the same way, and she relaxed against him.

He stroked her back, and it felt good. She lay her cheek against his shoulder. He smelled of siris webbing, air, and the wood scent she'd noticed when they were outside. That must be *his* scent. Her mother said every Edenist had a scent and some enhanced it with soap or oils of some kind. She liked how he smelled.

His face pressed on top of her head and another memory ignited of one of her fathers doing that. He said he kissed her head because he loved her. Did Keeva love her?

She pulled back, but he didn't let her go far.

"You are a remarkable woman, Mya." He lifted his hand and pushed her hair away from her face on one side. "If you were thirteen years-old then, would you tell me how old you are now?"

She gave him half a smile. "Tintysinin."

His brows lowered as he tried to understand her. She pulled up her free hand and held her fingers before his eyes. She closed her fist five times then held up only two fingers.

As understanding dawned, he smiled and his eyes crinkled. "Twenty-seven."

She nodded, matching his smile as she placed her hand on his chest. Immediately, tingles started up her arm, and she peered down at where they connected. Was it particular parts of his body? She looked up to ask him, but he scowled at her.

"By the Crius! Those lawbreakers deserve to be thrown into the Latzeran Sea with a boulder tied to their ankles!"

She didn't disagree, but she didn't like him looking so mean and his heart raced beneath her hand. She pulled out of his arms. "We go home."

He looked blank, staring near her but not at her. Then he rubbed the back of his neck. "Yes. Let us go to your home. If you have been on your own for..." He shook his head as if he didn't believe it, "for fourteen years, it must be a safe place."

It *was* a safe place. It was why she had stayed, first hoping one of her parents would escape the lawbreakers and then because they had always told her their home was safe. She had planned to live here forever.

She grasped his hand again. "This way."

He didn't say anything for a change, just fell into step beside her.

Her heart felt full, a feeling she hadn't had in a long time. That Keeva was angry at the lawbreakers because of what they did to her parents gave her that feeling. She'd thought all men in the jungle were lawbreakers, but in the last year she'd learned so much. Which was one of the reasons she'd decided to find her Naralinian grandparents and had stepped through a portal opened right outside her caves.

"Mya, why did your parents come here to live?"

At her name on his lips, she quirked a smile that he couldn't stay silent for long, but then she frowned. "Du nut new."

"You do not know." His hand in hers tightened. "Could it be that your grandparents and fathers had a fight?"

She shook her head vigorously. "No fight."

He didn't say anything else for a long time. She wanted him to. Maybe she should ask him a question. "What tingles men win tooch?"

He didn't respond so she looked at him. He frowned again, but he wasn't looking at her.

She slowed to a stop and opened her mouth, but he brushed his thumb across his chest.

He listened? For what? It was safe in her tunnels. She was about to tell him so when she heard it.

Footsteps.

Fear and anger collided inside her. Handing him the shiner, she ripped her hand from his grip and strode toward the sound.

"Ssht." Keeva's frustrated noise didn't deter her.

Someone was in her tunnels and they needed to get out! As she drew closer to the intersection where she needed to turn toward her home, her anger grew. If the lawbreakers were in her cave, she'd kill them.

The footsteps grew louder, but when she reached the intersection, she could tell they came from a different tunnel. That one led to a deep-water hole. Keeva's idea of drowning the lawbreakers with a boulder had merit.

The light from the shiner came closer, heralding Keeva's approach. Quickly, she headed down the tunnel where light shone close to the end where there was water. That could be convenient. Though the walls on this side of the water were sheer, the other side of the water hole had plenty of loose rocks she could use.

As she followed the curve of the tunnel and it dipped downward, she could see a man walking from one side of the tunnel to the other. It made her think of Geetic, the Strong Mind's twister man. The little man wasn't right in his head, what her mother called crazy.

Strong Mind controlled Geetic, playing with his mind and making him hurt people, even kill them, like her Air father. But the movement of the intruder wasn't Geetic. It was too methodical.

She walked quietly now, trying to see the man, but the light was behind him.

He stopped, picked up the light and moved it to the other

side of him then stepped around it. In that brief moment she recognized him.

Haldone.

She remembered him clearly. He had dark hair and dark eyes that went from gray to silver or gray to black. He had hair all along his jaw but it was very short, what her mother called a trimmed beard. On his hip was his birthmark, three dots straight across with two dots above, proclaiming him Kindred of Air.

She stopped. What was he doing this deep in her tunnels? He was supposed to be in Naralina. Last time she saw him she'd hit him over the head and when she'd been revealed by Akasha's blue light, he never stopped staring at her. She would have killed him if the woman named Toni hadn't explained they just needed some eyllen for the green table he made. It was a beautiful table and one she still wished to paint one day.

The light from Keeva's shiner started to reflect in the tunnel. Would Haldone hurt Keeva? When she'd first encountered Haldone, his gaze had been so intense, she dreamed of those silver eyes for two nights, even though he'd smiled and thanked her for the eyllen, which had softened his look.

She started to walk back toward Keeva when Haldone noticed the light.

"Who is there? Mya?"

He thought it was her?

"Who are you?" Keeva's voice rang through the tunnel and his pace quickened. "Mya, are you all right?"

Haldone picked up his shiner and held it high. "Keeva?" He strode past her to intercept Keeva. She quickly ran ahead. Keeva didn't need any more confrontations. He was still healing.

Keeva stopped. "Who is it?"

She ran faster to catch up.

"It is me, Haldone!"

Keeva's mouth broke into a wide smile. "Holy Bendis, what are you doing down here?"

She stopped a few paces away, her concern lessening.

Haldone came right up to Keeva and gave him a hug then stepped back. "What are you doing down here? Last I heard, you'd been exiled with no representation."

"You were there?" Keeva's anxiousness was palpable, and she stepped closer to him in case she needed to interfere.

Haldone shook his head, a frown on his face. "Not me, a member of Sandale's filoz. He said your father was angry. Last I was there, they were planning to search for you."

Keeva's worry was obvious in his brow. "I wish he would not. Grandall will exile him, too."

Haldone chuckled. "Not likely. The entire Ruling Circle has been overthrown. A lot has happened since you left."

Keeva's wide eyes told her he was completely surprised. She was happy that Toni and her friends had accomplished their plan. Toni had a lot of friends. That probably helped.

"I can tell you all the news this evening when I rest." Haldone motioned behind him.

"What are you doing?" Keeva's question was hers as well. She didn't like it that Haldone was so close to her home.

"I am creating air boxes so I can find Mya."

Keeva started to smile then stopped. "Why do you want her?"

She moved closer to him, pleased he didn't immediately reveal her presence.

"I need her help." Haldone stepped closer to Keeva, his gray eyes turning almost silver like the other friend of Toni's, Khaos. "How do you know Mya?"

She didn't like Haldone's gaze and shifted her weight to the balls of her feet, ready to make Keeva invisible and run away.

"How do *you* know her?"

Haldone crossed his arms. "I was here with the group planning Grandall's overthrow. We needed more eyllen and while I was working on removing some, we saw her."

"How could you see her? She is invisible."

She silently thanked Keeva for not revealing her vulnerability. Interesting that Haldone didn't mention she hit him on the head.

Haldone shook his head. "The man who was at your hearing, his name is Akasha, he can emit all the colors of the light spectrum. He used his blue light, and it revealed her."

Keeva looked as if he wasn't sure whether to believe Haldone. She stepped close but didn't touch him. Instead, she blew in his ear to let him know she was near.

He relaxed. "I know her because she saved my life."

That was a bit of an exaggeration. Yes, he was not doing well feeding himself and if direlots found him as she had…at the thought of Keeva dying, her heart squeezed. He was her first friend. She didn't want him to die.

"I knew it!" Haldone grinned, transforming his face into someone approachable.

Maybe she had judged him too harshly.

"Knew what?" Keeva looked as perplexed as she felt.

"I knew she was Crius."

This time Keeva laughed.

She was tempted to kick him in the shins. He had no business laughing, a phrase her mom used to use on her fathers, when he'd thought the same thing.

"Why are you laughing? She has to be." Haldone scowled now. "She is invisible, lives in these tunnels somewhere, and she cannot be an Edenist because she is female."

Keeva shook his head. "She is Kindred of Light. Her birthmark is on her ass. She reflects light so it appears she is not there. True, there are no men in Naralina who have this ability, but she is definitely an Edenist."

Haldone's mouth opened then abruptly shut.

"Why do you need her?"

She'd forgotten that Haldone had been looking for her, or maybe the better word for what he'd been doing was feeling for her. Now his movements made sense.

"I need to find the lawbreakers and discover what she knows about them. I am going to punish the one who played with Sandale's mind."

She gasped at Haldone's words.

His gaze snapped toward her. "Is she here?"

"Yes, she is here."

"How do you know? Can you see her? I thought you were Kindred of Eden." Haldone started to walk toward her, and she quickly stepped to the other side of Keeva and blew in his other ear.

"No, I cannot. Not right now."

Haldone stopped and crossed his arms. "Then how do you know she is here."

He turned his head toward her. "Mya, show him."

She didn't like that idea. "Safe?"

Haldone snapped his head toward her again. "Is she asking if I am safe?"

"Yes, she is. She has been through a lot. If she shows herself, you have to promise not to grab onto her. Understand?"

She wanted to hug Keeva again for saying that. If Haldone wouldn't grab her, she wouldn't mind showing him she was present.

He thought about it far too long, but finally nodded and sighed. "I agree."

She didn't like how reluctant he was. She didn't trust him.

Keeva motioned toward Haldone. "Go ahead. Show him."

Standing next to the two men, she grabbed Keeva's hand first.

"Wait, where did—"

She laid her other hand on Haldone's biceps.

He stared at her like he had the first time he'd seen her, his eyes turning lighter, more silver. It reminded her of a very fluffy dog she'd seen on Earth when she was little.

He didn't say anything, which unnerved her, so she withdrew her hand, unclasping Keeva's as well.

"As I said. She is here."

Haldone's glazed look cleared. "To be honest, I was afraid I'd imagined her last time I was here. She is so beautiful."

She smiled. She liked that.

Keeva nodded. "I know. It takes time to become accustomed to her."

Now she liked that even better. Her fathers always told her mother how pretty she was.

Keeva continued. "Mya, maybe we should all talk over some food. The more I eat, the faster I will heal."

She'd completely forgotten that he'd only had some berries when they woke up that she'd collected while he'd slept. "Yes." She took his hand and started for the end of the tunnel.

Keeva didn't move more than two steps. "Wait." He looked over his shoulder. "Just follow my shiner."

Heat rushed to her cheeks. She'd neglected Haldone. Her parents had taught her better. She waited until Haldone nodded then started forward again, this time Keeva walked with her.

Haldone followed the floating light back to the intersection he'd found. He'd explored two of the tunnels plus as far as he'd come in the one with the water hole. Every tunnel had paintings in them. At first, he'd tried to make sense of them, like some kind of story the Crius may have left behind, but the scenes were all different. Some from Eden and some from Earth. Now he could only think that Mya or someone in her family had painted them.

As they entered the intersection, they turned into the last tunnel.

There was no eyllen in the walls here, just more paintings. That made him feel better about Mya's home. Though he was disappointed she wasn't Crius, the fact she was a female Edenist was stunning.

She was stunning.

He'd thought over the weeks that he'd imagined she was as beautiful as he remembered, but now that he'd seen her, he'd been struck dumb all over again. She was even more attractive than he'd thought. Was it because she was an Edenist?

What kind of children would she have? He paused in his step at the thought. There'd never been a female Edenist who had a child. Would that child have multiple Kindreds and abilities? The idea was too new to fully grasp.

He strode ahead to catch up. Now that'd he'd found her, he didn't plan to let her disappear on him again. Not that he could see her now, but Keeva could. Though not jealous of the man, he was jealous that Mya trusted Keeva enough to hold his hand.

He wanted her to trust him, too. It was obvious she was intimidated by him. It was his fault. He'd always had that effect on women. It had taken months for a couple of women at the nearest Pleasure Temple to be comfortable with him.

It wasn't just with women. Men avoided his company as well, though if he was with a filoz of three or more, that worked fine. It's why he missed his brother so much when Sandale lived at Loraleaf and why he was determined to avenge him. Sandale had made it possible for him to function in Naralinian society.

But in the jungle, he had hopes that he may find his place.

Suddenly, the floating light seemed to get swallowed up by the darkness. Its feebleness moved to the side of what must be another large cavern. It hung there, then the whole space lit with small eyllen powered shiners that mimicked the eyllen dome he'd found the day before.

Keeva whistled, now visible and they both stood side by side to study the effect. Someone had gone to a lot of work, even painting teal and purple streaks in the doomed roof, the teal sparks reflecting the lights and the purple glowing. "It's an imitation of the eyllen cave."

"Yes!" Mya's disembodied voice came from across the room.

Her excitement that he recognized it made him feel connected to her in a way Keeva couldn't and he liked that. "Every light reflects the paint, just like it does the teal and purple striations there. Who did all this work?"

"Marder paded. Farder lights. Udder room denjir."

"What?"

Keeva touched his shoulder. "Her mother painted the ceiling and her father made the lights because the other room was too dangerous. If as you say it was eyllen, that would explain their concern." Keeva turned to face where Mya's voice had come from. "My guess is your mother loved the look of the other room, so your fathers wanted to recreate it for her."

"Yes." Mya's voice was closer now.

Mya couldn't speak correctly? He wanted to ask Keeva if she was unschooled, but he wouldn't insult her by doing so in her presence. "It is magnificent."

"Thank you. I lob." Her voice was very close to him, and he wanted to reach out to see her again, but as much as he wanted to touch her, he held back, accepting her hesitancy as his due.

He hoped he could win her trust like Keeva had. "I found the eyllen dome but thought it so dangerous I made a permanent air wall at the beginning of the tunnel."

"What?"

From her tone he could tell she wasn't pleased. "But I can take it down if you want. It is your home."

That seemed to pacify her because she didn't say anymore.

"I see a bed here. Do you sleep here?" Keeva had closed his shiner and moved to what looked like a very comfortable bed big enough for three grown men…or a filoz and their beloved.

"Yes. My mother and fathers bid. Mood from other room."

Stass, she learned fast. She'd already corrected three of her words since her last explanation. "I can see why you'd want to move the bed. Having it here makes it more like a home." He looked past the sleeping area to recognize a meal area with a cold box, food cabinet, table, and even a tiny stream running through it. Plus, there was a separate living area with a handmade longseat, chairs, and a floor covering. Yet, it was all in one open space beneath the lights.

Keeva had meandered to the meal area, obviously hungry. "Before I eat, is there a bathing room?"

Mya's voice came from near Keeva. "Yes. Turd tunnel."

"Third tunnel. This way?" Keeva pointed to another tunnel opening on the far wall.

"No. Nest."

"Next. So, this one?" Keeva moved to another tunnel right next to the first one. It was odd that two openings were so close together.

"Yes. Der."

Keeva moved into the darkness, then a light glowed from the opening. "I wish I had this size bathing room in my home." Keeva's voice carried, then the light disappeared.

Haldone wasn't sure if he should be concerned. "Mya, is he all right in there?"

"Yes. Door. Mother may fathers built." Her voice was closer to him now.

"Are your parents nearby?"

"No." Something in her voice told him to leave that subject alone.

"Would you like me to make a meal for us?"

"You woot cook?" Her surprise by his offer told him more than she knew.

Once again, he'd given an impression that he was not helpful. "Yes, I would like to cook for you and Keeva, if you have food."

"Yes. I have foot." Her voice came from the meal area, and he walked past the living area to see what she might have.

The cabinet disappeared before he could touch it. "Mya, if you could not touch the cabinet then I could see what you have." He waited to see what she would do.

The cabinet reappeared only the two doors were open. He was surprised by how well stocked it was. "You have a lot of food in here. Where did you get it all?" It hadn't occurred to him until now that she could very well be a lawbreaker herself.

"Jungle. Hund, pland and gother."

He hadn't missed that Keeva was repeating her words so she could learn them. He could do that too, if he could figure out what they were. "You get your food from the jungle. You hunt, plant and…" he wasn't sure what gother meant.

Mya's touch on his arm surprised him, but he didn't jerk away. With her other hand, she motioned. Her hand opened then her fingers closed and she pulled her hand toward her multiple times. Then she looked at him. "Gother."

At first all he could focus on was her violet gaze until her brows lowered in frustration. He forced himself to concentrate on the motions she'd made. "Gother, gother, oh, gather."

At her excited smile, he had to keep himself from pulling her close. "You hunt, plant and gather."

"Yes. I hunt, plant and gather my food."

He raised his brow in admiration. "Stass, you are very resourceful."

She nodded at him, still smiling. "I hag goot sills." Her chin lifted just a bit higher.

She was obviously proud of herself and he didn't blame her. "You have good…skills."

Her smile grew again. "I have good skills. My fathers and mother taught me."

"They taught you well. I am sure you can cook well, too. I will have to do my best to please you."

She turned her head away, as if she wasn't sure what he meant, and he had somehow embarrassed her.

"What I meant was I want you to like what I cook for you."

She let go of his arm, and it took all his willpower not to reach for her. He'd done or said the wrong thing again, though he was confident it had something to do with Mya this time.

He just didn't understand her yet. He wasn't good at intuitively understanding others like his brother was. Probably because there were few people he took the time to get to know.

Mya was definitely someone he wanted to know. Ever since Akasha's blue light illuminated her, he'd thought about her. He'd even dreamed about her.

Shaking his head, he refocused on the well-stocked cabinet. Maybe he could impress her with his meal. All Edenists cooked, and he was no exception. Crouching down, he opened the cold box. Once again, he was impressed. There was meat, vegetables and a variety of flavorings.

Taking out the meat, his first guess was havling pig, but upon opening the wrapping around it and smelling it, he paused. It couldn't be. He took a bigger sniff. It was feroon meat!

How could she have feroon meat? Yes, she was taller than

Earth females and probably stronger, but feroon were large animals, their backs coming to an average man's shoulder. Though they were supposed to be docile even in the jungle, he couldn't fathom Mya killing one.

Keeva exited the bathing area and strode toward him. "So, what are you making us for our midday meal."

He held out the meat. "Tell me what you think."

Keeva lowered his head and sniffed. "It is feroon meat."

"Exactly." He waited for Keeva to think about it for a moment.

The man's eyes rounded. "Mya, where did this feroon meat come from?"

"I hunt feroon." Her voice was at the table where a chair had disappeared.

He looked at Keeva who in turn looked at him before returning his attention to Mya. "How do you hunt? What weapon do you use?"

The chair reappeared, but there was nothing else disappearing. Haldone scanned the area but couldn't tell if something was missing because he didn't know her home.

A noise preempted the disappearance of the table and then it reappeared with something on it. Setting the meat on the preparation area attached to the cabinet, he moved to the table with Keeva. "What is it?"

Keeva lifted the weapon and examined it. "I believe this is an Earth crossbow. It is very modern, and it uses a metal tipped arrow if I remember correctly."

Having not paid enough attention in school, Haldone just nodded. He had no idea how it worked. Turning away, he returned to cooking. He wasn't sure what to think.

When he'd first met Mya, he'd thought of her like any other woman only beautiful and possibly Crius. But now she was far different than any other woman in all of Naralina, possibly in all of Eden.

As he cut the meat with the sharp knife he found among her other utensils, he tried to reconcile the hesitant, feminine woman with the strong hunter. Nothing in his experience helped him understand such a contrast.

Choosing some of the sauces she had in the cold box, he mixed them together and slathered the meat. There was no inducer, but there was an eyllen cooktop. Turning it on to the desired heat, he threw the three cuts of meat on it then turned to the vegetables.

Behind him, he half-listened to Keeva teaching Mya how to say her words correctly. When he'd finished preparing the dally greens and pegwa squash, he flipped the meat then stepped closer to the table where Keeva sat talking to the invisible chair.

He interrupted. "Mya, you are obviously very smart. I do not understand. Did you not learn how to speak when you were younger?"

Keeva frowned at him, clearly indicating he should have kept his question to himself. Scrat, how was he supposed to know what he should and shouldn't say. He had a hard-enough time around typical women.

"I have not spoden in fourdeen yers."

He stared in shock. "Fourteen years?"

"Yes."

"Why not?"

There was just a long enough pause that he could imagine her shrugging her shoulder. "No one to seed to."

He looked at Keeva in question.

The man recognized his need to know and rose. "It is smelling pretty good in here. Mya, you can wash and I will help Haldone serve."

The chair reappeared as she left it and a minute later the bathing room light turned on. He didn't waste any time, lifting the pan with the vegetables, he turned toward Keeva. "Why has she been alone here for that many years. She had to have been a child."

Keeva nodded and kept his voice low. "Her parents were taken by the lawbreakers and killed when she was thirteen. She hasn't explained exactly what happened, but I think she saw it all."

He sucked in his breath as rage filled his veins.

"Haldone, you're bending that handle." Keeva pried the pan from his hand and he stepped away, taking deep breaths. If Sandale were here, he'd be calm already, but he'd had to learn to control his own emotional spikes while his brother lived in Loraleaf. Focusing on the little stream of water that ran on the ground at the back of the meal area, he took a few more deep breaths before he could unclench his hands.

Keeva continued with serving their meal, even pouring cool water from the cold box into cups. There were four cups, four plates, four everything, a testament to the family that had once lived here and the care Mya took of her possessions.

The bathing room light shone again, and he stifled any more questions he wanted to ask…for now.

Chapter Six

Keeva sat on the longseat. He was positive that Haldone had a lot more questions for Mya, but he was aware of Haldone's lack of grace. The man was like a wild grendal in a flower garden, but unlike a grendal did not actually mean any harm.

He was also brilliant when it came to combining eyllen with an ability. Of course, creating boxes for eyllen out of solid air that had no air in them was a very handy skill to have on a planet dependent on the energy mineral.

The other side of the longseat dipped, letting him know Mya had joined him.

The light in the bathing room behind them flickered before disappearing, heralding Haldone's approach. His step was heavy but assured as he joined them. He paused when he noticed the indent on the couch and moved to the chair opposite.

Keeva planned to control the conversation for Mya's sake. "Now that our hunger is satisfied, I think we need to discuss what we are all doing here. Maybe we can help each other."

"Yes." Mya's soft voice came from his right, while Haldone nodded.

He turned toward Mya. "I know you can see us, but it might be easier if we could see you. Would you mind?"

Instead of answering, she moved closer until her thigh touched his. His abdomen tightened at the pleasurable feel of her skin, but he forced himself to ignore it.

Instead, he looked at Haldone. "If you can pull your chair closer this way and leave your foot out, I think Mya could comfortably touch you as well.

He barely finished speaking before Haldone was moving his chair. He sat back down and stretched one leg all the way to the long seat.

Keeva, stifled a chuckle. It would not be appreciated. Mya tentatively rested her calve against Haldone's. As before, the man appeared a bit stunned when he looked at Mya.

"I will begin." He waited for Haldone to acknowledge him. "Since I was exiled, my goal has been to get back into Naralina. Originally, I was desperate to do so in order to stop Grandall, but now that I know he has been stopped, my urgency is less, though I do hate to worry my father and my filoz. What about you, Mya? What were you doing so close to Naralina when you found me? From our walk through the night and the time we traversed these tunnels, you were decods away from your home."

She glanced at Haldone then turned toward him. "I wanted to ender Naralina to finte my grandparents. I not finte a pordle." She looked at Haldone. "I do not have a creesus chep."

Haldone relaxed a bit. "I do. I have a Crius chip but we need two." He moved his gaze. "Keeva has one."

Both he and Mya shook their heads. He placed his hand on the clear hesta strips wrapped around his upper chest. They would have to be taken off soon so he could clean his wounds, something he wasn't in a hurry to do because he knew it would hurt. "Grandall removed my chip, but when lawbreakers knocked me unconscious, they didn't know that and cut into both my sides looking for one."

Haldone's brows lowered. "They already have one Crius chip, my brother's. When Sandale was rescued, he discovered he had no chip left though he has one now. If they obtain a second chip they could escape to Earth."

Keeva felt his blood chill. Lawbreakers could do too much damage on Earth and humans would eventually capture them and learn about Eden. It was part of Criuson Law that no one reveal Eden to those who lived on Earth.

It was why women who were brought to Eden had the choice of their filoz or a Pleasure Temple. It was also why filoz, a group of men who were close friends, watched their prospective mate for years on Earth before approaching her and eventually bringing her to Eden. They wanted the women to bond with them so when they went back to Earth, they would keep the secret.

He stared hard at Haldone. "If they catch you and take your chip, Eden could be doomed."

Haldone shook his head. "Or we could get back my brother's chip."

His gut tightened at Haldone's proposal, but Mya's eyes lit with excitement. "Two Crius chips and we ender Naralina."

"That is a very dangerous proposition. We do not know how many lawbreakers there are, what abilities they have, and who has the Crius chip, never mind getting it out. I do not see any of us taking a knife to one of them like they did to me."

"I could." Haldone's scowl was so harsh, he believed him.

"We go to seddement. More Edenists there." Mya's hesitant suggestion, surprised him.

"There is a settlement in the jungle not comprised of lawbreakers?"

She nodded, but Haldone spoke up. "It is made up of men like you. Those falsely accused while Grandall was on the Council. After he exiled Wareson and Nassic, they gathered these men together, but now those two are back in Naralina with some of the men from Haven."

Haldone took a deep breath. "That is where I portaled to. I walked to these caves from there. It is about half a day walk, but we will not find any help in Haven."

Keeva did not want to hear that. "Why not?"

Haldone rolled his shoulders. "Haven's leaders have lost their beloved to the participating in orgies. Nothing is being done there. The only functioning person is their healer, Jerumbala. He has contacted people in Naralina, but it does not appear they will be arriving anytime soon."

Keeva's stomach tightened as the man across from him looked away. What was he not telling them? Was it worse or better than the way he explained it?

"What about this Jerumbala. Cannot you and he open a portal for us?"

"We could, but then I would be left here since whoever opens a portal must close it."

That was true. He was still willing to figure something out. Going to Haven sounded a lot safer than tackling the lawbreakers.

Haldone continued. "I came here to punish the lawbreakers. They have the whole jungle, yet they have preyed upon innocents. Look at you. You were no threat to them. All you wanted was to get back into Naralina, yet instead of asking you about your chip, they decide to cut into you."

He'd never thought of himself as an aggressive person, but he'd be the first to admit he was angry that he could have died in the jungle because of them. The heartbreak it would send through his family almost took his breath away, but he did want to get back to them soon.

"And you, Mya." Haldone's loud voice lowered. "I understand your parents were taken by them, leaving you alone."

Mya nodded. "They did. We were hunting and gathering. My mother and Air father were gudding a pig. My Mind father was hunting another. I was gathering burries." She paused looking at the wall behind Haldone. "When my mother skeemed, I look. A tornedo heet my Air father, teerding him to picses. Strong Mind gab my mother and told another to find my other father."

She finally looked at them. First, at the stunned Haldone and then at himself.

"Mya, I am so sorry. You were so young to see that. What did you do?"

She grasped some strands of her hair and held onto them as if they could help her. "I starded my transion and dispeered."

He laid his hand on hers, his heart aching for her as the reality of her young life became clear. "Have you been invisible ever since?"

She nodded.

His gut twisted and a deep-seeded anger gnawed its way up

his throat. For the first time in his life he understood what rage was. He looked at Haldone, whose own rage was barely controlled if the storminess of his eyes was any indication.

At the moment he wanted to unleash Haldone on every lawbreaker that ever lived. He glanced at Mya, whose eyes had turned a deep purple, the glistening over those beautiful orbs too heartbreaking to resist. He wrapped his arms around her and held her head against his shoulder.

He was surprised and pleased when she returned his embrace. He stared at Haldone over her shoulder and gave the slightest of nods. They would punish the lawbreakers for what they had done, to him, to Haldone's brother, but mostly for what they'd done to a young girl on the verge of her transition.

Haldone reached across the space that divided them and grasped his arm at the elbow. He lifted that arm away from Mya and grasped his in turn. For whatever happened from now, they would be there for each other and Mya.

She lifted her head and noticed their clasped arms. Gently, she laid her hand on top of them. Whether she understood, he did not know.

Haldone's surprised gaze rested on Mya's hand until it raised to her face. "For you."

"For you." He echoed Haldone's sentiment.

She glanced from one to the other. "For you."

Mya led the men a bit faster than when she'd brought Keeva home. The day was almost over and they would have to travel back at night, but Keeva appeared much better. After another good sleep and a long time in the rainshower, he'd had her rewrap his torso with clean hesta strips.

She'd purposefully ignored how her fingers tingled when she touched him. She liked how smooth his chest was and how it was mounded.

Haldone's was different. It was also mounded, but he had a small line of hair that ran down the center all the way to his cock. Since the hairs were so dark, it was hard to miss.

It was odd that she wanted to touch Keeva so much. She'd seen many Edenist men while living in the jungle, but she'd never wanted to touch them. Her mother had touched her fathers a lot, but they loved each other.

She slowed her stride as they drew closer to the area she considered lawbreaker land. It was easy to find because it had the blood sign on many trees. The round circle with an X over it always gave her the chills. She inadvertently squeezed Keeva's hand and he squeezed hers back.

He was always reassuring her and comforting her. She did like him, but the only people she'd ever loved was her family. It didn't feel like that at all.

Keeva tugged on her hand and she halted. Looking back, she found Haldone crouching down and looking at something on the ground. Curious, she walked toward him. Before she could see what he'd picked up, he stood.

"It is not worth looking at." His voice was so quiet she almost couldn't hear him.

She tried to look anyway, but Keeva pulled her back and spoke close to her ear. "Let us keep going. If as you say Strong Mind is near Naralina, we should take every moment he is gone to discover all we can."

She looked at him then Haldone, who nodded.

That did make sense. She strode forward. She didn't know for sure if Strong Mind could sense other people. Her father always could and he was Kindred of Mind, but he'd also told her of someone he'd worked with in the Naralina Library who was Kindred of Mind but couldn't sense others. That Edenist's ability was he had a photographic mind.

She couldn't imagine being able to look at something and remember every detail like the cameras they had on Earth. She was glad she had the actual photos of her parents and grandparents. She'd painted them on the walls of her caves, but she couldn't very well carry those with her. The photos meant she could show Naralinians what they looked like hopefully find her grandparents.

At the sound of a stream, she slowed. They were close now to the lawbreakers "camp," what her mother called it when people lived outside. She stopped and lifted Keeva's hand in hers to point. Since they were all holding hands, they were invisible, but they still could be heard, sensed and touched.

Haldone moved past Keeva turning them around. She frowned at him but he frowned right back at her. For some reason, that made her want to chuckle. She kept quiet but looked back at Keeva and rolled her eyes.

His answering grin warmed her.

For such a forceful man, Haldone moved quietly, bringing them through the trees, stepping around anything that would make noise. Finally, they were close enough to see the camp.

The clearing was not natural. It looked as if a tornado had whipped through it, throwing trees and rocks to the sides creating an embankment. The entire circumference had a small hill around it as high as her breasts.

In the very center was a large pit, no doubt where they cooked with eyllen, as she had when she'd fed Keeva. There were six lean-tos as her mother would call them, branches and vines stacked at an angle against a large boulder of savinstone to provide shelter. They were set-against the far edge, so there could be more on their side.

Sandwiched between the men, much like her fathers had treated her mother, she felt safe, but it also rankled. She was the one who knew how to survive in the jungle, not them. Still, she grasped their hands tightly. She didn't want them to be seen.

There was no movement in the camp, and she began to think it had been abandoned, when sound came from one of the lean-tos. A lawbreaker rolled out onto the ground, his long hair matted. He stood and scratched at his balls before holding his penis in his hand.

As if he thought better of urinating in front of his lodging, he walked to the next lean-to and urinated outside it. She wrinkled her nose. The man was disgusting. When he was done, he moved toward the center pit. Pointing his finger at something on the ground, an orange light shot from it and smoke rose before he stopped it. He was obviously Kindred of Light.

Bending over, he picked up a dirty piece of meat and threw it on the pit. This time, he faced his palm toward the center of the pit and held it there as a large swath of orange light hit what was in there. Smoke rose for a few moments before he stopped.

He walked away, leaving the meat and crouched by the stream that ran through the camp. He pulled a cup from it and drank before dropping it back in the water. Returning to the pit, he lifted the meat out with his hands, the outside charred black.

Mya shook her head. Just the thought of what that meat would taste like had her clamping her jaw tight.

Another lawbreaker crawled from his sleeping quarters. Even from where they were, she could see the soft edged heart birthmark on his left shoulder. He went straight to the stream and splashed water on his face.

The two men ignored each other. One chewing on raw, charred meat and the other washing himself. Either they hated each other, or each thought the other was too good to speak the first word. She remembered a fight her parents had where no one would speak first. That had ended with her scolding them. She'd only been nine.

She grinned at the memory. It had been so long since she'd thought about it.

Noise coming through the jungle on the opposite side of the clearing drew her attention. Haldone and Keeva tensed beside her. If she'd been alone, she would have left, but having them there made her feel safe. She mentally kicked herself. One man was still healing and the other she'd been afraid of only a day ago. As her mother used to say, she needed her head examined.

As soon as she could tell the lawbreaker moving through the jungle didn't have the white and black hair of Strong Mind, she relaxed. She believed he was the only one who could sense their presence, but as the man emerged, she recognized him, which had her squeezing Haldone's and Keeva's hands.

They both looked at her, but she kept her gaze on Womer, Kindred of Water.

He strode toward the man eating meat. "Churi get a fire going. There is more than just you who needs to eat."

"Go bond with a boarox." The man punctuated his statement by flicking his hand down his forearm.

Womer grabbed Churi by the neck. Immediately, the meat dropped from his hands and he started to thrash around. Womer let go. "I said start the fire."

From where they were, she couldn't hear what Churi said beneath his breath, but he obeyed.

Womer turned away and strode toward the man in the stream. She'd seen Womer do something similar to another lawbreaker and that man had screamed as if in excruciating pain, which scared her, but she had no idea what he actually did to them.

According to her fathers, Kindred of Water generally could make water appear, or make it rain or control the humidity. None of those abilities would have caused the meat-eater to struggle so. Womer tapped the man in the water on his shoulder. "Go get us some dinner."

The man stood up immediately. "Yes, Womer."

Womer headed for the man at the pit, a scowl on his face. He opened his mouth then closed it. His gaze snapped to the trees where they all stood, but they were invisible. Still, she shuddered.

Womer clapped a hand on the other man's shoulder. "Someone's here."

Keeva's hand immediately rose and a branch snapping sounded behind the lawbreakers' camp, causing both men to turn. In the next second, Haldone's hand rose.

Suddenly, she could no longer hear the lawbreakers. The Kindred of Light man scanned the trees on the opposite side and Womer pointed in the direction of the sound Keeva had created as a distraction.

Womer gestured, but the Kindred of Light man shook his head. Womer moved toward him and he waved Womer off, striding toward the jungle.

Mya did not like Womer. He was dangerous.

Womer lifted his hand toward where they stood. Cocking his head, he frowned before walking toward them.

She tried to back away, but Haldone shook his head. "He cannot sense us. I created an air box around us that will keep all Edenist abilities from penetrating as well as sound."

Keeva stepped around her to face Haldone. "How big is this box? Will he bump into it? Can I create another distraction from inside?"

"He could bump into it, and no, you cannot use your abilities beyond the box while inside it. Only I can because mine can flow into the box and out."

Mya tugged his hand. "What about air?"

Haldone smiled, putting her at ease. "I pulled in extra air as I created it, so we have plenty."

He had the best smile. The transformation in his stern face continued to surprise her. The skin at the corners of his eyes crinkled and his gaze turned a warm smoky gray. It made her want to make him smile more.

"He is coming closer." Keeva's voice had lowered.

She didn't blame him. Though Haldone was confident in his box, it was hard to stand still when a very dangerous enemy approached.

Womer stopped at the edge of the clearing and stared hard at the spot where they stood. She held the men's hands tighter. If they separated at all, Womer would see them.

Womer looked back across the camp, then gave one last look in their direction before striding back to the pit as the Kindred of Heart man walked into view, a dead havling pig thrown over his shoulder.

She took a deep breath. "What is Womer's ability?"

Keeva answered. "He is Kindred of Water and from what he did to his fellow lawbreaker, my guess is he can suck the water from a person's body."

She gasped. "Damn, that mud hurd."

"I imagine it does hurt. There are a few men in Naralina with that ability, but they do not use it that way. The Discoverist I know uses it for experiments on dead animals."

She shivered but didn't let go. The more she learned about the lawbreakers, the more she hated them…and feared them. "Go home now."

Haldone brought her hand to his chest. "I think we should wait until they are busy eating. I can get us away by creating more air boxes, but I have never had to create them to travel through. If I make a mistake, I'd rather the Womer lawbreaker is distracted. I have no doubt he keeps checking this area with his senses. Since he is Kindred of Water, he can probably sense the water in our bodies."

She'd never thought of that. She always thought it was Strong Mind. Maybe he couldn't sense others. She didn't like the delay in going home, but if it would keep them safer, she'd wait.

Haldone's heart tightened at the disappointment in Mya's eyes, but he'd rather she was safe. He looked up to find Keeva watching him. The man nodded as if to validate his decision. He'd never needed or wanted anyone's validation, which was one reason why he wasn't part of a filoz, but right now he appreciated it.

He turned back to watch the lawbreakers. The dynamics between the men were almost the opposite of what was the norm in Naralina. Instead of eating their meal together, the Kindred of Light man took his food and ate it like a starving dog. The other two sat near each other but did not appear to speak.

As he predicted, Womer continued to glance their way. He'd sensed them, but now he couldn't. It had to be the water in their bodies. His father Fripp was Kindred of Water, but he couldn't sense people like this man did. It was no different than the fact Nassic, who was Kindred of Mind couldn't sense others nearby, yet Grandall, also Kindred of Mind, could sense people and know who they were, but that was all he could do.

He was happy he'd been born Kindred of Air. He'd been able to create not only rainboxes and windows for the people of Naralina, but he'd created other things, like the chairs and table in Theron's portion of Mya's cave or the table for Loraleaf's guest house. Thankfully, once he'd mastered using eyllen with his ability to make what he created last, he hadn't had to depend on anyone else.

It was odd to be depending on Mya with her knowledge of the lawbreakers and the jungle. He'd been taught that it was men's responsibility to care for women, which he'd always had a problem with.

His brother's beloved, Toni, was a perfect example of a woman who didn't need to be cared for. That woman could handle anything. A niggling guilt crept into his gut. He hadn't wanted her to be a part of Sandale's life. His little brother had just reentered his life, completely altered, and she took over.

His brain wanted whatever made Sandale happy, but he'd missed his brother. He still did.

"It dark now. Bendis rise soon." Mya's soft voice had him refocusing on her.

He looked past her toward Keeva, who also looked expectant. Another glance toward the camp showed Womer moving outside it to relieve himself.

He raised his hand creating a long narrow box as far as he could see and reinforcing it like the one they were in. He glanced back toward the camp but didn't see Womer anywhere. "Where did he go?"

Keeva pointed.

The man was walking around the perimeter of the camp as if to make sure nothing lurked beyond it.

He waited as the man slowed as he neared them. Again, he studied the jungle then finally moved on.

The next part of the box transfer was the trickiest. If he didn't make the next box's walls exactly the same density, their transfer to it might be sensed. It might only appear as a few small animals to Womer, but he had to make it perfect.

He waited until the man returned to the fire, so he could watch his expression. "Keeva, you step through first. I might have to make quick adjustments."

"Where do I go?"

He pointed to the end of his box. "Walk that way with your hand out. You will feel the wall. When it vanishes beneath your fingers, lead us through quickly."

Keeva did as requested and waited.

He looked back at Womer and watched him as he eliminated the wall between the boxes. Immediately, he was tugged forward by Mya. He followed, keeping his gaze on the lawbreaker. Not seeing any change, he quickly closed the new box and eliminated the old.

Womer suddenly rose and he froze, keeping his companions from moving forward.

The lawbreaker walked to the middle sleeping shelter then turned toward them again. He stared for a long time before finally crouching down and crawling inside.

Haldone let out a breath and turned to Mya and Keeva. "I'll lead. This box is longer and narrower. Follow me in this form until we are far enough away."

His new friends nodded, and he started them back the way they'd come. Finally, he determined they were far enough and allowed Mya to direct him, but he wasn't about to give up her hand.

When they arrived at Theron's entrance to her cave, he finally relaxed. The second night of the Bendis moon made the jungle light up like the city of Naralina, but instead of gold it was pink. Once inside, Keeva opened a shiner.

He brought his companions with him to the cold box. "I think a celebration is in order." He pulled out the ambrosia and set it on the preparation shelf of the cabinet.

Keeva's eyes lit. "You have ambrosia? Here?"

"Thanks to Haven. When we gathered here last, Theron brought it, but we did not have time to enjoy it because my fathers were accused by Grandall." There was ale, too, but he'd rather not mention it. His conscience rose. *Like you didn't tell them about Loraleaf and the many people who could have portaled them to Naralina?* He pushed away the guilt and took out three cups.

Mya's worried gaze caught the light. "Did you safe them in tine?"

"Did I save my fathers in time? Yes, I did. They were to have a hearing and if Grandall had continued to rule, they would have been exiled. Instead, they helped us capture the man and round up all of the Ruling Circle."

She gave him a relieved smile that made his inside tighten. "What is ambrosia?"

He grinned. "It is a favorite drink of all Naralinians. You have not tasted anything as good, I promise."

He hated that he would have to release her hand to pour the drinks, but he forced himself to. When he'd poured them, she leaned against his arm of her own accord and accepted a cup.

He raised his drink. "To surviving our first encounter with the lawbreakers." He pressed the cup to his forehead and drank.

Keeva did as well, but Mya frowned.

"What is it?" She hadn't even tasted the ambrosia, so he knew it wasn't the drink.

Her eyes were shimmering again. "My fathers uzed to do that. I forgod."

He wanted to take all her pain away but didn't know what to say. He lacked the ability to say the right thing. Helpless, he leaned in and kissed her on the cheek.

When he pulled back, she was staring at him. "Do that again."

If she wanted, he'd kiss her a hundred times. He leaned in to kiss her cheek and she turned her head to face him. The second his lips touched hers, his gut tightened. Careful not to scare her, he gave her two light kisses, wanting more than ever to part her soft lips and taste her.

She pulled her head back a little and brought her finger to her lips. "That tingles, too." She turned her head to address Keeva. "It tingles when I wrap your cuts, too. Why?"

His throat closed at her statement. Tingles could only mean one thing. She was attracted to him.

He wanted to create the largest air slide and ride it. He wanted to yell out to the jungle that his most fervent wish had come true, but instead he looked at Keeva, who asked without speaking if he should answer the question.

Haldone nodded, preferring that Keeva explain, since he was so much better with words.

"The tingles you feel mean your body is interested in our bodies."

"What does that mean?" She turned to him for more explanation.

He cleared his throat. "It is why people bond and have families."

He let out a relieved breath as she looked back at Keeva. "The tingles are good then?"

Keeva's mouth quirked up on one side. "They are very good. You said that you moved your parents' bed into the main dome, but it was somewhere else, right?"

She nodded.

"That is because they were enjoying each other's bodies and since you were too young and didn't have anyone else, they did so in private."

She didn't say anything for a long time. Then she turned back to him and placed her hand on his chest. "Does it tingle for you?"

He swallowed hard in order to speak. "Yes."

"And you lide it?"

"I like it very much." He opened his mouth to tell her how he'd dreamed of her ever since he'd first saw her, but snapped it shut. Instead, he laid his hand on her chest above her breast.

Her eyes widened and her breaths shortened. "That makes me…" She frowned. "Eggsided?"

Keeva brushed her hair from the side of her face. "Excited, yes. That is important when a woman and men join their bodies together."

She disengaged her hand from Keeva's and ran it up his arm. "Tingles for you, too?"

He nodded, his Adam's Apple proving he was having an equal reaction to her. "Did your mother ever talk to you about bonding?"

She started to shake her head then stopped. "Bonding. A filoz and a beload."

"Yes, when a filoz of men take their chosen one together in a certain way, they bond and she becomes their beloved."

The conversation was getting too far ahead in his opinion. "But that is only one way men and women bring their bodies together. First, they need to see if they each feel great pleasure."

He thought he'd said that well, but Keeva frowned. Either he said it wrong or Keeva didn't intend to act on his attraction for Mya.

Mya looked at him. "Pleasure? Like food on my tong?"

He grinned. "Even better."

She returned his smile. "I want pleasure."

He was in love. "We can give you pleasure."

Keeva spoke up. "I know you feel tingles, Mya. I just want to be sure that you trust us."

She looked at Keeva then at him a long time before answering. "Yes. You my frens. Not have frens sin liddle."

Keeva repeated her words correctly as usual. "You have not had friends since you were little? Were those here on the planet?"

Haldone ground his teeth. Keeva's curiosity never stopped. Now was not the time for more questions about her childhood in his opinion.

"No. On Earth. Visited grandparents and payed with friends." She looked at him. "You are my first friends on Eden."

His heart tightened at her words. That she was forced to be alone for so long tore at him. He liked to be alone but that was his choice. He returned her hesitant smile. "Yes, we are your friends and always will be."

Her smile brightened. "You are my friends." She leaned in and kissed him on the lips again.

Then she turned to Keeva and kissed him on the lips.

Haldone smirked at Keeva's stunned expression. Maybe now there would be no more questions.

Mya turned back to him. "Can we have pleasure now?"

"Yes, we can." Now that his dream was coming true, he wanted to savor every moment. "There is a bed this way." He didn't want to break the mood by taking the long trek back to her dome.

Keeva swayed, taking a step to right himself.

That wasn't from a kiss. "What is wrong?"

The man looked longingly at Mya then shook his head. "I am still healing. I need to rest. I will lie down on the longseat here."

Keeva faced him. "As much as I'd like to join you, I do not want to ruin the first time."

The man's message was loud and clear, be careful because all of Mya's future sexual encounters would be influenced by what he did with her now. He gave a short nod to affirm he understood and resolved to keep his usual exuberance in check.

She placed her hand on Keeva's cheek. "Rest. We will have pleasure when you are well."

"Yes, we will." Keeva, gave her a tired smile before moving away from her touch to stretch out on the longseat.

Haldone doubted he could have stepped away no matter how hurt he was. His obsession with Mya was far too strong. Still, it was better that Keeva rest so he could be fully healed when they attacked the lawbreakers.

"Come." He took her hand from his chest and held it, wishing that Keeva could be with them even if just to make sure he did not say something to ruin it. It was the first time he'd ever wished for a brother of his heart. What a ithio he was. Without a filoz, he could never claim Mya as his beloved. Shaking off the surge of anger that sparked, he walked to Theron's old sleeping room and opened the shiner near the door.

Once inside, Mya turned and faced him, flipping her hair over her shoulder with her head. "Now I can have pleasure."

"Yes." He stepped up to her and cupped her face in his hands, her violet gaze sending warmth through him. Lowering his mouth, he kissed her as he had before then licked at her lips, coaxing her to open her mouth.

When she did, he gently pushed his tongue inside to stroke her own. Her free hand, which rested on his arm, tightened as her breathing grew faster. When her tongue pushed into his mouth, he allowed her in to explore his own, letting her experience the joy of giving pleasure in return.

She pulled away, her breathing fast. "I like that."

"I like that, too. Now I would like to kiss your whole body." He didn't want to speak so much, but he wanted her to understand so she didn't become fearful. Women's orgasms could be intense, and he wanted her to enjoy every part of the excitement beforehand and the satisfaction afterward.

Her cheeks immediately flushed, but she didn't say no. Instead, she nodded.

He moved to the side to kiss her ear and jawline, trailing his mouth along her smooth skin so as not to startle her. Next, he let his tongue glide over her shoulder before pressing small kisses along her collar bone.

She tilted her head back as her hand grasped his arm tighter.

Slowly, he moved his mouth lower to give a lick between her breasts.

She seemed to freeze in her position, waiting, anticipating. As he moved his tongue across one breast, just beneath the areola, her breath caught. He switched to kisses as he made his way around her pert peak, ignoring it as he tasted her skin, his own hand on her waist tightening.

Her fingers moved into his hair and gripped tight, urging him on. He was confident she had no idea what it was she wanted, just that she wanted it. For her, he would prolong her need, letting her grow used to his touch.

At her insistence, he pressed a light kiss on her nipple then flicked it with his tongue.

A tiny moan emerged from the back of her throat.

Mya's grip in his hair grew tight, but he ignored the pain as he finally sucked on the large hard nipple. Keeping it in his mouth, he stroked his tongue around it before taking it between his teeth and rolling it.

The grip in his hair suddenly changed from pushing into her to pulling him away and he reluctantly obeyed. This first time had to be on her own terms. He would do whatever she wished, even walk away with his hard cock throbbing.

CHAPTER SEVEN

Mya gasped for air as she held Haldone's face away from her breast. Her tummy roiled and the place between her legs had moistened. She had to know if this was bad, once she caught her breath.

She stared at the opposite wall, needing to calm herself which wouldn't happen if she looked at him. His eyes made her excited and anxious. What he made her feel when he touched her was pleasure well beyond what she received from food. Licking her lips, she finally asked her question. "I have a hart time breeting and my papaya is moite. Is this good or bad?"

"This is good. You are excited which causes your heart to race and makes your breathing go faster."

When he didn't say anymore, she glanced at him. His eyes had turned a deep gray like gathering storm clouds. "And my papaya?"

He cocked his head. "I do not understand papaya."

She took his hand and pressed it between her legs, but the moment it touched her a zing of pleasure speared her deep inside, and she jumped back. "What was that?"

He looked surprised then brought his hand to his mouth and kissed it, making her tingle without even touching him.

"I think I understand that your papaya, that which is moist, is sensitive. When you put my hand against it, your pleasure nub reacted. Did it feel good?"

She wasn't sure. It didn't feel bad, but how would she say that?

He didn't wait for her answer, instead he took her hand and placed it on his cock. It was silky smooth, but hard, sticking straight out from his body. "This is my pleasure nub. It grows larger and harder when I am excited."

"It's your cod." She'd never touched one, so she explored it with her fingers, stroking across the veins and up under the ridge near the cap. When she pressed a finger on the tip, it came away wet. That helped her relax. If he was wet too, that must mean what she was feeling was what he felt.

She looked up at his face to find his eyes closed and his jaw tight. "Yes, that."

At her words, he opened his eyes. "What?"

"That is what I felt."

He took a deep breath. "That is good."

She grinned. "Will you suck on me some more?"

His nostrils flared at her words, and her insides tightened. She didn't know that pleasure could be felt without touching.

Haldone didn't say anything. Instead, he took her hand and walked her to the side of the bed and turned her away from it. They stood before a reflection square hanging on the wall but they weren't in it. It showed the bed and the door to the bathing room.

"Touch the reflection." Haldone's voice seemed deeper as it whispered past her ear.

A shiver raced up her spine, but it wasn't from fear. It was more excitement. Anxious to discover what else he would show her, she did as he requested.

As soon as she touched the frame, she stared transfixed. "Oh."

It was herself. Much clearer than her reflection when she washed in her underground pool of water. She could see her whole body at once. She liked it. Haldone stood behind her, his hands resting lightly on her waist. She lay her other hand on one of his. Hers were more slender and smooth while his were broader.

He raised his other hand to cup one of her breasts and the tingles started all over again. She watched, fascinated as his thumb and finger held her nipple then rolled it. Excitement shot from her nipple to between her legs, but not on the surface where moisture gathered. Somewhere deep inside her.

He moved her hand to do the same to her other nipple and the same thing happened. It made her feel alive and empty. How strange.

She grasped his hand and moved it to the juncture of her thighs. "Touch me."

At first, he didn't move, so she looked at his face in the reflection. His eyes had turned to almost black, but instead of frightening her, it sent pleasure from her chest to that deep place inside her.

There was so much that caused her to feel. "Please."

Haldone moaned quietly as his gaze moved to their joined hands. "Whatever you wish." His hand slipped out from under hers and his fingers brushed across the smooth mound between her thighs. Then he slid two fingers lower, across what he said was her pleasure nub and into her moisture.

Her eyes wanted to close at his touch, but she refused to let them. She needed to learn.

He stroked between the folds of her flesh there, sometimes grazing her pleasure point and sometimes not, though why he avoided it, she couldn't imagine. It was very hard and sensitive and made her excited.

Her body tightened with pleasure but it still felt empty. She moaned with her need, tipping her pelvis forward, wanting something more.

Frustrated, she stopped. "Why doz it fill good but emty."

He stopped his fingers and looked at her in the reflection. His Adam's Apple moved up and then down before he spoke. "Why does it feel good but empty?"

She nodded, still staring at his neck.

"Because I have not brought you to satisfaction yet. It is more enjoyable if the pleasure builds inside you."

She wasn't sure what he meant by satisfaction, but the pleasure was definitely building. "I want satisfaction then."

His whole body at her back stiffened and his cock jumped against the top of her butt. "And I will give it to you."

But instead of touching her more, he let go of her and crouched to the ground. "Open your legs."

She did as he requested. Anything to make the need in her be happy. It was like being hungry and seeing food, wanting it, but not be able to reach it.

Haldone slid between her legs with his back to the reflection.

His face at the spot his fingers had just left and another spurt of shivers raced over her skin.

She looked down just as his tongue shot out and licked her pleasure point. She came up on her toes without even thinking about it.

His hand clamped down on her butt, which brought her heels down but another shock of need raced to her center.

She looked in the reflection just as he raised his hand to her flesh again. Seeing his dark hair at the juncture of her thighs, had her body producing more moisture. His finger began to stroke through her folds with his tongue darting out whenever he wanted, his beard sensitizing her.

Her whole body tensed and she grabbed his hair, wanting more yet wanting it to end in some more pleasurable way, looking for the satisfaction he said he would give her.

When his tongue stopped, his finger pushed inside her. Her natural reaction was to close her legs, but she couldn't. That alone sent another flush of feeling flooding her lower body.

Slowly, his finger moved farther inside her. She wanted to crouch down onto it but he was in the way. This could lead to satisfaction. She could feel it.

When he removed his finger from her, she almost cried. "No."

He didn't say anything, but he did fill her again, only this time she felt fuller. This felt right. "Yes. Do that."

A noise that sounded slightly like a strangled chuckle came from him. He pulled his fingers almost all the way out and then pushed them in again.

Oh, she liked that. A lot.

His fingers began to move inside her in a regular rhythm that she couldn't help but move her hips to meet. Her body tightened, getting more tense, building toward something she wanted more than anything. She gasped for air as she reached for something she didn't understand.

Haldone's mouth moved against her and his tongue twirled her pleasure nub.

The tension in her body broke as she shattered into a million pieces, but she didn't care as ecstasy washed over her even as his tongue continued to drive it on.

As she panted, she managed to pull his head away from her, her heart beating faster than a rhybat's in fear of its life. When she'd finally calmed enough to open her eyes, she stared at the rock ceiling. Looking down, she found she'd fallen back on the bed with Haldone still kneeling between her thighs.

He gazed at her, his eyes black as night, sending a thrill up her spine. Instinct kicked in. She had reached satisfaction, but he hadn't. He still had that burning need that she had had.

She swallowed to get her voice to work. "You need satisfaction, too."

His face tensed before he gave her a quick nod.

"Dell me what to do."

"Tell you…lay all the way back on the bed."

She moved back until even her feet were on the bed. As if she could help him faster, she lifted her arms while he rose to stand at her feet.

"Holy Bendis you are so beautiful." His words, barely above a whisper slid into her heart before he crawled onto the bed between her legs.

Her body seemed to melt, accept whatever he wanted to do to give him his satisfaction.

He took his cock in his hand and opened his mouth but didn't say anything. She stared at his cock and suddenly she understood. That could fill her better than his fingers and he would have satisfaction, too.

Even at the thought, her belly contracted. She reached forward and took his hand from his cock. Then she gave it a tug. "Now."

Haldone fell forward onto his hands, wanting to give into his need and her request, but he refused to hurt her. Thank the Poetess, Mya had no hymen like most Earth women. His fingers had encountered no barrier while bringing her pleasure for the first time. Still, she was untried, her sheath narrow, and he was not.

The frustration and hunger almost brought tears to his eyes, but he was made strong for a reason. Pulling back, he latched onto her nipple and gave her some light bites. She arched her back, pushing her breast to his mouth as her hands rifled through his hair.

He moved to her other breast, sucking it lightly before increasing the pressure. Her moans of pleasure told him how hard he could go. That she liked and took more suction than the Earth women he'd been with had his control slipping.

She was more everything to him. More height, more beauty, more ability, more intelligence, just more Mya. It was as if he'd waited his whole life for her. He lifted his mouth from her breast and kissed her.

This time he plunged his tongue into her mouth, demanding a response, and he wasn't disappointed. As he came down onto his elbows, she ran her hands over his back, her feet rubbing his calves as if she was anxious for more.

He lifted his hips and found her wet entrance with his tip. Despite his normal mode of plunging in, he nudged her opening and lifted his mouth from hers so he could gauge her comfort. This was her first time.

She lifted her hips, blowing air from between her lips as if frustrated. He understood that, but he wouldn't let her hurt herself either. Slowly, he pushed in a little. This time she stilled, but she didn't open her eyes.

Watching her face, he inched in more, her tightness slowly giving way to accommodate him, much to his relief. If they couldn't fit, he'd be lost.

Her hands moved down his back and pulled his ass.

Scrat! She would break his control if she kept that up. Though her body opened to him, he had to give her time to adjust. Again, he let his hips lower, sinking into her tight sheath a very small amount at a time.

Her legs spread wider and before he knew what she was about, she lifted her pelvis.

He quickly pulled back just as far. She might think she wanted all of him at once, but she didn't know what to expect.

"Dammit Haldone. Get inside."

Her outburst released his humor and gained him the control he needed. "We need to go slow this first time or you could be hurt."

"No. I'm strong. I want all of you."

It was her last sentence that broke him. He'd happily give her all of him, his body, his heart, his soul if she wanted it. Giving in to her, he slowly glided the rest of the way in.

Complete. The word flew through his consciousness for the first time in his life before Mya grabbed his attention again.

"All." She shifted her hips, bringing her legs up around his waist, causing him to sink in deeper.

This woman was made for him. If she wanted him deep, he could think of a couple other positions she would like as well, but first he wanted her to know how it felt to join with him.

He started to lift his hips, but she tightened her legs around him, keeping any separation from happening. The woman was as strong as she claimed.

"Mya, you need to let me move in and out of you. It will make you feel good and reach satisfaction again."

She looked at him skeptically, one delicate eyebrow raised, but she finally loosened her legs, sliding back along him until only his tip was inside.

Her glide to the bed had him gritting his teeth, his own release just a few strokes away. Angling his hips, he slid into her again brushing her sensitive clit, his need rushing to the fore as her eyes widened with excitement.

Pulling out again, he pushed forward a little faster, forcing himself to watch her. But after a few thrusts, her eyes closed and the soft moans coming from her slightly parted lips caused his own pleasure to spike.

He gripped the bedding as he gritted his teeth to hold on to a steady rhythm, keeping his thrusts long and regular.

Mya's moans changed to short high-pitched noises that grew in intensity, urging him on faster. As her noises gained in volume, his balls tightened until she let out a scream and her orgasm burst over him.

He was a man of control, always reaching for perfection, but at her joy, he lost all control and shouted his release for all of Eden to hear, pumping into her frantically as her sheath accepted what he had.

When his pleasure subsided, he lifted his head to gaze at her, concern for her edging out his lethargy.

Rounded violet eyes stared at him as if he were a Crius. "I lub that." Her hand came up and stroked his beard. "You give me the bet pleasure edder."

"I loved that, too. You gave me the best pleasure ever."

She kept her fingers in his beard as if she'd never touched anything like it, focusing on her hand. "I your best?"

He took her hand, brought it to his lips and kissed her finger tips. "Yes. The best. I like you very much." *In fact, I love you. I have since I first saw you, but I can't tell you that.*

Her finger moved across his lips. "I like you very much. You are my best friend."

His heart squeezed with hope and anguish, both for her and him. That she had no one to talk to, lean on, or share life with for so long gnawed at him to never allow that again. Yet, his lack of a filoz, made that impossible.

Unless…

Mya yawned, her pink tongue calling to him again, causing his cock to harden inside her.

She widened her eyes even as her sheath contracted around him.

He wanted to make love to her again, but his gut told him it may not be a good idea. He'd never had sex with a woman who was pure before, so he wasn't sure how her body would react to the intrusion.

Ignoring the squeezing of her sheath as she did it again as if discovering a new muscle movement, he started to pull his hips back, his intent to let her rest, but her legs around him tightened.

There was no way he could resist without her help. "Mya, I need to take myself out."

"No. I want more pleasure."

His cock jumped inside her, and she answered with a squeeze of her sheath. This was not a good idea.

"I know you do. I want more too, but this was your first time. If we do it again, you may be sore and then we will not be able to have pleasure for days."

Her brow furrowed. "I want pleasure airy day."

Again, his cock jumped and even his breath caught. If ever a woman was made for him, it was her. He had to find a way to keep her. "I promise that you will have pleasure every day you want it."

She started to smile, but it turned into a yawn instead.

Quickly, he pulled out before she could keep him from doing so.

She moaned, and he had to swallow his own. Rolling to the side of her, he pulled her close, so her head rested on his shoulder. She curled her legs up, bracing her knees against his side.

As much as he wanted her to wrap her arm around him, her position, with her hand tucked under her chin, reminded him of exactly how little experience she had, not only with sex, but with people.

It wasn't long before her breathing fell into a regular rhythm, telling him she was sound asleep.

Sleep was still far away for him. Despite his body feeling

satisfied and content, his mind and heart were not. He had to find a way to keep Mya.

He'd been accused of being too intense, but it was nothing compared to his feelings for her. The moment Akasha's blue light revealed her in the darkness of the cave, he was struck dumb. Even then, he'd sensed it was far more than her beauty. All this time he'd thought her a Crius who had used her power to force him back to her.

He grinned. There she had stood, a large rock in her hand after hitting him on the head and ready to do it again, and he stared at her in awe. He had Toni to thank for not being knocked unconscious. Even then, he'd recognized that Mya trusted women more than men.

Still, he had firmly believed that like the Sirens of his culture's ancient past, she had forced him to return so she could finish what she started and kill him. Discovering she was an Edenist threw all his ideas into the mythological Valex pit.

He could see two possibilities for keeping her. His first choice was to simply live here with her after he rid the area of lawbreakers. He would, in essence be a lawbreaker himself as it was against Dickinson Law for a man to have a woman all to himself. Though Grandall had made an exception to that law for Ruling Circle members, the new Council had made striking that exception from the scrolls one of their first priorities.

Though he'd prefer to not have a filoz, it wouldn't be fair to Mya. Women deserved more than one man, and as she was an Edenist—he glanced down at her—with an Edenist appetite for pleasure, it would be wrong for him to try to satisfy her by himself.

Which meant he needed another man. The problem with that is he didn't get along with anyone else except his brother Sandale, but even then, he wouldn't want to, nor was it allowed to have his brother in his filoz.

His frustration made him anxious to move. Carefully, he held Mya's head as he pulled his body out from beneath her, then he slowly lowered it to the bed. At the movement, she curled into a tighter ball, looking young and vulnerable.

The need to protect grew stronger inside him. He knew himself. That need would grow until all the lawbreakers were expelled from the area.

Slipping out of the bed, he strode for the door. Once in Theron's old living area, he turned to find Keeva standing at the food cabinet.

The man held up a cup. "Ambrosia?"

He nodded, striding forward to take the proffered drink. It was well known that the citrusy-nutty drink with the spicy after taste had not only healing properties but energy ones as well. Though he'd just had the most satisfying experience of his life, he didn't feel drained at all. Rather, he felt ready to tackle all his problems at once.

"How is she?"

At Keeva's soft spoken question, he grinned. "She is fine. Though I fear she may be insatiable."

"Why, do you think that?"

He strode to the chair across from the longseat and sat. "First, she wanted me to go a lot faster than I was willing, given her inexperience. Second, after I brought her to completion twice, she wanted more."

Keeva smiled. "It sounds as if you were the perfect one to introduce her to pleasure."

He studied the Discoverist. He'd worked with him on a few projects and though he wouldn't call him a friend because he didn't have any of those, Keeva was one of the few people he hadn't argued with or infuriated. "I expected you to be asleep."

The man returned to the longseat where he was supposedly resting. "I was not tired. I just thought for her first time, she should start with one man, not two."

"You are a better Edenist than I am."

"I know."

He snapped his gaze to the man's face, but he was smiling, obviously meaning his statement as a joke, not a reprimand. He relaxed. "I admit, for all my control, I could not have given her up."

Keeva stared into his cup and spoke without looking up. "You seem particularly focused on her."

He should have known a Discoverist would be observant, not that he'd hidden his attraction to Mya. He wasn't good at pretending or lying for that matter. *But lying by omission worked.* Again, he ignored his conscience. "I am. Ever since I first met her, I have been…" He wasn't sure how to put it. Obsessed sounded too harsh for how he felt. "I have been fascinated by her."

Keeva nodded. "I can certainly understand that. When she first helped me, I couldn't see her and thought she was a man. When I saw her for the first time, I was stunned."

Which brought up something that had been bothering him. "Do you think she can make herself visible, or will she always be invisible. Is it because she is a female Edenist?"

Keeva shrugged. "I do not know. There has never been a

female Edenist in the entire twelve-hundred-year history of Naralina. I have so many questions for her, or rather I did when I first saw her."

"And now?"

Keeva took a swallow of his drink before answering. "Now, she is less of a curiosity and more a…I guess the best word would be the one she used. She is more of a friend."

He understood that. "She is unique, special, and my one fear beyond her safety is that if those in Naralina discovered she was an Edenist, she would have no life of her own." He rolled his shoulders. "It is just a feeling, but I can almost see them putting her on display in the Discoverist Oasis."

Keeva chuckled. "I do not think you would have to worry about that. She may be unique, but she is first and foremost a woman. I hope that our society would treat her better than as an object of curiosity."

Haldone raised his eyebrows. He had serious doubts.

"You think that us Discoverists would be anxious to discover all there is to know about her?"

He nodded.

"I am sure they would be excited. And yes, they would want to ask her thousands of questions. Maybe take a blood sample. Maybe test her ability. Maybe…" Keeva trailed off.

"You see my concern."

Keeva started to shake his head but stopped and sighed. "I do."

It had been a concern he'd had since he'd seen Mya. Luckily, Toni had agreed with him, for which he'd been thankful, and had convinced Akasha and Sandale not to say anything to anyone until she investigated further, which with her new position as beloved of two Ruling Circle members, was the farthest thing from her mind.

He caught Keeva's eye and held it. "I would request an oath from you."

"I think I know what you would say."

"I wish to keep secret that Mya is an Edenist."

Keeva frowned. "That is a difficult oath to make. As a Discoverist I am sworn to investigate anything that might benefit Eden even if it hurts Naralina itself."

Haldone held his breath, not prepared to think about what he would have to do if Keeva refused.

The man looked away, his body tense as he held his cup with both hands. After many moments, he finally faced him again. "I know that your connection to her is strong. I admit to feeling a certain responsibility to her as well." He paused as if trying to find the right words.

His patience was at an end. "Just tell me if you will keep it a secret or not."

Keeva's mouth quirked up on one side. "Yes, I will."

He closed his eyes in relief.

"It means that much to you?"

He opened his eyes. "Yes, it does."

Keeva looked away, uncomfortable with where his mind kept going. Haldone's absolute surety regarding his feelings for Mya shook him.

He didn't feel that way about either of the chosen ones his filoz had been watching for the past five years. He was also sure that at least two of the three other men in his filoz did feel that strongly but another did not, which was why he hadn't thought about it much.

But in the face of Haldone's focus on Mya, he had to question his own feelings. That was what he was trained to do, question. His two fathers seemed equally enamored of his mother, so why did not his entire filoz feel the same about the women they had chosen. Was it the women or them? Was it impossible when there were four men in a filoz?

Haldone stood and set his cup on the cabinet. "I need to do something. I am going to Mya's to bathe. I do not want to wake her by doing so here."

He grinned. "You just want to use that innovative rainshower."

"Scrat, yes. I am curious how it will work. You already enjoyed it."

"I did but I did not just enjoy a woman. I *am* still recovering from my wounds." He raised his arm to look at them, clearly visible through the clear hesta strips. "I think another day I should be back to normal." He lowered his arm.

"Good. We need you healthy if we are to tackle the lawbreakers."

Though he considered himself anything but an aggressive man, he too felt keenly the need for retribution on Mya's behalf. He couldn't think about what had happened to her without anger surging up his throat. "I will be ready."

"You may want to join her. I know she has lived alone a long time, but now that she has us, one of us should be with her always."

He nodded. He had the same thought. "I will go in and sleep with her."

"I will come back and join you." Haldone grabbed the shiner

off the cabinet and pulled open the middle door on the back wall. After he closed it, the room was left in darkness, except for the beckoning light coming from beneath the sleeping room door.

He swallowed the last of his ambrosia and set the cup on the small table next to him. Standing, he stretched his arms above his head carefully. His sides were stiff and sore, but he was confident he could take the hesta strips off in another day.

He stepped around the longseat, holding onto the back so as to guide him through the dark room toward the light. Opening the door, he found the shiner far too bright and closed it some more.

He moved to the bed, which appeared empty, but Mya was on it somewhere. Studying it, he could see a small dent in the sheeting beneath the hesta that he knew to be on top and that moved up and down slightly. Not sure which position she was in, he felt his way to sitting on the edge then reached his hand toward the center.

The moment he touched her, she appeared, his hand against her ass as she was curled away from him. Immediately, his cock woke up, much to his chagrin. She'd just had her first sexual encounter. He would not hurt her by entering her again…no matter what she might want.

Plus, he didn't want to accidently bond with her. Two Edenists one after another was enough to cause a lifetime bond, and he couldn't risk that. No matter how much he cared for her, he had a filoz back in Naralina and as soon as they eliminated the lawbreakers threat and obtained the second Crius chip, he would be going home.

Slowly, so not to wake her, he lay down behind her and pressed himself against her back. His whole body sighed in contentment.

Wrapping his arm over her, he held her gently, purposefully ignoring his hardening cock as it pushed against her ass.

This felt good…right. It had never felt this way at the Pleasure Temple, but then again, he didn't stay overnight with any of the women. While he was thankful for the Pleasure Temple near his home teaching him how to make a woman orgasm and for allowing him to stay in practice, he was never about a particular woman. He'd always treated them with respect, making sure they found their ecstasy before him, but he never stayed the night.

The night before, he and Haldone had left Mya to her bed alone, her comfort with them not at the level it was now. She trusted them now. A part of him feared her trust. Would she feel betrayed when they arrived in Naralina and he went home? He had no doubt that Haldone would keep her with him, but he couldn't keep her forever unless he found another to make a filoz.

His gut churned at the thought of another man joining with Mya and Haldone. Already he felt a loyalty to them, but he was also loyal to his filoz and that took precedence.

He needed to stop thinking if he was to rest and get well. Inhaling the floral scent in Mya's hair, he closed his eyes. She was soothing in her sleep and breathtaking when awake. She was both strong and focused, yet feminine and fragile. It was an intoxicating combination that made him feel more confident in himself. Very odd.

He let his mind drift, imagining her in her home, inhaling her scent and dreaming of making love with her, of satisfying his curiosity about how her mouth tasted, how hard her nipples turned when touched and the many colors that were between the folds of her sweet feminine entrance.

He could feel his cock sliding into her moistness, her sheath tight, a soft moan coming from her mouth and vibrating up his shaft.

What?

Opening his eyes, he stared at the dark hair between his legs trying to reconcile it with his dream. But he wasn't dreaming and Mya was wide awake, her mouth enveloping his cock, mimicking the thrusting he'd been seeing in his dream. To his right lay Haldone on his back, his breathing deep as he slept.

Not wanting to hurt her, he forced his hips to remain still and touched her head. "Mya?"

Her sweet mouth pulled up his length, small teeth lightly grazing him until they reached his ridge and jumped over it, sending shocks of pleasure through him.

Finally, her mouth released him, and she looked up at him with violet eyes so dark they appeared black in the low lighting. "Yes."

"What are you doing?"

She motioned with her head toward Haldone. "He shod me what feels good after he bathe, but after I drink ambrosia, he was already asleep. I wanted practice. Does feel good?"

He swallowed hard to clear his throat. "Very good."

She grinned, one corner of her mouth going a little higher giving her a seductive gleam. "Good, I want to be good for you too."

He let his head fall back against the head puff, his heart beating at a speed that defied breathing.

Mya must have taken that as a sign of consent, because she immediately resumed what she'd been doing, taking him into her mouth as far as he could go before stroking upward.

He forced himself to lay still, allowing her the freedom to explore and "practice." Obviously, she must have woken when Haldone returned and he'd showed her how to pleasure him.

Keeva didn't mind being practiced on. His only hope was he could hold on long enough for her to be happy with her time. To that end, he tried to think of anything else, the experiment he'd been working on in Naralina, the voices of the lawbreakers who had cut into him, but it was no use.

The feel of Mya's tongue stroking his cock while it was deep inside her mouth forced his brain to one spot. Then she moved and for one brief moment, he thought she'd stop. Instead, she reached her hand beneath his ball sac and gently massaged him as if coaxing him to release.

He didn't need much coaxing, his balls tight, slivers of excitement racing up his ass, encouraging him to let go. He reached down, intending to lift her head and tell her she didn't need to taste him, when she released his cock.

She looked at him as she sucked on her own finger as if practicing how to please him. He tried to tell her she did very well, but his throat wouldn't release. She made licking that one finger seem like an erotic journey all its own.

A knowing look came into her eyes, making it impossible to tear his gaze from her. Then he felt her finger squeeze between his ass cheeks and find his anal hole.

He widened his eyes in surprise just before she penetrated his ass. Everything stiffened at once before her mouth found his cock again and sucked, demanding he release. His moan filled the air as he tightened around her finger and his seed shot through his cock into her waiting throat.

It had been a long time since he'd been with a woman and his body reveled in his ecstasy. When he finally calmed enough to view the woman who had commanded his release, he found her smiling as she licked him clean.

She stopped when she caught his gaze on her. "You liked it."

He nodded, still amazed at how quick she'd become an expert.

She continued to lick him until she'd cleaned every last drop, then she scooted off the bed before he could blink. When the adjoining bathing room door disappeared then reappeared closed, he relaxed.

He glanced at Haldone, who except for turning onto his side away from them, still slept on. The man had to be a heavier sleeper…or Mya had worn him out "practicing."

When the bathing room door disappeared and reappeared open, he waited to feel her. The bed dipped before she brushed up against him.

To his surprise, she laid her head on his shoulder and looked up at him. "I am happy I make you feel good."

His heart skipped a beat. "I am supposed to make you happy."

She nodded. "You will."

He chuckled silently. "How do you know?"

She motioned with her head toward Haldone. "He gave me pleasure two and he only had one, so I made him shod me how. Now fair. Now I gave you one pleasure, so you will give me one." Her full lower lip jutted out. "But you have to weet. Haldone said I cannod until morrow."

Holy Bendis, he was thankful Haldone had convinced her because after what she'd just done, he wasn't sure he could resist her if she asked him to give her pleasure. He rested his hand on her hip and gave her a squeeze. "That is right. You need to *wait*. I know that Haldone *showed* you how to give us pleasure, but I promise we will show you many more ways to experience it."

Her eyes lit with excitement, but as she opened her mouth, she yawned. "I am sleepy now."

He gave a small nod, his heart warming with the joy that was Mya. "Then close your eyes and sleep. We all need to rest."

She did as he suggested then her lips formed a secret smile. "Need to rest for more pleasure."

He gave her another squeeze to let her know he heard her and continued to watch her as she fell asleep. As her breathing evened out, her legs curled up, resting her knees against his thighs.

Protect screamed through his consciousness so hard he had to force himself to relax. Silently, he swore that no matter what the future held, he would always protect Mya and everyone else would simply have to accept that fact—his filoz, his chosen one and Haldone.

CHAPTER EIGHT

Mya spoke softly despite the air box surrounding them. "That is Geetic. Kindred of Air. He makes mini tornatoes. His mind is not stedi. I think Strong Mind odors him." She knew some of her words weren't right, but at least she was getting better.

Haldone turned toward her. "Who is Strong Mind?"

She studied the men around the camp then shook her head. "He is not there. He has back and wide long hair. Kindred of Mind." She looked into his eyes. "He plays with minds."

Haldone's hand in hers tightened. "He is the one who put the evil mind into Sandale."

She nodded. "*He* is ebel."

"Haldone, control yourself. This box is dependent on you." Keeva's voice from beside her had a calming effect on Haldone.

She gave Keeva a grateful smile before returning her gaze to the camp. Churi was not present either, but another Kindred of Light was building something out of wood. "The one biding is Ickis. He is Kindred of Light. He makes pickures in the air."

Keeva repeated her words correctly. She loved that he understood her so easily.

Haldone nodded. "We had someone like that creating images for some of the rainboxes we made. With eyllen, you can make the image last forever, but the only images he could create were ones he'd seen."

"What about that man there, with the Kindred of Heart birthmark?" Keeva gestured with their joined hands.

"I do not know what his ability is. He banages ones hurt."

"Ah, a healer then and perhaps the one that saved your brother's life, Haldone."

Haldone frowned. "Then what is he doing with lawbreakers."

Keeva sighed. "It may be that like me, he was exiled unfairly and was caught by them."

Oh, she hoped not. How awful to be trapped into serving Strong Mind. The idea that some of the men in the camp may have no choice bothered her.

"We have to consider every one of them a true lawbreaker first." Haldone's voice brooked no argument.

Movement on the stream side of the camp caught her attention. As the black and white hair of Strong Mind appeared, she gripped the men's hands tighter. Though the man had wrinkled skin, his gaze was sharp. Beside him, as usual, was his pet boarox. He never went anywhere without that brutal creature by his side.

"Holy Bendis, it is a boarox." Keeva's surprise was mirrored in Haldone's face.

"I'd heard that Theron had been attacked by one outside his cave, but they belong on the polar caps." Haldone turned to look at her. "I wonder if this is the same one or another one. How can the man keep it from ripping into his followers?"

It was a question she'd had as well when she'd first seen the animal with Strong Mind, especially because she'd seen one open its mouth and devour two feroon at the same time. It had two rows of jagged sharp teeth that her mother had said were like the Great White shark on Earth. But this animal was land based and its large bulbus lips covered its enormous mouth, the upper one hanging past the lower one, making it look sad.

"I did not realize how big they are. This one's back is as high as that man's head, and its brown leathery skin is smoother than I expected. Its eyes are so far apart on its flat face, I do not see how that can be of any benefit. The fact is, it looks too ugly to be as dangerous as its recorded to be."

She and Haldone stared at Keeva. Haldone responded. "You do realize that is the whole point. They are deceptive animals that pretend to be hurt until their prey move too close. If that mouth opens, a man could almost stand inside."

"I know. I just expected something so dangerous to hint at its true nature."

Haldone lifted an eyebrow at Keeva. "You mean like Grandall."

Keeva's face froze for a moment. "Point understood."

The beast left Strong Mind's side and wandered over near the fire pit. Laying down, it looked hopeless. She glanced at Keeva whose gaze darted about from one man to another. For him, this was as much a knowledge builder as a plan for attack. His eyes lit with his interest, making them a warm amber-brown.

She looked at Haldone. His jaw was set as if he'd locked it and near his ear a slight tic pulsed with his anger. His energy radiated off him.

Her own feelings were different. She wanted revenge on the lawbreakers for what they had done to her family. She'd dreamed of it since she was young, but she had no one to help her and had no idea how to accomplish it alone.

Now, she had friends who could help her drive these particular lawbreakers away, though she had a feeling that Haldone was bent on killing at least one of them. She supported him in that. In her gut, she knew Strong Mind would never leave.

But as usual, she was well aware of the danger of their goal. Though now she had friends to help her, she also had friends to lose and after being alone for so long, she didn't want that to happen.

And what if they didn't find the Crius chip. What if Strong Mind hid it in the Boarox until he obtained a second one? Or what if it was destroyed like her Air father's was when he was torn to pieces by a mind-controlled Geetic?

Keeva's hand squeezing her own had her blinking the moisture from her eyes.

"Are you ready to go home?"

She nodded and looked at Haldone who was also focused on her. It was odd to have two people in tune with her after living alone, but it was a good kind of odd feeling. "Yes, let's go home."

She let Haldone lead, his preferred position, as they walked through the long airbox he'd created on their way in. Keeva followed behind her, content to observe and protect her from behind them. It reminded her of her parents and a new dream began in her heart. For the first time since her family was taken from her, she could see the possibility of having a new one.

Halfway home, Keeva lifted them all into the trees before a pack of grendals ran through, snorting and destroying any plant life in their path.

They had to wait until the animals were far away before

Haldone created a long air slide and she had the pleasure of sliding back to the ground. She'd wanted to ask to do it again, but it was too dangerous a time to be playing.

It was almost dark when they reached her cave. In the small clearing before it, everything looked gray, like Haldone's eyes when he was satisfied. At that thought, her mind raced. Keeva had promised her they would show her more ways to feel pleasure. And he owed her one.

A pale pink started to infuse the landscape, and they all turned to see the very beginning of the Bendis moon.

Keeva sighed. "It is the last night of the pink moon until Selene completes her journey again. It always rises early on the last night as if it wants to make the most of the dark."

Haldone chuckled. "I think you mean chase away the dark."

The area grew brighter as they watched, their hands clasped as they enjoyed the moonrise. She loved that she could share this with friends.

A shadow fell over them and she looked up, expecting a cloud, but it was no cloud.

"By the Crius, what is that?" Keeva pointed.

Against the growing pink light was the largest animal she'd ever seen, but it had huge wings like the pictures of Earth bats her mother had shown her and its body was furry like the bats, but it wasn't a giant bat.

"I'll be a Logar's ass, it is a dirgon." Haldone's whispered words meant nothing to her.

"It cannot be." Keeva's voice was no louder.

She kept her gaze on the huge creature as it moved toward the rising moon. She distinctly made out four legs and a long furry tail before all she could see was a black outline as the large wings carried it farther away.

When it finally disappeared beyond the trees, she looked at Haldone. "What's a dirgon?"

He blinked as if still in shock. "Let us go inside and I will explain."

"Please do because that mythical creature does not exist." This time, Keeva led them as they entered the cave.

Once inside, Haldone made straight for the cold box and poured three cups of ambrosia. She didn't mind. She liked the taste of it. On Earth it would be considered a mix between coconut and mango with a spicy after taste like an Indian chai. She didn't remember drinking it as a child, but it could be because her parents couldn't make it.

"Explain." Keeva hadn't even sipped the delicious drink.

She wasn't surprised by that. When it came to learning something, the Discoverist was impatient.

Haldone took a large swallow before answering. "I'd heard that the dirgon was mythological as well, but a man at—that I know claimed to have seen one. Of course, his filoz believed him, and two other Edenists did, but no one else. My friend Konala believed Cordtz because he found prints in the ground that he believes to be dirgon. He can also speak to animals as he is Kindred of Eden, so I do not wonder that he is right."

"And what about the other person?" Keeva barely let Haldone pause.

"That would be Khaos. His ability is like no other in Naralina. He can see parts of the future."

Keeva's eyes widened. "I have never heard of that, but if he could see the future, what would that have to do with an animal believed to be a myth, or at the very best, from so long ago in Eden history that some Discoverists consider it extinct?"

Haldone scratched his beard. "I do not know. But if Khaos believes a dirgon exists, it could be because some event in the future will reveal it."

Mya enjoyed watching the two men converse. Their interactions with each other in this particular conversation the reverse of their norm. Usually it was Haldone who was the aggressor and Keeva the calm responder. She liked that they had so many sides to them. "Why is the dirgon contitert myth?"

Keeva turned his attention to her. "The dirgon is supposed to be a legend about the combining of two races who had once been at war. In ancient times, before the Crius populated Eden with humans from Earth, there was only animals and plant life on Eden."

"And water creatures." Haldone moved to sit on the longseat.

"Yes, and water creatures. In the few moving images left behind by the Crius, it was stated that the two largest of the species had become sentient and began a long battle over territory. Though we have oceans here, it is possible to travel the entire planet on land, which made the carving out of living space difficult. Both animals required a lot of resources to sustain their survival."

Mya joined Haldone on the longseat, being sure to sit close enough to touch, fascinated by the story. Her parents had never told her about a dirgon. "What kind of animals were they. We have feroon and boarox libing on the panet and there's still plendy of food left for the other animas."

Keeva sat in the chair opposite them, stretching his legs out in front of him.

She moved her foot to touch his, so he could see them.

He looked at her instead of past her and smiled, obviously happy to tell the tale. "These animals were far larger than even those. Their names are unpronounceable in our language, but the closest our Discoverists could determine based on the descriptions was they were like dragons and direwolves."

Direwolves? Her mom had told her Earth stories of princesses who needed to be saved from dragons because they didn't know how to save themselves. Her mom had always said that she had no use for princesses. Mya liked that. But she'd never heard of the other animal. "What's a direwolve."

"A direwolf is a giant canine. They look like the direlot except they have only one tail, one head and they are furry."

"Like a tigran?" She enjoyed petting the tigrans and listening to the rumble deep inside their chest.

"Yes and no. They are bigger than a tigran and their fur never changes color. It is the color of the tree trunks to help them hide. They also have a pointed snout which stands out farther than a tigran nose does. Or I should say they did."

She tried to imagine the image. She would paint what she envisioned and then ask Keeva how close she was. "What happened?"

Haldone answered. "They were killing each other off and were soon to go extinct, which in hindsight was a good outcome as it allowed the other animals we have today to flourish."

Keeva nodded. "Yes, but these beasts were not ready to give up the fight. A few saw what was happening and they tried to negotiate a peace, but it was useless. Both sides were too caught up in their own needs and importance, so a small group decided to join together and mate to produce a new species that could live after they had all perished."

Ah, she understood the name now. "The dirgon, half direwolf and half dragon." It made perfect sense. "What happenet to the dirgons?"

Keeva shook his head. "That's why they've always been considered a myth. There was no record, not even a story of one having been born. But the few records found from the Crius were moving images with sound and once the early Edenists figured out how to view them using the Crius chips, the records began to deteriorate. They are long gone with only the notes of our early Discoverists who viewed them, as a testament to what they revealed."

She turned to Haldone. "Then how can what we saw be a dirgon?"

"It could not be, but Cordtz said he saw one as well, which means either the dirgons have been hiding for centuries, or what we saw was not really a dirgon."

Keeva's eyes lit. "That also begs the question, if they were in hiding, why come out now? Or if it was not a dirgon, what was it?"

She shook her head. "We do not have the anders. I think we shood tell others when we go to Naralina."

Keeva nodded. "I agree."

"So do I." Haldone rose. "And now, I think we should move to the green table and plan our attack on the lawbreakers."

~~*~~

Mya's fears eased. Haldone's plan was a good one. For someone who'd never lived in the jungle, he had a good sense of strategy. Keeva's suggestions had added a level of safety she didn't think would have been included had Haldone decided on his own.

Inside, her heart warmed. Every suggestion Keeva had made was met with stony silence at first, but he knew how to phrase his ideas in a way that Haldone could accept. She envied Keeva his ability.

His hand moved from her wrist, as it lay on the beautiful shimmering green table, to her upper arm, sending delicious shivers along her skin. "I believe it is time I pay back a debt I owe to Mya."

"You owe her a debt?" Haldone's question echoed her own.

"Yes. Last night after you were asleep, she practiced what you taught her with me."

Haldone's lip quirked up. "She did?"

At the memory of Keeva's taste, her body came alert. "Yes, I did. So now he owes me pleasure."

His hand moved to cup her neck and he rose. "And I am very willing to pay my debt."

He held her neck as his lips brushed hers. She opened for him, inviting him in, but he didn't taste her. Instead, he pressed a kiss to her cheek before kissing her shoulder then lifting away.

His eyes had turned a darker brown, closer to the color of soil. That simple change caused a spike of excitement to race through her heart.

"No time like the present." Haldone pulled her hand up and she rose.

She'd been sitting at the end of the oval table, but he and Keeva walked her around to one side of it and stopped. "Aren't we going to my dome?"

The two men looked at each other and some type of silent communication passed between them. She was positive if she knew more about pleasure, she would know what they said, but she didn't.

Haldone turned her to face him as Keeva let go of her hand. How could Keeva give her pleasure if he couldn't see her?

Haldone placed both his hands on her waist and lifted her so she sat on the table. Its cool, hard surface beneath her butt felt similar to the rocks outside the bathing pool where she usually sat to dry off.

Immediately, Haldone let go of her and Keeva, sliding his hand along the table surface, touched her thigh. "I do not want to wait another moment to give you pleasure."

"Oh." His words sent shivers across her skin. Was there such a thing as a Kindred ability that made words give pleasure?

Keeva stroked his hands along her thighs from her hips to her knees and back, focusing her total concentration on the telltale tingles moving between her legs.

Haldone's hand found her back and moved up to her shoulders. She looked back to find him on the other side of the table.

"Lay back."

She glanced down to see his cock was hard and straight, and she licked her lips. That part of the men's bodies almost made her salivate when it was in that state. Happily, she did as he requested, liking how he kept one hand beneath her head until she was fully flat.

She shivered slightly as her back came into full contact with the cold table, but it warmed quickly. She smiled up at Haldone as he pulled her hair away from her body and let it hang over the edge.

"Your breasts are far too beautiful to be hidden."

It was his stare more than his words that had her nipples hardening. She would have to try that on him, too. There was so much to learn about pleasure.

Keeva's hands had moved from the tops of her thighs to the insides, causing her folds to fill with moisture.

She spread her legs wider, offering him whatever he wished to do to bring her that indescribable feeling she'd experienced with both of them.

He accepted her invitation with his finger and his eyes, sitting down on the chair and blowing over her moistness. "I want to learn all there is to know about you, Mya."

That he spoke to her feminine spot wasn't lost on her and more moisture pooled at her opening. Could he see it?

As Keeva's tongue touched her folds, Haldone clasped both her hands in his. She looked up at him, her eyes widening when Keeva's tongue found her opening. Haldone's knowing smile was all she saw before he lowered his head to suck a nipple deep into his mouth.

She arched upward toward him, trying to move her hands to grasp his head, but he wouldn't release them. Instead of being upset, a zing of excitement ran from her heart to her sheath, and she tightened it just as Keeva's tongue pushed inside.

His moan vibrated through her and she brought her knees up, wanting him to do more.

Haldone nibbled at her hard nub with his teeth as his hands clamped her own in place, making her feel helpless as need shot from her nipple to where Keeva's tongue invaded.

The man between her thighs seemed to understand what

Haldone did to her, and his tongue pulled out to lave her upward to the small pleasure point she'd just learned about.

Haldone released her breast and grinned. "I think we both enjoy your hard points."

Keeva didn't stop the swirl he'd started with his tongue on her pleasure nub. He simply moaned against it, sending tiny vibrations through her and causing her to gasp.

Haldone's chuckle made her glance at him before he took her other nipple in his mouth and purposefully hummed against it. The vibrations seemed to meet somewhere in her center, her stomach tensing.

Again, she tried to move her hands but Haldone's strength had them secured to the hard table beneath her. Instead of feeling trapped, like she had the time a tree had fallen and caught her hair beneath it, forcing her to break her hair to escape, this made her feel both helpless and excited. Their main focus was her pleasure.

She had so much to learn and was more than willing to let them show her.

Keeva's finger moved between her folds to her opening.

Yes. She held her breath, anticipating his invasion.

Then as Haldone began to roll her nipple between his teeth, Keeva inserted his finger to its end.

She moaned loudly, wanting more. He didn't disappoint, his finger retreating only to insert two fingers inside her. She pressed her pelvis up, wanting more, wanting him. But his mouth played faster with her nub as Haldone's kept up a steady teasing at her nipples, one then the other.

Her sheath tightened against Keeva's stationary fingers inside her. She arched again as her body stole her breath from her, the feelings building inside until both men hummed against her at the same time and the ecstasy she'd reached for poured over her and through her.

Keeva removed his fingers only to press his tongue inside her, moaning as she slowly gained the air she needed. Haldone let go of her hands and massaged her breasts. It was a calming yet stimulating feeling.

Keeva stood and licked his fingers, the action setting off tiny sparks inside her. If he felt like she did when she'd licked him the night before, then she understood why he closed his eyes.

Haldone bent over her and gave her an upside-down kiss. His tongue dominated her mouth like he'd dominated her breasts. When he finally broke the kiss, his breathing was as rapid as hers, but he didn't move away from her lips. "May we pleasure you in any other ways?"

His smile was seductive, promising more than she had knowledge of, which brought to mind another curiosity for her.

"Yes."

He raised both eyebrows and slowly stood. "And what would our new pleasure virgin like to request?" He seemed not only curious, but utterly confident in his ability to grant her wishes.

She loved that about Haldone. Whatever he focused on had his absolute attention. She'd seen it when he'd worked on this very room, as he watched the lawbreakers, and when he'd pleasured her the very first time.

"I want what you both had last night."

Keeva frowned. "That is what I just did for you."

She shook her head. "No. I want to feel full in both places."

Keeva's eyes widened as he stared at her. Had she asked for

something not done? She looked up at Haldone. His eyes had grown dark, his nostrils flaring. "Are you saying you want us both at the same time?"

Her entire body lit up like a shooting star. She'd never considered that possibility. She'd only wondered why it felt so good to the men to have her finger inside their butts. At the idea of being taken by both men at the same time, to have twice as much pleasure, made her head feel light.

She nodded uncertainly, not even sure if that was something acceptable.

Haldone's lips quirked into a seductive smile, and her toes curled as her body flooded her sheath again.

She looked back at Keeva to find him squeezing his cock in his hand. Before she understood why, he pushed himself deep inside her in one long stroke.

She gasped at the full feeling, her heart racing all over again. "Is that yes?"

He pulled her up and took her mouth with his, his tongue sweeping inside hers as his arms grasped her tightly to him. Having him around her and in her mouth and sheath made her happy.

Haldone strode to the open door to the living area. "Before we say yes, I need to see if there is shilla in the cabinet."

She broke the kiss. "What is shilla?"

Keeva rested his forehead against hers. "It is a slippery coating so one of us can fit into your ass. That area does not self-lubricate like where I am now."

"That's why I had to spit so much on my finger to push it into you?" That made sense.

Keeva's Adam's Apple moved as he swallowed. "Yes."

She pulled her head away to look at him, concerned by how hoarse he sounded.

Haldone strode back in with something in his hand. He unhooked the shiner and opened the door that led the way into the caves where she lived. "If you would bring our woman through here."

They weren't going to give her both?

Keeva didn't ask Haldone what he planned, as if he could see what was in Haldone's mind. She knew he couldn't. Her mind dad could talk to her in her mind, but he couldn't see what was in hers. Only what she said to him in her head.

He began to walk, and she locked her legs at the ankles around him, enjoying the feel of him inside her too much to focus on anything else. When he sat in a green chair outside the room, she unhooked her ankles, sitting more securely on him and liking that she could adjust herself as she preferred.

Keeva grasped her hips. "Stop." His jaw tightened like Haldone's usually did.

She froze. "What?" Did she hurt him?

Haldone stepped past Keeva, found her and wrapped some of her hair around his hand. "He wants to save himself until we can all three find pleasure together in your dome."

She blinked. That was a long walk. She opened her mouth to say so, but suddenly the chair moved, and she held on tight. It was if they were gliding on air, but though Haldone was Kindred of Air, he couldn't levitate.

She looked below them and the chair did appear to be slightly above the cave floor. Behind Keeva, Haldone pushed them, but he didn't seem to have a difficult time doing so.

He grinned at her over Keeva's shoulder. "Air slide."

Excitement of another kind filled her and she lifted her arms. "Yes!" She hadn't felt so free and happy since she was a child.

Keeva's mouth on her breast brought her back to her new reality, one she liked more and more each day. Her sheath tightened at his suction, and he groaned before he let go. "Does it hirt."

"Not exactly."

She refrained from tightening around him. Though he said it didn't hurt him, she could imagine what it would be like if she wanted pleasure and then delayed it for one of her men.

Her men. Were they? Like her fathers and mother? Did she want them to be? She looked from Keeva's pained face to Haldone's smiling one. Now that they were in her life, she couldn't picture life without them.

Then again, when they entered Naralina, she may have so many people in her life, they may not want to be in hers anymore. That thought bothered her.

"Here we are." Haldone stopped in the living area of her dome and unwrapped his hand from her hair. He walked to the wall with the shiner that hung from his wrist and turned on her dome lights, then he shut the shiner and set it on the ground.

Keeva stood and walked with her to the bed. He was stronger than she realized. "Leave your legs to my side."

She nodded, anxious to see what he'd do next.

What he did was sit on the edge of the bed. The bounce sending him in deeper, but this time she was the one that groaned. It felt so good in this position. Her legs had folded under her so she was kneeling on Keeva. Like this she could pull up and down like Haldone had done with her.

Keeva laid back on the bed. "Come." He nudged her shoulders, pulling her toward him.

She gladly lay on top of him. She liked that she could brush her nipples over his smooth chest.

Haldone's hand on her back surprised her, and she looked back at him. His gaze was focused on her ass and suddenly she understood. Her sheath around Keeva's cock filled with her excitement. She looked back at him as her arms lost all strength and she collapsed against him.

He lifted her face with his hands. "Are you sure you want us both at the same time?"

She swallowed hard, but her heart was racing and she couldn't speak. She nodded her head vigorously.

Haldone chuckled behind her, but it sounded more seductive than funny. When cool liquid ran between her butt cheeks, her sheath tightened in anticipation. She hadn't meant to and looked worriedly at Keeva, but a slight smile curved his lips.

"Relax."

Relax? She was so excited she wanted to yell. Instead, she tried to get her sheath to loosen.

Haldone ran his finger down the path of the cool liquid and it stopped at her anal hole. As he played around it, she held her breath, wanting him to push into her. When he finally did, her sheath tightened and her pleasure nub pulsed, taking what little breath she had.

Haldone stroked her back with his other hand. "Relax. It is not time yet."

She didn't know how to relax. She wanted that feeling she'd had before only doubled.

"Shhh." He continued to make circles on her back until she felt her body calm. He withdrew his finger then pushed two into her.

"Oh." She snapped her head up, arching her ass in the air, pushing her pelvis into Keeva.

Haldone stopped. "I do not know, Mya. You are tight. Maybe we do just this tonight, and I can enter you here another day."

Though that was all she had asked for, now that she knew she could have both men at once, she didn't want just his fingers. She looked back at him. "No. I want both."

"I do not know."

She faced Keeva. "Please."

His eyes warmed to their lighter color and his hand cupped her cheek. "Kiss my nose."

"Your nose?"

"Yes. Just a light kiss."

She did as he asked.

"Now kiss this cheek." He pointed to his right cheek, and she kissed him there. Then he pointed to his left cheek, and she kissed him there. As she kissed everywhere he pointed to, she felt Haldone remove his fingers and insert them again. Though she tensed with the pleasure that shot through her, she was able to relax as half her attention was taken with doing as Keeva asked.

Then Haldone pulled his fingers out, and she felt him spread one of her ass cheeks to the side. Her body immediately responded, her sheath contracting around Keeva's cock as excitement raced to that spot.

More cool liquid flowed across her anal hole.

"Kiss me." Keeva's words caught her attention.

"Where?"

He pointed to his mouth.

Finally. She lowered her lips to his, and he nudged them open. Gently, he explored her mouth, running his tongue along her teeth, wrapping it around her own. He sucked on her tongue just as Haldone pushed his cock forward against her ass.

She moaned into Keeva's mouth but didn't stop kissing him. Haldone slid in deeper, spreading her and pushing against Keeva's cock inside her. She tried to focus on Keeva as he thrust his tongue into her mouth.

She arched more and Haldone's balls hit her even as she ground against Keeva and ripped her mouth from his on a hiss. "More. More." She could barely catch her breath, but her body was on fire everywhere. Her pleasure nub throbbed, her sheath sent sparks of sensation through her body and her anal hole seemed to energize everything.

Keeva groaned. "Move Haldone."

As if he'd been waiting for the command, Haldone pulled halfway out and then pushed back in. His movement sent her against Keeva, pushing him as far as he could go inside her. The dual sensations set her sheath aflame, heat pulsing through her body.

But Haldone didn't stop there. He pulled halfway out and rocked back in again, starting the conflagration all over again. She pushed her hands deep into the bed as she arched and grinded, prolonging the pleasure.

Keeva's fingers caught her nipples and began to roll them, sparking more flames, not letting the last burst subside. And then Haldone rocked forward again and Keeva lifted his hips pushing into her, and her pleasure exploded from her body, ripping a scream of pure rapture from her as the heat engulfed her.

Whimpers of bliss pushed past her lips as the blaze continued to throb through her, its intensity far surpassing her bodily knowledge and sending her consciousness floating along a sea of joy.

Eventually, her body demanded air and she gasped. Pulling in long draughts, she filled her lungs as she reconnected with her body and the slowly fading feelings from the touch of the two men in its wake.

Haldone had collapsed on top of her and her face lay against Keeva's shoulder. A small niggle of disappointment crept in because she hadn't heard or felt the men's pleasure, too. She wasn't sure she could have and still remained conscious.

Keeva kissed her temple.

She turned her head farther to the side, only to feel Haldone shift as he caught her lips with his. The kiss was gentle before he whispered against her lips. "You were destined for me."

Happiness floated through her at his words. That he wanted her, thought it destiny they were together thrilled her deep in her heart. It made her feel as if she belonged. She glanced toward Keeva, but his face was turned away. Did he feel the same?

Haldone stood again, his hands holding her waist. "I need you to relax now."

She quietly chuckled but didn't say anything. She felt as if she'd been on a two-day run with no food or water. Every muscle in her felt like the drooping leaves of a salis bush.

As Haldone slowly pulled out, she felt a few sparks ignite, but she couldn't have moved if she wanted to.

Keeva's hand came up and stroked her back. "Did you enjoy having both of us? Was it all you had hoped for?"

She wanted to look into his eyes to gauge his mood, but his head remained turned away. "I liked it. It was more than I imginned. Pleasure dubbed. Every part of me is happy but feel weet."

Haldone's voice came from behind her. "What you need is some ambrosia, a warm wash and a meal.

She smiled against Keeva's shoulder. "Then we can do it agin."

Inside her, she felt Keeva harden at her words. That he would be ready to pleasure her again, warmed her heart.

"You are my kind of woman." Haldone's voice came from farther away, and she opened one eye to see him on his way back into the tunnels.

"I will return with ambrosia."

She closed her eyes and gave in to the sleep her body demanded.

CHAPTER NINE

Keeva lay still, not wanting to disturb Mya. His mind raced faster than a scared welchet and his heart ached. It made no sense considering the amazing pleasure he'd just experienced. Something far surpassing any other sexual occurrence.

And that was the crux of his problem. The pleasure the three of them derived from each other wasn't typical. It was special, like a gift. Not only was he in tune with Mya's feelings, needs and happiness, he was also sensing what Haldone was thinking. That only happened among filoz members after years of being together. It shouldn't be happening at all for him. He was already part of a filoz.

Could it be because Mya was an Edenist as well and so the connection went beyond friendship and into the physical? And if he was correct, what did it mean for him? He'd be lying to himself to say his feelings for Mya were no more than what any man on Eden would feel for a woman not his.

She is mine.

He tried to push away the thought. This wasn't how men found their chosen one. They watched her as she acted on Earth, becoming aware of her wants and needs, her flaws and strengths, her acceptance of the idea that life existed on other planets.

But Mya wasn't from Earth. She was very much alive on another planet. Her strengths were both physical and intellectual. Her reactions purely honest, her needs very few and her wants… he swallowed. Her craving to learn about pleasure with him and Haldone had him feeling as if he could take out the lawbreakers with a flick of his hand.

No one had made him feel that way. Even in his filoz, he felt like the weak link, as if all his thinking was unneeded. But with Mya and Haldone, he never felt that. In fact, in the few days they'd been together, he could see a change in Haldone. The man even asked his opinion on a couple ideas already, something he would never have expected from him.

And Mya, she looked to him as if he was the most knowledgeable man on the planet. It was a heady feeling. He was well aware that he looked upon her with a bit of awe as well. After all she'd experienced, all her years living alone with no one aware she existed and to have survived and grown into a confident woman, impressed him more than any discovery he'd ever had.

And soon they would take on the very people who forced her into a life alone. At first, all he wished was to punish the lawbreakers, but the more he learned about Mya, the more he wanted to kill them.

But in his gut was a deep seeded fear they would hurt her. The plan kept her from being in too much danger, but the chance was real. He didn't want to lose her.

How do you expect to keep her in Naralina then?

At the sound of Haldone's footsteps, he ignored his own

conscience. First, they had to battle the lawbreakers, then he could figure out what to do about his growing love for Mya.

He stiffened. Love? As a Discoverist he should look into this idea, explore his own feelings, but he was a coward. *Not now.*

"I brought half the stock back." Haldone walked into the dome, keeping his voice low. He loaded some of the drink into the cold box then poured three cups. "We will need to wake her."

"I know." He reached his arm out. "Give me a hand up."

Haldone felt around on the bed until he touched him then grasped his hand and pulled him and Mya to a sitting position.

She blinked.

Haldone handed him a cup, and he put it to her lips. She grasped it and drank.

Keeva accepted a cup from Haldone and let the cool liquid soothe his dry throat, reminding him of exactly how intense their pleasure had been.

"Are we ready to use the rainbox?" Haldone sounded like he had more energy than he and Mya combined.

Mya shook her head and handed the empty cup to Haldone. "No. Bathing pool."

He didn't remember seeing baths in her bathing room. "Where is your bathing pool?"

She pointed outside the dome. "Where we find Haldone."

He looked up at the man. "That is not far is it?"

He shook his head. "No, but Mya, is that water warm enough?"

"Yes. Bring tools and shiner."

Haldone frowned. "Tools?"

He grinned. "Towels."

"Yes, towels." She moved her leg from the bed and pulled back, obviously forgetting he was still inside her. "Oh." She wavered a bit as she stood.

Any discomfort he felt was washed away by the bereft look on her face. "Do not worry. We will have pleasure again." He rose, ready to steady her.

She studied him for a moment then stepped closer and wrapped her arms around him. "Thank you."

Haldone joined them, towels from the bathing room thrown over one arm and a shiner in his other hand.

He reached out as the man approached so he would see they were standing in his way. Haldon quickly grasped Mya's hand and led the way out. When they reached the pool at the end of the next tunnel, Haldone set the shiner on a rock high on the side, to give them the most light.

Even so, the water looked cold and black. Mya released their hands before they could stop her and the water moved.

"Feels good. Wait." The water moved, and he could tell she'd gone to one side. Suddenly, the entire rock pool was flooded with orange light. He could see the bottom now, but it was deep, and all along the sides were very large rocks that started wide and came closer and closer the deeper it went, making the pool look like a funnel.

The light was from eyllen glowing just beneath the rock surface. There must have been a hand sized rock covering it and Mya simply moved it to allow the light to shine. Even if the eyllen was scratched to where its pure form came through the rock, it wouldn't explode because the water kept the pure oxygen of the planet's air from contacting it.

"Come in." Mya's voice came from the back center of the pool.

Haldone didn't hesitate, jumping into the water and making a large splash.

Mya's laughter filled the space and his heart skipped. Her reactions were pure, not tainted by either Earth or Eden societies. A strange urge to keep her from everyone forever had him shaking his head at himself. That was beyond possible.

"Keeva, you come, too."

He couldn't see them, but her voice made it sound as if she didn't want to be apart from him for any longer than she had to. Trying to brush away his fanciful thoughts, he stepped into the pool, walking down the rocks until he was submerged.

Immediately, he felt Mya's hand on his arm, her appearance almost a relief, as if he'd doubted she really existed.

Her hair was wet and slicked back over her head and her smile was wide. "Warm, right?"

He nodded. "It is. I am guessing it is the eyllen in these caves that makes it that way."

"Yes, that's what my Mind father said. Steam in meel area warm too."

She always referred to her fathers by their Kindred which was common among young Edenists. "Do you know your fathers' names?"

Haldone frowned at him, but he ignored it. If they were to find her fathers' parents, knowing their names would make it easier.

She shook her head. "I don't remember. But I have picdure of them with names on bad." She pointed down the tunnel. "I also paint them with mother in painting on thad waw."

He smiled. They couldn't bring that to Naralina with them,

but at least she had their names somewhere. "Are all these paintings yours or did your mother paint some, too?"

She shook her head. "She paint on Eard and dome. I paint here."

Haldone dove underneath her and came up between her legs, bringing her above the surface as he found purchase on a rock.

She squealed with delight. The water dripping down her skin made her seem like a water nymph of his ancient ancestors and her long hair pooled in the water around them, some of it lying on Haldone's shoulders. The man grinned, able to live in the moment far better than he could.

Mya surprised them both by throwing herself off him backward and disappearing from sight. "Marco."

He looked at Haldone, but the man just shrugged.

"What is Marco?"

The water before them moved and Mya emerged between them, her hand on each of their shoulders. "You don't know Marco Polo gane?"

"I have never heard of this *game*. Is it from Earth?"

Her brows lowered. "I don't know."

That wasn't the first time she'd used an Earth contraction in her speech. She must have been close to her mother if she used it so naturally. Naralinian speech tended to be more formal. He'd also noticed she used a word he didn't know that he was sure was an Earth swear of some kind.

Haldone continued to grin. "It does not matter. Tell us how to play it."

As Mya gave instructions, he couldn't help but think

she had a distinct advantage with this game. Did her mother teach it to her after she'd started her transition, or had it been a coincidence?

After almost half an hour of the game, he finally figured out that she was cheating by climbing out of the water completely. He watched the water carefully, not easy to do with Haldone constantly moving trying to brush against her.

Finally, he called "Marco." Her responding Polo was exactly where he thought she would be. Haldone raced to the spot, but he jumped out and caught her as she tried to run around the outside. "Got you."

She squealed then laughed and he picked her up and swung her around. When he put her down, the laughter was still in her eyes. She reached up and pulled his head down, giving him a hard, exciting kiss, her tongue delving into his mouth.

"I found you." Haldone stepped behind them, and pressed against her, pushing her closer.

She giggled and broke their kiss. Though she kept her arms around his neck, she looked back at Haldone. "That's my tickish place."

He wiggled his brows. "Good information for me to know."

"Oh!" She pressed closer to him, Haldone having pinched her ass before throwing a towel over her shoulders.

As much as he wanted to listen to his cock, which was growing harder by the moment, he was sure that they should eat first. "I think we need to feed this woman before we explore her any further, be it to find ticklish spots or pleasure spots."

That woman in question, ground her pelvis against him.

"It appears I must take matters into my own hands." Bending

his knees, he scooped his arm under her legs and lifted her in his arms.

"What? Wait." Her arms tightened around his neck. "Put me down. We fall."

"We *will* fall, which we will not." He strode down the tunnel, the sound of Haldone's chuckle assuring him the man followed.

After a few strides, Mya's hold lessened a bit, but she was very quiet. His guess was she was remembering something from her childhood again. He hated to see her sad. "Have you tried to be visible?"

She perked up at his question. "You think I can?"

"Yes. Your invisibility is your ability as an Edenist. Just like I can make the plants obey me, or Haldone can make air hard, you can make yourself invisible. That means you can make yourself visible again.

"How?"

"It starts with your mind. You need to think yourself into visibility. However, many of us use our hand as it is a way to focus our ability. I cannot show you as there are no living plants down here and I do not want to bother the roots." He looked over his shoulder. "Haldone, can you show Mya how you create something hard out of air?"

Haldone strode closer, his hand out until he touched Mya. "I can create anything, but without green light, you would not be able to see it."

Of course. "Then I guess we will have a lesson on using our ability when we go outside again."

"I'd like that." Mya smiled tentatively.

Was she embarrassed? She shouldn't be. It was the lawbreakers that took her family before they could help her through the transition. His family had been a great support for him.

When they reached her dome, he let her stand and pulled out a chair. "Now you sit and I will cook you dinner."

She nodded as she pulled the towel about her. "I like that. I always cook dinner."

"What?" Haldone pulled out a chair and sat next to her. "I just cooked you dinner two nights in a row." He ran a towel over his wet hair.

"I mean before you two came here."

Keeva caught the towel Haldone threw at him and wiped down his limbs. "You *meant* before you two came here." He opened the cold box then looked over his shoulder.

Mya rolled her eyes. "Meant. I think I like learning pleasure more than speaking."

Haldone laughed, but he was focused on Mya.

The look of happiness on her face because she'd made the man laugh just reinforced his determination to go after the lawbreakers. She had so little happiness in her life.

Unwrapping the havling meat, he cut into it. Would he be one to cause her more pain when he returned to his filoz in Naralina?

~~*~~

Mya followed Haldone through the jungle with Keeva protecting her back. In their planning for the attack, Haldone kept trying to figure out a way to avoid using her, which she thought silly. It made sense for her to help. She was invisible and she was good with her bow. It was a good weapon and the fact the arrows were invisible until they left her hand, made it even more deadly.

But Haldone told her to only wound the men because he didn't want her to have to live with having killed someone. It was nice to be cared about so much that he worried about her. If Haldone was able to create air boxes around Womer and Strong Mind, she had no doubt they would succeed. Removing the Crius chip from Strong Mind, if that is where it was, might be another matter.

There were only six lawbreakers. They had agreed Strong Mind and Womer the water-sucker, were probably the most intelligent. Geetic, the twister, and Churi, the orange light man, they considered the most uncontrollable. The picture-maker and Kindred of Heart were probably the least threats.

As they drew closer, Haldone created his air box, but that would only be temporary. In order for Keeva to help, he had to draw some of the men into the jungle. She didn't like that Keeva would be exposed before she and Haldone. But once Haldone had an air box around Strong Mind and Womer, there would be less danger.

They stood farther north than usual, not wanting to reveal they had come from the south, in case any of the lawbreakers escaped. Helios had not broken over the horizon yet and the camp remained quiet.

Damn, they'd forgotten about the boarox. She shivered as the large creature snored contentedly. Hopefully, when Strong Mind's abilities were nullified, the creature would turn on one of the lawbreakers or just escape.

Haldone had wanted to attack while they all slept, but Keeva had suggested another strategy. He said if they did as Haldone suggested, they wouldn't have as much control, having to react as others woke. She'd agreed. This was better.

Haldone looked at Keeva. "Are you ready?"

The man nodded then squeezed her hand. "Are you ready?"

"Yes." She kept her voice low though no one could hear them. Finally, she would be able to avenge her parents' deaths without risking her life by trying to do so herself. For too many years she'd lived in fear of these men.

"For Mya's parents and my brother." Haldone held up her hand in his and Keeva held up her other one.

Too soon, Keeva let go and moved to the edge of the box with his hand against it. Haldone nodded and Keeva slipped into the jungle. Then Haldone moved his hand to close the air box.

Mya stepped closer to Haldone instinctually wanting comfort, her heart having started to race as she watched where Keeva had disappeared. Once again, she worried like she had after her parents were taken. She needed to remember that Keeva was strong and had the jungle plant life at his command as well as she and Haldone to help him.

When she turned back to look at the camp, the boarox had woken and looked in the direction of Keeva. Did it smell him? With Keeva's abilities, it wouldn't be hard for him to avoid the creature.

A vibration in the ground from where Keeva had headed rumbled across the area. Within seconds, Womer, Strong Mind and the Kindred of Heart exited their shelters.

She grasped Haldone's hand harder.

Womer looked at Strong Mind and spoke, pointing in Keeva's direction.

Strong Mind spoke to Kindred of Heart and gestured toward Churi as he crawled out of his shelter.

Kindred of Heart nodded to Strong Mind and soon he and Churi were headed for Keeva.

She glanced at Haldone to see his jaw tight and the small tic at the side of his cheek moving. He hated Strong Mind.

She watched the older man who caused so many of them misery. He motioned with his arm and the boarox followed the two men.

She whispered. "Only two went into the jungle." They had hoped for three.

Haldone held up his hand. A few moments later all the lawbreakers's heads snapped toward Keeva's direction.

Haldone smiled. "Keeva is having success."

Then Strong Mind nodded to Womer.

Damn, that wasn't what they'd hoped for. He and Womer needed to stay together for Haldone to imprison them.

He squeezed her hand. "Mya, I have to go now. You know what to do?"

She looked into his darkened eyes, unafraid. "Yes."

"When I release this air box, Womer will be able to sense you, but he cannot harm you unless he touches you, so stay away from him."

She nodded, her emotion suddenly clogging her throat at the danger Haldone would be in.

He pulled her toward him and kissed her. It was quick and heartfelt, then he let her go. "It is time."

Releasing her hand, he raised his and ran in the direction of Keeva before jumping over the camp boundary.

Womer turned at his appearance, but Haldone ignored him and ran directly toward Strong Mind He lifted his hand and the man yelled, but no sound could be heard. He'd done it!

She raced over the embankment, taking aim and letting her arrow fly.

Geetic, who had just emerged from his shelter, howled as her arrow found his thigh.

Haldone turned toward where Womer had been, but that man had raced into the jungle. She stopped and aimed at her next target, cringing as it hit Ickis in the leg. He yelled as he fell to the ground.

Three incapacitated, but three were unaccounted for. Womer could kill Keeva, but if Haldone left the area, Strong Mind would escape. Suddenly, the boarox bounded over the camp boundary strait toward her.

Her heart stuttered in fear. Pulling another arrow from the quiver on her back, she tried to take deeper breaths. She needed to pretend it was just another a direlot. But the beast's large lip flapped as it bounded closer, exposing its jagged teeth.

"Mya, shoot it."

She notched the arrow with shaking hands.

Mya run!

She froze at the voice in her head. "Daddy?"

Move!

The urgency of the tone snapped her into action, and she dove away from the oncoming beast.

She rolled to a stop and stared as the beast tackled Womer who would have grabbed her. "Daddy, where are you?"

Beast.

Haldone's heart spiked in his chest as Mya suddenly became visible, the boarox and Womer both converging on her. No! Lifting his hand, he ground his teeth. "By the Crius, Mya, move!" She finally dove to the side and he quickly incased Womer and the beast in an air box. He ran toward her.

"No!" she raised her bow and shot, but the arrow hit his hard wall.

He wrapped her in his arms, his heart still beating so fast he could barely take in air. "Thank the Poetess, you are not hurt."

She turned on him with a snarl. "Take down the air box!"

He stepped back. "Why? Mya you are safe now."

"Boarox is my father! Take it down!" She slapped his face. "Take it down!"

Stunned, he raised his hand, releasing the box. It couldn't be Strong Mind playing with her mind because he was still well trapped.

Mya spun, took aim and hit Womer. The man howled but refused to let go of the boarox.

The boarox was her father?

She pulled another arrow from behind her when an orange beam hit the ground at her feet.

He spun and threw a hard wall up between them and Churi, who ran out from the jungle toward them. The orange light rebounded off his wall and hit both Womer and the boarox.

The two broke apart as they were hit and Mya ran for the beast. He raised his hand to entrap Womer, but the sound of a tree falling behind him switched his aim and he incased Mya and the beast instead. The tree fell on Womer, crushing him, while the branches that would have hit Mya had spread a part, obviously Keeva's work, leaving her untouched, even without his air box.

"Daddy? Daddy?"

Mya reached toward the beast, her hand seemingly disappearing into its flesh.

"Daddy. Please daddy. Don't die again."

When there was no response, she grasped the animal with both arms. "Please daddy."

"We need to go." Keeva's voice as he spoke to Haldone behind her was urgent.

Mya turned to face them, her tears causing pain to slice through his heart. "My daddy needs hep. Please. Don't let him die."

When she broke into sobs, Keeva crouched down next to her. "Why do you think this boarox is your father?"

She looked at him. "He talks to me in my head."

Keeva's eyes widened before he examined the animal. He lifted a front paw where a strap was tied around it. "Haldone, I need a knife."

Startled back into functioning again, he stepped forward and handed Keeva his knife. "Make it fast. I cannot hold them all for long."

He kept scanning the lawbreakers, two wounded, two in air boxes, one hopefully dead and one not accounted for.

He glanced at Keeva when he heard the knife cut through material. The beast disappeared and in its place was Mya's father. "Holy Bendis!"

"Daddy? Please be alive."

Keeva touched her hand where she held her father's. "He is breathing, but he is not well, and we need to leave here."

"Not without my father."

"No, not without him. But you will have to help me move him."

Haldone wanted to help, but he couldn't create anything more and still contain the lawbreakers. He'd had to release the wall against Churi to protect Mya but had quickly enclosed the man when the tree was down.

Mya stood. "What do you need?"

"Help me get him into the jungle. I can have him carried once there." Keeva pulled Mya's father into a sitting position and motioned her to the other side of him. Slowly, they lifted him, his lack of movement not a good sign. What if they saved him only to lose him? She'd never be able to live with that…or them.

She glanced at him as they walked to the edge of the camp.

"Go." He nodded. "I will follow."

She turned her head quickly and moved her father beyond the camp.

He waited, making sure they were far enough that none of the lawbreakers, except the one missing, could harm them. Then he focused on the men under his control.

Churi kept trying to burn his way out, only to be blasted by ricochets. The man was not smart. Geetic just stared at his leg as if he didn't understand what had happened and Ickis had crawled into his shelter. Only the Kindred of Heart man was misisng, but that could mean that Keeva had him tied up somewhere.

He raised his hand toward the air box holding Strong Mind to increase its stability to hold for several hours. The man smiled at him and crossed his arms as if to say he'd still won.

He didn't have time to kill the man. For that he'd have to create a different air box and with Mya's father so harmed, he had to get them to Haven quickly.

"I will be back for you." He pointed at Strong Mind.

The man laughed, though no sound could be heard.

He turned away and strode out of the camp. He *would* kill him. He had no choice now. There was no doubt in his mind that Strong Mind would scour the jungle until he found him, Keeva and Mya. He would have to get to him first.

Once he'd gone a few steps into the jungle, he ran the opposite way that Keeva and Mya took her father, then circled around and found them halfway to the cave.

Keeva was moving Mya's father through the jungle with vines, gently transporting him. They stopped when he joined them.

"How is he?"

Mya, still visible, ran to him. He embraced her, his heart finally slowing to a normal beat as he inhaled her floral scent.

Keeva shook his head. "We have stopped three times to dribble water into his mouth which he did swallow, but it was the only sign of life we've seen."

"We need to go to Haven."

Mya pulled away. "Why? I thoudt all there in bad shape."

"They are, but they have a healer." He looked at her father's unconscious form. "And if the lawbreakers track us, I would rather they track us to a place with high stone walls like Haven."

"Then we go there." She said it as a command and stepped to her father's side.

Keeva looked at her and gave her half a smile. "Yes, we will go there." He turned to Haldone and opened his arm. Lead the way."

CHAPTER TEN

Mya sat in Jerumbala's living area twisting and untwisting her hair. She couldn't help it. Though the healer assured her he would do everything he could, the side look he gave Haldone made it clear he wasn't sure he could save her father.

She couldn't believe they made her wait in Jerumbala's house while they took her father to the baths. They said she'd be in the way, and they weren't sure about the reactions of those in there. She'd still insisted, but Haldone had put an air wall outside the door.

Dropping her hair, she rose and walked into the other room where one of the leaders, a man named Lennix slept. He'd almost starved to death and only Jerumbala's intervention had kept him alive. She'd been told he'd lost his beloved to the lawbreakers.

Before today, she wouldn't have understood that, but if she lost her father again, she wasn't sure she would want to live either. It was hard enough the first time.

She stood before the reflection glass, amazed to see herself in it without touching it. Haldone said she appeared when the boarox started running toward Womer. He thought it was because she was afraid, but that was the moment her father had spoken to her.

It had been odd when a couple of men had stared at her as they passed when they came into Haven, but other than that, it didn't feel any different to her. Keeva had promised to teach her how to use her ability.

Her lip quirked up. She could tell Keeva liked teaching her things. She was grateful that he'd listened to her about the boarox.

Mya?

"Daddy!" She ran out of the room and threw open the front door.

"Wow, that is quite a greeting." Jerumbala entered first, followed by Haldone and Keeva carrying her father on a litter.

She stepped to his side. His eyes were still closed and it made her question if she'd just hoped to hear him, "Daddy?"

His eyes opened. "Mya. My treasure."

She didn't understand why she broke into tears, but she grabbed his hand and didn't let go, even as they settled him into another bedroom.

"Do not strain yourself too much, Tauren, or I will ban her from this room." Jerumbala's voice held no real threat.

Her father glanced toward the man.

"Good, I am glad to hear that. I will let you visit for a little while, but then it is back to sleep." Jerumbala nodded then ushered Haldone and Keeva out of the room.

"Daddy, I can't believe you're alife."

Only because of you.

"Me? But I didn't know you were with the lawbreakers. Why? How come they let you lid?"

My sweet girl. You were my reason for living. Yanek penetrated my mind before I knew he could and discovered I had a daughter.

I quickly shielded myself from him after that, but the damage was done. I had to stay and make sure you were safe.

But he had never told her. "Why didn't you bisit me?"

You would have run from me. Once Yanek knew I'd rather die than tell him where you were, he created that bracelet with eyllen and had Ickis make me appear to be a boarox. I tried to get it off once, but he promised if I ever succeeded, he'd have Womer kill me. So, I lived with it. I could live with anything if I knew you were still alive.

Her heart filled. He sacrificed so much for so long. "How did you know I was still alive? I was invisible. I couldn't turn back."

I am so sorry I could not help you with your transition. I could feel you with my mind, but I never revealed that. Did you not wonder at the wounded feroon and havling pigs you discovered not far from our home?

"That was you?" The memory of her excitement at finding the wounded animals and being able to shoot them for food filled her. "Did you leave that grendal for me, too?"

I did. He was a victim of Geetic. There would have been more, but not much survives that man.

At the mention of the lawbreaker, she sobered. If it hadn't been for Haldone and Keeva wanting to avenge her family, she wouldn't have ever discovered her father. She owed them so much. "I'm so glad I made friends with Keeva and Haldone."

Her father's brow lowered. *Have you bonded?*

She shook her head. "No. I don't know how." She didn't like admitting she still didn't know that, so she changed the subject to what she'd been thinking about since finding her father. "What hattened to mom?" Her voice came out in almost a whisper and when he didn't respond, she wasn't sure he heard her. "Daddy?"

Your mother was traded to some other lawbreakers. Yanek cannot access Earth women's minds, so he trades them whenever he gets his hands on one, which is not often, thank the Poetess.

Happiness and fear cascaded through her at the news. "So mom's alife?"

Again, her father didn't answer right away.

This time she waited, almost afraid to hear his answer.

I do not know.

She squeezed his hand. In her heart, she knew if her mother was alive, she would be missing her and her father as much as they missed her. Now that she had her father, she didn't need to go to Naralina until he wanted to and then they could go together so she could meet his parents. Maybe she could—

The door opened and Haldone stepped in. "Jerumbala says it is time for your father to sleep if you want him to grow healthier."

She nodded and stood. "I'll be back as soon I'm awlood." She bent over and gave her father a kiss on the cheek. "I love you, daddy."

He squeezed her hand before letting go. *I love you, too, Mya.*

She walked toward Haldone and took his hand. She wanted to tell him and Keeva exactly how thankful she was they were in her life.

~~*~~

After two days of enjoying her men and showing them exactly how happy she was, she opened the door to her father's room to find him sitting up. "You look better."

He smiled. "I am better and having you visit me makes my day complete."

She gave him a kiss on the cheek then pulled her chair up to the bed. "Your injugies made an impession on the men here in Haven."

He raised his brows. "They did? Are they making the walls around this settlement stronger or have they all decided to go back to Naralina?"

She shook her head. "Neither. They finally realized that having ordies and drinking ale was not a life worth living."

Her father coughed. "That is good to hear."

"Yes. They have started to resume some of their duties."

"How are the two leaders doing?"

She shook her head. "Not good. I think I should tell them that Strong Mind, I mean Yanek, trayes women and doesn't kill them."

Her father nodded but didn't say anything. She listened inside her head, but he didn't communicate there either.

"Jerumbala also said that the help he requested of his brother will arride soon. I think maybe they pick new leaters."

"Have you been practicing your abilities?"

His change in topic meant he didn't want to talk about it anymore, so she didn't. She'd noticed that happened often after he stopped talking. "I have. But it still takes a lot of thinking."

"You mean concentration?"

"Yes, that." He opened his mouth but she held up her hand. "I'm practicing with Keeva on pro—saying my words. I'm practicing with you on controlling my abilities."

"That is fair." A gleam came into his violet eyes. "And what are you practicing with Haldone?"

She blushed, but Haldone's words the night before came to her mind. "Nothing. He thinks I'm perfect."

Her father's laugh filled the room, making her happiness complete.

The door opened and the very man they'd been discussing walked in. "Tauren, you sound much better."

"I am. I doubt you are here to help my daughter control her ability. From what I hear, you think she is perfect."

Haldone gazed at her with so much caring, she was afraid her father would notice. Her dad hadn't yet asked her about the two men besides wondering if they were bonded, but her gut told her he would eventually.

"I do think she is perfect, perfect for me."

She sucked in her breath. He'd never voiced his feelings in front of anyone but her and Keeva.

Her father nodded. "I see. So, you just came to see if her imperfect father is doing better?"

Haldone closed the door, his face turning serious. "I came because I wanted to know about Ickis and the Kindred of Heart lawbreaker."

Her father's smile faded. "What do you want to know?"

"Are they true lawbreakers, or were they, like Keeva, falsely accused and exiled."

Her father sighed. "They are not lawbreakers. Ickis was said to have projected images of another filoz and their beloved in a public place, but he told me it was not him. As for Donte…"

She frowned. "Is Donte the Kindred of Heart?"

Her father nodded. "He had been a very good healer until a fatal accident at the eyllen deposit. There were so many wounded and many did not live. Donte's ability is he can feel the pain of others. It was too much for him. He escaped to the jungle, only to be caught by Yanek." Her father's lip quirked up. "Even Yanek did not want to be in Donte's mind and told him he could go, but Donte stayed because he saw what Yanek did to others and wanted to help in some way."

Haldone nodded as if all her father had said was what he suspected. "I imagine that Donte is who saved my brother's life."

"Yes."

"As I thought. Do you think if I neutralized Yanek, Ickis and Donte would attack me or stay neutral?"

Her heart lurched at his words. "What do you mean neutrise? You can't go back there."

Haldone faced her. "I have to. What they did to your family, your father, my brother, even Keeva. That must be avenged. They cannot be allowed to hurt others again."

Her gut tightened and she rose. "No. You can't. I don't want you to. I don't want to lose you."

He strode to her and took her hand. "I promise to come back to you. I have to make it safe here. Yanek will not stop until he finds us. I do not want to live every day with the fear he could harm people I love."

She swallowed hard to clear her throat, her fear escalating. "We can live in Naralina. We'll be safe there."

"And what about those out here? What other atrocities will Yanek commit? How many more helpless women will he trade to other lawbreakers? How far will he go to track us down?"

She shook her head, ignoring the determination in his eyes.

"No. You tode me you would do anything for me. Do this for me. Don't go." Her heart squeezed making it hard to breathe.

"Once I rid Eden of Yanek, I promise you, whatever you ask, I am yours to command. Do not ask me to forgo this. I made a vow to avenge my brother before I met you. I must fulfill that. My conscience demands that I make this area safe."

Frustrated, she pulled her hand from his. "You say you care about me, but then you won't stay. You breek my heart."

He grabbed her hand again. "No, I will keep your heart safe. I promise, once I return."

Tears gathered in her eyes as fear raced up her spine. "*If* you return."

He brought her hand to his lips. "I will do everything in my power to return. If it pleases you, I will not request a kiss as I leave, but rather one when I come back."

Her heart hitched at his words, tears cascading down her cheeks. "No." She flung her arms around his neck and kissed him with all she felt. If it was love, it hurt.

He wrapped his arms around her and held her as his tongue met her own. Finally, he lifted his face to stare into her eyes. "I love you, Mya."

No sooner had he said the words than he dropped his arms and left the room, taking her heart with him.

Haldone steeled himself against Mya's tears. He did the right thing. Maybe if he could have explained it better. She was his life and he *would* come back to her. He'd been thinking about this for two days and he'd made his decision.

Mya was safe now and had her father. The man would never

let her be in danger again. He could be confident she wouldn't follow him.

Still, as he opened the door to leave, he couldn't help looking back at the closed door to her father's room. Never had he felt so strongly for another, not even his brother. Though he traveled to avenge him, his motivation had changed the moment Mya suddenly appeared in the lawbreaker camp standing there as if she'd been frozen. As she stood there vulnerable to Womer and the boarox, he'd felt true fear for the first time.

Turning away, he closed the door behind him only to find Keeva waiting for him.

"You are going back for Yanek." The words were spoken without emotion.

"I have to. Come with me?"

Keeva's gaze moved to the house where Mya was. "What did she say?"

He took a deep breath. "She did not want me to go. She does not understand. Do you?"

"I do." Keeva's gaze returned to him. "Yanek must be stopped."

Relief washed through him unexpectedly. That the one man he could call a friend understood, somehow validated his instinct. "Then you will come?"

"And if we both perish?"

His gut twisted at the thought of Mya left alone. She had her father, but would she feel as if she'd traded one family tragedy for another if he failed? He nodded. "You are right. Stay with her. I can handle Yanek and Churi."

"And Geetic?"

He'd forgotten about Geetic. "He is wounded. For one who

must stand to use his ability, I do not think he will be an obstacle. Tauren assures me that Donte, the Kindred of Heart and Ickis are not lawbreakers. I will succeed."

Keeva's brow furrowed. "I know you believe this, but do not underestimate them."

"I will not."

Keeva nodded. "Be successful my friend." He held out his arm.

Haldone grasped it at the elbow and pulled him close, hugging him like a brother. *A brother of his heart.* He closed his eyes against the thought then opened them again and pushed away. I will return by the rising of Selene." *If I return.*

"I will watch for you."

He forced himself to give a nod of farewell before striding down the center of Haven toward the door that would open upon his destiny. What a different feeling it was from the last time he'd left Haven.

Keeva watched Haldone until he disappeared beyond the cyndis-tone walls of Haven. He wished he was as confident of the man's success as he was. If Haldone failed, he wouldn't survive. This was clear. Yanek was not one to simply punish someone for attacking his camp. He would kill. That Haldone planned to kill as well made him swallow hard.

Killing had long been a forgotten art in the cities of Eden. From all he had studied and observed, only lawbreakers had that tendency. But Haldone was different. He was neither lawbreaker nor content Naralinian. He was caught somewhere between or was before he'd met Mya.

His breath caught as he imagined the pain Mya would endure

if Haldone did not return. Or was it his own feelings for the man that had his hands fisting with frustration. Despite his longtime connection with the men in his filoz, his bonds to Mya and Haldone were stronger and they had not even bonded.

There was no possibility that Haldone would come back if he attempted revenge on his own.

He looked to the house where the woman he'd come to love waited while the true brother of his heart left to battle what everyone feared. And if he didn't come back, not only would Mya and he be left with half a heart, the lawbreakers would have a second Crius chip to use to enter any city on Naralina or worse, travel to Earth.

A new purpose rose within him. He'd always thought as a Discoverist he was a servant of Naralina, focused on helping it to evolve, but now he needed to be its defender, even if the city never learned of his efforts.

He took two steps toward the house to say goodbye to Mya then stopped. If he saw her, he wouldn't be able to leave. He didn't have the strength Haldone had to resist her pleas, and because she was honest with her emotions, there would be pleas. If he stayed, he could not forgive himself.

Turning away from seeing the woman he loved one more time, he strode after Haldone. The only chance they had was if they surprised the lawbreakers. And if he was wrong, if Haldone could vanquish Yanek alone, he'd protect his back.

Slipping out through the door of Haven, he let his mind wander back to Mya. *I love you, Mya.*

~~*~~

Mya paced the confines of Jerumbala's house, wrapping her hair around her hand then letting it loose to grasp it and repeat the process. After a thorough search of Haven, it was clear that Keeva was gone, and she knew exactly where. He'd joined Haldone.

Part of her was relieved that Haldone would not face the lawbreakers alone, but another part felt betrayed by them both while her heart ached with fear. She wanted to consult with her father, but he still slept as the afternoon waned, drawing closer to the time of day when all was black and white.

Haven was only half a day's jog to the lawbreakers' camp. If her men were successful, they should have returned by now. What if they were dead or worse, had Yanek in their minds. The man was ruthless, and she could imagine him pitting Haldone and Keeva against each other for fun then killing whoever survived such a battle.

In that camp, Keeva would be at a distinct disadvantage, but if Haldone hurt him, the man's intensity would make it impossible for him to live with himself. There was no positive scenario that she could think of for why they hadn't returned.

Mya.

At her father's call she rushed into the room. "Daddy? You're awake. Do you need something?"

Her father pulled himself up into a sitting position and studied her. "Yes. I need you to tell me what is happening beyond these four walls. You are obviously distraught."

She let go of the hair still gripped in her hand. "Keeva left with Haldone. They should have been back by now if they were successil."

Her father laid a hand on her arm. "Mya, it is not easy setting up an attack, especially with two against many. They may have waited until just the right moment. Maybe when the lawbreakers are asleep."

She shook her head. "We determined that would not be a good stradeict move because we could not prelict the use of the lawbreakers' abilities."

His eyes widened before he lowered his brow. "I know this is hard, but you need to remember, they did this to keep you safe."

She stood, irritated with her father though she had no idea why. "Who is going to keep them safe?" She faced her father. "What if they don't come back?"

He looked away from her and she finally understood what his torture had been. Her other fathered killed and her mother lost to lawbreakers somewhere in the jungle. Her heart hurt for him now that his reality could become hers.

She knelt at her father's feet. "Daddy, what should I do?"

He returned his gaze to her and for one unshuttered moment, she glimpsed the raw pain in his eyes. He cupped her cheek. "Did you want to bond with these men? Do you love them?"

She pressed her fist against her chest. "It hurts here." She moved her fist to her stomach, her eyes watering. "In here it's all tight like a dead knodded infragile vine. That's what I feel. Is that love?"

Her father stroked her hair and sighed. "Yes."

"Why does it hurt, daddy? I thought love was happy."

His eyes widened and his lip quirked up. "Oh, it is, my treasure. It is, but only when we are all together." He looked away a moment then seemed to have come to some kind of decision. "You must go find them. You will never forgive yourself if you do not."

"I'm afraet. Afraet they are hurt and afraet of the lawbreakers. That's why I never found you."

"Fear is good. It keeps you alert. Take some of the men from here and go look for your men. Then come back to me. I cannot bear to see you gone for long."

She rose. "I will."

"First, disappear for me."

She fisted her right hand and knew from his smile she'd done it right.

"Now reappear."

She fisted her left hand and his gaze found hers again.

"That is my girl. Remember, any spike in your emotion could cause you to disappear or appear without your control. Be aware of that."

"I'll try." She looked around the room and found her crossbow where she'd set it after showing her father how well she'd kept it. Strapping the quiver of arrows on her back, she lifted the bow.

"Be sure to take some men with you. I do not want my daughter captured by the lawbreakers, too. Yanek cannot control the minds of Earth women, but he can control the minds of Edenists, and you are both woman and Edenist. I do not know what he could do to you."

She nodded, her fear and excitement closing her throat. As afraid as she was, she couldn't stand the thought of staying inside Haven's walls while Haldone and Keeva could be hurt or worse.

Bending over, she gave her father a kiss on the cheek then turned. The faster she left, the faster she'd find out what had happened to her men. *Her men.*

Slipping out of the house, she looked around for men to come with her. The only man about was Sarach, the ale maker who sat on a longseat outside his home, probably relieved to be able to rest. She asked him to gather men and told him where they should go then spun on her heel and headed out the door of Haven, unwilling to wait one more moment.

Though the older man called her as she exited, she ignored him. Only one thing mattered now and that was getting to Haldone and Keeva. Squeezing her right hand, she hoped she was invisible then started running through the jungle.

As she crossed a stream, she looked down onto no reflection. Satisfied she was undetectable, she continued her run. By the time it was dark, she arrived near the lawbreakers' camp, the fire in the center like a beacon through the underbrush.

With Womer no longer alive and her father in Haven, there was no one to alert Yanek to her presence. Her father's assurance that Yanek could not sense others had given her the courage to venture forth.

As she drew closer, she heard voices near the north edge of the camp, so she moved around it, keeping as silent as possible until she reached the far west side. When she could finally see the camp clearly, she sucked in her breath.

Hanging from a tree just outside the northern perimeter of the camp was Keeva, a vine around his neck, his feet dangling in the air as his hands grasped at the vegetation. It was as if he was making his own vine strangle him.

It wasn't hard to deduce that Yanek played with him. She scanned the camp for Yanek and found him smiling at Haldone, who sat on the ground gasping for air, his hands pounding against an invisible wall. Holy Bendis, he was suffocating in his own box!

Her arrow couldn't penetrate an air box and the vine from this far away would be a difficult shot, but the man with the black and white hair was an easy target.

Fury rose from her tight gut and threatened to take her over, but she swallowed it down. Her father said emotion would reveal her, and she needed her invisibility now. All their lives depended on it. Fisting her right hand just to be sure, she moved within range, boldly walking over the embankment of the camp.

Pulling an arrow quietly from her quiver, she strode closer, then halted as Churi, the man with the burning orange light, looked her way. There was no way he could sense her, but his gaze was on the ground behind her.

She glanced back. Dammit, she was so used to her cave floor where no foot prints could be seen, she'd forgotten the dirt would give her away. Quickly, she stepped far to the right and took aim at Yanek. Just as she let her arrow fly, a burst of burning light hit the ground to the left where she'd been standing.

Yanek howled as the arrow penetrated his thigh, and Churi turned toward him.

She pulled another arrow out and struck Yanek in the abdomen.

He yelled again. "Find her!"

Churi held his hand up and began a giant sweep with his light. Running up the embankment, she jumped into the jungle and ducked behind a large tree trunk. Once the beam had passed, she sprinted through the jungle toward where Keeva had been. When she arrived there, he was gone. Where?

Running to the edge of the camp, she found him. He was

helping Haldone stand, half dragging him away, but Churi had given up on her and turned toward the men and raised his hand.

Grabbing another arrow, she yelled as she released it. "No!"

Churi turned, his orange beam just heading out, meeting her arrow. She threw herself to the ground and the burst of light went over her. She jumped up again, but her hand stilled as she reached for an arrow.

Churi swayed on his feet, her arrow glowing bright orange and sticking out from his forehead. The sight turned her already churning stomach and she doubled over, her last meal spraying the jungle floor.

She didn't want to look again, but the sound of her name forced her to.

"Mya run!"

She couldn't see the camp anymore as a swirling cloud of dirt headed straight for her.

Frantic, she sprinted through the jungle around the embankment, desperate to get away from Geetic, but the man kept on her trail. Just as she realized she must be visible, she was lifted into the air and high into the tree tops.

Grabbing hold of the vines that cradled her, she hung there as Geetic continued by before pausing. Whipping the air up around him, he headed back the way he'd come as if he wanted to make sure he hadn't missed her.

Silently thanking Keeva, she quickly fisted her right hand, then swung down from the tree to land on the embankment of the camp.

At the center was Haldone and Keeva. Haldone's hand was raised and Yanek snarled at him though no sound could be heard.

She avoided looking at Churi, who now lay on the ground and proceeded to walk toward her men.

Fisting her left hand, she let them see her so they would know that she was unharmed. Keeva strode toward her and wrapped her in his arms. "By the Crius, you are safe." His voice was barely above a whisper, but she didn't care. As long as he still breathed, that's all that mattered.

He let her go partially but kept one arm wrapped around her waist as he walked toward Haldone. The relief in Haldone's eyes told her all she needed to know. Careful not to bump his arm, which kept Yanek imprisoned, she hugged him.

He rested his chin on the top of her head. "I love you."

His voice too was scratchy, which made her lift her face to look at him. "Finiss this."

He gave her a silent nod.

Turning her back on Yanek, she walked away toward the end of the camp and into the jungle.

After a few moments, Keeva joined her. "It is done."

Still, she wouldn't look. She'd never killed anything besides an animal and that was only to eat. That she'd killed Churi, despite his evil nature, left her feeling sick.

"Mya?" Keeva lifted her chin. "You saved our lives, but you should not have come. It was too dangerous." Despite the softness of his voice, his words were still clear.

She touched his throat with two fingers. "I did not want to live without you."

"I did not want to live without you either." Haldone's voice as he strode through the jungle, had her turning. "But I also did not want you to risk your life. How could you come here by yourself?"

His angry scratchy tone caught her off guard. "I didn't. Men from Haven are on their way."

He raised his brows. "Are they invisible, too, because I do not see them."

Keeva grabbed Haldone's shoulder. "I do not see Geetic either."

They all froze, listening for the whirring sound that always preceded the twister Edenist. Instead, they heard footsteps approaching.

Mya fisted her right hand then gabbed both men's hands. They stood silent, watching the jungle as the footsteps grew closer.

Finally, the greenery gave way and Jerumbala, along with Sarach and five others moved toward them. She let out a breath of relief and let go of her men.

Jerumbala stopped at their sudden appearance.

To be polite, she squeezed her left hand before she spoke. "I'm gad you came."

Haldone grumbled something next to her, but she ignored him.

"We found these two not far from here." Jerumbala moved aside to reveal Donte and Ickis.

Haldone stepped forward. "Yanek has been vanquished, as has Churi."

Donte looked past them. "Are you sure?"

Haldone nodded. "I am, but you are free to confirm it."

"I must." The man started to walk past them and Haldone nodded with his head for two more men to go with the man. She liked how quickly they listened to Haldone.

"What about Geetic?" Ickis looked to Haldone for his answer.

"He is still alive and spinning."

Ickis shook his head. "I am not sure Geetic will survive without Yanek."

"Why?" She couldn't help asking. It seemed like Geetic would do better without Yanek controlling him.

"Geetic, does not think like us. His brain is scattered. I am not sure he can focus long enough to obtain food. Yanek may have controled Geetic and made him do as he wished, but he also made sure the man stilled long enough to eat the food we provided."

"I doubt it was a kindness. Yanek just wanted his weapon of death to live so he could control him." Haldone's harsh thoughts seemed at odds with their success.

She looked to Sarach. "Do you think someone from Haven mide be able to provide food here for Geetic for a wyle. We still don't know if he was a lawbreaker or falley aqueed. I don't like that he mide stard to death. Yanek is the one that made him an intumint of death."

The gray mustache of Sarach lifted. "I think we can arrange something. It would be like feeding a pet animal. I hear Theron did that to get his tigran to follow him to Loraleaf."

Theron? He was the man who built the home at the opening of her caves and created the reflection that looked as if there was no opening. She knew of Theron's tigran and had wondered where it had gone. "Is Loraleaf close then?"

Sarach smiled at her. "Of course. It is only a good day's run from Haven, but now that we can use our portals again, it does not matter where it is. Haldone came to Haven from Loraleaf. I have not seen that settlement yet, but I hear it is very unique."

A long day's run? Haldone had come from there? A place with men who had portal chips that could have transported them to Naralina in an instant? Betrayal and hurt gnawed its way up from her belly and into her heart as she turned to face Haldone. Her fury was so raw, she could barely form the words. "Loraleaf is close." Her voice was deceptively soft.

Haldone's eyes widened. "Yes, but I knew we had to—"

"Had to what?" Keeva's scratchy voice as he stepped next to her still conveyed his anger. "Had to risk our lives for your revenge when we could have been portaled safely to Naralina?"

"It was not *my* revenge. You too wanted to punish the lawbreakers for what they did to Mya's family. It was our revenge and we were successful."

Her heart squeezed. Fearing for Haldone's life was one thing, but he had kept this information from her. "You lied…to me." Tears filled her eyes. "You were my friend."

He took a step toward her but she backed away. "I still am. I love you, Mya."

She shook her head as she stepped back again. "Friends don't do…" She pressed her fist to her chest, "this." She didn't know what to call the pain she felt.

"Where did she go?" Sarach's voice behind her told her she'd become invisible again.

Good, she didn't want to share her pain.

Keeva reached out toward her but she ducked away.

"Mya, come back." Keeva's voice pulled at her, but she couldn't be around Haldone right now. Turning away she started to run, her tears making it hard to see, but she didn't care. She just wanted to be alone.

She swallowed the hysterical laugh that threatened. After all her years alone, she finally found one positive. She couldn't be hurt by others.

Chapter Eleven

Haldone slammed his fist into the wall of the guest quarters he and Keeva had been given. After two days with no sign of Mya, he was beyond thinking. He had to find a way to make her see.

"I doubt Mykl and Lennix will appreciate the extra hole in their guest house." Keeva's voice, which had returned to normal, stopped him from yelling out his frustration.

He spun around. "Neither of them is in a frame of mind to care."

"Mine enemy is growing old, I have at last revenge. The palate of the hate departs; if any would avenge, let him be quick, the viand flits, it is a faded meat. Anger as soon as fed is dead; 't is starving makes it fat."

Haldone stared. "You would quote the high poetess to me?"

"I would." Keeva held his ground. "She was wise and warned of the spoils of revenge."

All his anger seemed to seep out of him at Keeva's words. The man was much smarter than he was. "Keeva, I need to find her. I need to make her see what I did was right."

Keeva's eyes revealed his own pain for a moment before he

spoke. "Did you not just hear the words of Dickinson. What you did was not right. It was wrong."

"How can you say that? We vanquished the lawbreakers. The jungle is safer and no one needs to fear Yanek, especially not Mya. We even found her father."

"You can try to justify what you did to yourself for the next turn of Selene, but that will not make it right." Keeva shook his head. "What if Mya pretended to like us just to get us to help her eliminate the lawbreakers. That we accomplished that, would not make her actions right."

His heart constricted. "You think Mya only pretended to care for us?" He could not reconcile that idea with the Mya he knew, yet she had not come to Haven and though he and Keeva had gone to both Theron and her living quarters in the caves, it was obvious she wasn't there either.

The thought that he had driven away the one woman he could love because he'd wanted to avenge the wrongs done to her and his brother, killed a part of him. He slumped into a chair. "I would do anything to have her back." He looked at Keeva, allowing the man to see his own pain. "Anything."

Keeva sat on the longseat across from him and leaned his elbows on his knees. "Even apologize and admit you were wrong?"

His ego sparked up, but he suffocated it. "Yes." His shoulders slumped. "She means more to me than breathing. If I had not vowed to avenge my brother before I met her, I would not have gone after Yanek."

Keeva nodded. "I know. But now you must accept that you were wrong and beg her forgiveness."

He sat straighter. "I will. I just have to find her and—" He paused, looking at Keeva's slumped shoulders. "Will you forgive me? I put your life in danger, too. I—when I saw you hanging there and there was nothing I could do…." He shook his head. "I have been an ithio."

Keeva sat back, studying him. "Yes, you have. I can forgive you, but it will not do us much good if we cannot get our woman back."

His mood brightened. "*Our* woman?"

Keeva nodded.

"What about your filoz?"

"It will be hard telling them, but I cannot ignore what I feel for Mya."

Inside him, peace began to fill the holes in his soul. "Are you saying you do not mind establishing a filoz with me?" He swallowed but forced himself to say it. "Even after what I have done?"

Keeva's mouth quirked up. "As hard as that is to believe, yes."

Haldone smiled, a new feeling of belonging flooding his psyche. It was so new, he was almost afraid to breathe. "I thank you."

"Now, we need to discover where our chosen one might be."

He jumped up and rolled his shoulders. "Yes. We know she has not been in her dome or in Theron's living quarters or here. Could she have attempted to find Loraleaf on her own, out of curiosity?"

Keeva rubbed the back of his neck. "I do not think so, in that she and I are very different and that is something I would do."

"Point well made."

"Do you think she could be at Haven?"

He scratched his beard. "You mean be here and not reveal herself?"

"She might come here to see her father. I cannot believe she would stay away from him long."

He sighed, wishing with all his heart that he could have made it so she wouldn't stay away from him. Somehow, he had to prove to her that he was worthy of her.

"I suggest we start by asking her father if he has heard from her."

He raised his brow in disbelief. "First, knowing that we have searched for her, do you think the man would have told us? And second, why would he betray his own daughter to me after what I did?"

When Keeva remained silent, his gut clenched. He'd made a true mess of so many people's lives. "She was also very upset that she killed, Churi."

Keeva rubbed the back of his neck. "We should be with her to help her through that."

"Yes, we should. At least Donte recovered the one Crius chip Yanek had before we buried him. That Donte has a lot of courage. To deny implanting the chip in Yanek unless he received the second one was a risk."

"Maybe not. If what Tauren said was true, it was a brilliant maneuver. Since Yanek tried to play with Donte's mind once but found it too bleak that he never went back, it gave Donte the freedom to challenge the man. I think Donte was somewhat safe from Yanek."

He nodded. "And if he healed the man's followers, he was valuable."

"Yes. Has he agreed to go to Loraleaf and meet with Jahl and Khaos?"

Absently, he nodded, then he stopped. "What about the other tunnels?"

"Why would she be there instead of in her dome where she has all that she needs and comfort as well. The tunnels are solid, smooth rock and dark." Keeva shook his head at him as if he'd become addled.

He crossed his arms. "Her painting?"

Keeva's gaze snapped to him. "Her painting?"

He started to pace. "Yes. When she explained some of the paintings to me, she always linked it to an event in her life. The havling pig being butchered the day her parents were taken, the city of Naralina the day she decided she needed to find her grandparents because too many people knew about her caves, even the painting of the welchet sitting on her bed was because it had died."

Keeva's eye lit with hope. "So, you think between finding her father, his brush with death again, her saving us, and your betrayal, she might need to paint…a lot?"

He swallowed the lump in his throat at the reminder of how he'd hurt her. She wasn't like other people. She'd never been lied to before. This was new, and he had to be the logar's ass that introduced her to such a sickening feeling. "Yes, I think she is painting…a lot."

Keeva rose. "We may be wrong, but we need to—"

The door to their guest house banged open and Mya's father stood in it. "Where is my daughter?"

Obviously, the man was feeling better. "We were just leaving to get her." He was relieved to see Tauren's face relax.

"Good. I need to see her before I leave."

He glanced at Keeva who shook his head in confusion.

"Where are you going?"

"To find my beloved. Ickis has volunteered to help me look. He feels bad about making me look like a boarox."

"I doubt he had a choice."

Tauren shook his head. "No, he did not, and I do not blame him, but he does want to help me, and he knows where to find the men Yanek traded with. I may never find her." He paused as if trying to reconcile his heart with that fact. "But I have to try." He gave them both a stern look. "I am assuming you will bond with my daughter and take care of her."

They both nodded, but he felt compelled to be honest. "If she will have us."

"My daughter has survived this long because she is intelligent, but from what I understand, you have hurt her. She has little experience with emotional interactions beyond those she had with us. Too long she stayed in our home alone." He shook his head. "We always told her it was safe and it was, but we never expected what happened."

He stepped up to Tauren and put his hand on his arm. "Thanks to you, she survived. I promise you, we will protect her always."

"Haldone, one other request." Tauren looked at Keeva as well. "Be careful about revealing her nature to Naralina. We had not made a decision about whether to let anyone know she was an Edenist."

Keeva took a step closer, keeping his voice low before the open door. "I have to know. How did this happen?"

Tauren turned and closed the door before answering in a low

voice. "We were never absolutely sure. Mya was born on Earth. Ember, her mother, had been pregnant before and lost the baby. We had gone back to Earth many times because Ember was an only child and her parents were much older. When she discovered she was pregnant, she insisted on staying on Earth until the baby arrived."

Keeva's eyes grew round. "You think that being born on Earth instead of Eden means this planet somehow keeps female children from being born?"

Tauren shrugged. "I do not know. All I know is that Mya was born on Earth."

He'd never been very attentive in the bodily sciences classes he'd had in school, but he had a feeling Keeva would be happy to explain it to him.

First, they had to find Mya. Then they had to convince her to forgive him. And then they had to see if she would be their beloved. They had a few hurdles to tackle. "I think we should leave now. I do not like the idea of being apart any longer than necessary." And he didn't want Tauren to realize they did not know for sure where Mya was.

"But you will consider revealing her as an Edenist carefully?"

"You have my vow on that." Especially, since he wasn't sure he wanted to share her with an entire city anyway, or rather the whole planet.

Tauren looked Keeva in the eye. "Do you agree as well?"

"As I swore to Haldone week's ago, I will keep her secret as long as we can. I love discovering new things, but I love your daughter more."

Haldone felt the tension in his body subside. If he had needed any proof that Keeva was the brother of his heart, he'd just received it.

Tauren smiled. "Good. Then go fetch my daughter."

~~*~~

Keeva smiled with relief as they turned the corner into one of the tunnels far from Mya's dome to see a light near its end. He quickly closed their shiner and kept his voice to a whisper. "We've found her."

"Finally." Haldone's relief was more than his own, based on his voice.

He wasn't surprised. The man was being eaten alive with guilt, worry, and love. At least he had only two of those. "I know you are anxious, but remember to let her talk, too."

Haldone nodded before waving his hand at the entrance to the tunnel.

He wasn't sure putting an air wall up was the best idea, but he wasn't in a hurry to lose Mya again either.

Quietly, they strode toward her. The tunnel was so black that her shiner only cast a dim glow. As they drew closer, he noticed there were images on the wall, but the light was so focused on where she was painting that he couldn't tell what they were, but he had no doubt they were paintings.

He moved his gaze to Mya who studied her artwork as she lifted the brush and stroked it against the cave wall. He glanced behind her and noticed a hesta and her bag. He hoped she'd been eating. He grinned as a memory came to the fore of her bringing him hennys, his first real meal in the jungle. Mya could take care of herself, at least physically.

"Mya?" Haldone's voice sounded both tortured and pleading.

She started before holding the shiner up in front of her. Her gaze focused on Haldone, and she put her paint brush on a box at her feet.

"Please, Mya. I came to beg your forgiveness." Haldone's words were just above a whisper.

Mya tore her gaze from Haldone and smiled at him. "I missed you."

His heart sored at her words, but for them to become a family, she had to accept Haldone as well. "We missed you, too. We were worried. We looked everywhere for you."

She frowned. "Why?"

Haldone took a step. "Because we love you, Mya. We were afraid you could be hurt and we would not know where you were."

Her gazed snapped back to Haldone. "You betrayed me." Her hand came to her chest. "Hurt me. Why worry about me being hurt?"

Haldone's hands curled into fists. "I did not mean to hurt you. I thought I could have you and avenge you. It all seemed to fall into place."

She shook her head, her chin lifting. "You lied to me."

"I did not exactly…"

Keeva laid a hand on Haldone's arm. "You did."

Haldone snapped his head around, his anger palpable.

He raised his eyebrows and shook his head.

As Haldone's shoulders fell and he faced Mya, it was clear he understood. "You are right. I lied to you. That is why I am here. I hurt inside because I caused you pain. I never want to cause you pain again."

"When I was alone, no one caused me pain." Her logic was almost too simple to argue with.

Still, Haldone tried. "But then you had to do everything yourself. You had no one to talk to."

"But now I can talk, and I have my father."

"But he is at Haven."

She shook her head. "I can go to Haven. Talk to him there."

Luckily, he didn't mention her father leaving. That was sure to be another painting.

"We could be with you, always."

Keeva could see this going back and forth forever. His Discoverist friends who focused on Edenist behavior had once shared a study they conducted where they used the "common enemy" theory to bring families back into concert.

For the first time since they entered, her demeanor changed from confident to unsure. "How can I trust you? I don't want to hurt again."

His heart squeezed at her admission and at the look of devastation on Haldone's face. Though he hadn't done anything, he suffered to see their pain. He stepped forward before Haldone said the wrong thing and bridged the space between the two. "Mya, your decision to forgive or not forgive Haldone is not just about his lie."

"What are you saying?" Haldone's voice was almost a growl now. "I have not done anything else wrong."

He ignored him, keeping his focus on Mya. "Haldone and I have formed a filoz and we want you to be our beloved. You are our chosen one. This means we want to bond with you for the rest of our lives."

"You do?" Her violet eyes lit with interest, which gave him the confidence he needed to continue.

"Yes, but you have to understand that Haldone will hurt you again."

"What?" Haldone stepped closer and lowered his voice. "This does not help."

"And you will probably scare us by disappearing on us again."

Mya, cocked her head, her brows lowered, clearly confused. "It is my ability."

"And I am sure I will ask so many questions that both of you will wish I would sleep through the entire day."

Mya smiled softly. "Maybe."

"What I am saying is that we are not perfect. We descended from humans and though we have evolved, we are not like the Crius machines we have found. We will make errors and sometimes inadvertently hurt each other. That is what happens with families, but it is all worth it to have each other. We can work together, love each other and stand together against others who might want to harm any one of us like we did in the lawbreakers' camp."

Mya nodded, but she didn't say anything.

It had to mean she understood what he meant. She was a smart woman. "Others in your family like your grandparents, even your father, may in the future say something that will hurt you, but they still love you."

"No, my father would not hurt me. He protects me."

His heart ached at what he knew was going to break her heart. "I want you to think about all of this, because it is more than forgiving Haldone for one lie. It is about being willing to risk the tough times for the joy of being together. You need to think about this because if you accept us, it is for the rest of your life. At the end of today, we will return for your answer. No matter what you decide, at that time you will need to go back to Haven as your father wants to speak with you."

"I understand."

He turned to find Haldone glaring at him. "And if I do not wish to leave this to her to think about?"

He leaned in and whispered. "Do you want her for today or for forever?"

The man was clearly torn.

Keeva gazed at Mya. "When we come back at the end of the day, we will ask you for your answer. If you do not want us, we promise to never bother you again."

At her look on consternation, his stomach lightened. She didn't want to live without them anymore than they wanted to live without her. She simply hadn't figured that out yet. He just hoped the rest of the day would be enough time for her to do so.

Haldone's hand shot out and gripped his arm. He didn't say anything, but from the shiner's reflection in his eyes, Keeva knew the man barely held himself in check.

Not bothering to lower his voice he addressed Haldone. "Trust me."

The new brother of his heart looked to Mya then to him and let out the breath he'd been holding. Finally, he released his arm and turned away, striding back the way they'd come.

"We will return when Helios has gone to sleep." He gave Mya a hopeful smile then forced himself to follow Haldone.

Haldone waved his hand and turned the corner, but he didn't walk much farther.

Keeva found him barely ten steps from the entrance to the tunnel. "What is it?"

"I was thinking. If we have today with her, we can spend it convincing her that she is meant to be with us. I think we should go back in."

He linked his arm around Haldone's. "Not a good idea. Then we are going back on our promise."

"I did not make a promise." Haldone resisted him as he pulled him forward.

He sighed and faced the man. "We did. We are a filoz now."

"Then I should have a say in what we promise."

"I think we need to go to Theron's living quarters in the cave and have a drink?" Maybe even a little kerasi juice, if there was any. Haldone needed to relax.

"No, I do not need a drink. I am not leaving until after Mya makes her decision. I am waiting right here."

Keeva grabbed Haldone by the arm and tugged. The man tried not to move, but they were equally matched, until Haldone used his ability to fashion a hard air block and jammed it against his chest.

He could have resisted, but instead he let Haldone go and fell back on the cave floor. He let out a grunt as he hit.

"By the Crius, are you hurt?" Haldone reached down his hand, his worried countenance exactly what Keeva expected.

He wasn't hurt, but Haldone didn't know that. "I think now *I* could use a drink."

Haldone helped him up. "What were you thinking?"

"I was thinking about a cold drink." He grinned as Haldone led the way back to Theron's living quarters which was not a short walk.

~~*~~

As Helios left the sky, Haldone stood. "It is almost dark. It is time to talk to Mya." He was anxious to find out her decision, but a part of him was as afraid as a rhybat of its shadow. He'd never thought there could be a woman for him or a filoz for him and now that he'd found both, he was desperate not to lose them.

That was one reason he'd stayed with Keeva instead of rushing back to the tunnel Mya painted. He was too afraid to learn that Mya decided she could not forgive him for his mistake or for any future mistakes.

He shook his head, still not sure why Keeva had to connect one error with their entire future. He would have preferred to deal with each problem he caused as he caused it. That was how he'd always muddled through life.

Keeva rose as well. "Yes, it is time to hear our fate."

He felt the blood drain from his face. "Could you use a different terminology? You are the one who is supposed to be good with words."

"And what are you good with?" Keeva swayed a little, proving the ale he'd decided on instead of ambrosia may not have been the best decision on his part.

"I am good with actions. I get things done." He grabbed a shiner to light their way.

Keeva appeared to think about that then nodded. "I agree." He grinned, the right side of his mouth going higher than the left side.

In any other circumstances, he would have found the sight amusing, but their life was being decided in a matter of moments.

As he followed his slightly swaying friend out the door, he halted. Was Keeva as afraid of Mya's decision as he was? He caught the door as it swung toward him and pushed it back to step into the tunnels.

Now his fear had escalated beyond control. He strode forward, finally breaking into a run.

"Hey." Keeva ran after him past the tunnel that led to Mya's dome and farther through two more intersections until he reached the one Mya was in.

Keeva stopped next to him. "That is one way to dissipate the fog in my head. Are you ready?"

"No, but I have to know and I need to know now." He walked to the tunnel and turned the corner. Fear turned his stomach into a connar boulder. The tunnel was dark. "She is gone!"

Keeva looked suddenly alert. "Again."

"She could be anywhere." He couldn't keep the panic from his voice. "We need to return to Haven."

"I agree." Keeva started back the way they had come and this time he followed.

What if this meant she didn't want to be their beloved? What would they do? They couldn't make her forgive him or love them. A growing feeling of dread filled his insides until he felt bile coming up his throat.

When they exited the cave, Keeva pulled them through the forest with his vines, making the trip to Haven in half the time. He had to admit, it felt good to be part of a filoz.

Reaching the outside wall of the settlement, Keeva had the vines lift them over and inside as he had done with the injured Tauren. It wasn't as if anyone patrolled the walls, though there was a bit more activity since Tauren had appeared.

Keeva released the vines. "I am sure she is here."

"I am not." He walked up to Jerumbala's house and knocked.

The man opened the door. "Ah, here you are." He turned his head. "They have finally arrived."

He walked past him to find Mya and her father sitting on the longseat together. She had obviously been crying. He glanced at Tauren who nodded. He had told his daughter he was leaving.

"Mya?" He opened his arms to her, wanting to comfort her, but afraid she'd reject him. He held his breath as she looked up.

She blinked at her tears then rose and threw herself into his embrace.

His heart eased as he comforted her, hoping this meant she accepted his and Keeva's offer to be their beloved, but not willing to ask outright. He looked to his side to find Keeva smiling. That had to mean all was good.

Tauren rose from the longseat. "I was just waiting for your arrival. If I am to leave, I wanted to make sure Mya was taken care of…this time."

Keeva responded. "We would have been here sooner, but Mya did not tell us she was coming here."

"Mya." The stern tone had her lifting her head and looking at her father.

"What, daddy?"

"These men are your family now." He glanced at them with his stern look, the message clear. They had better be her family.

They both nodded.

Tauren continued. "You cannot disappear on family without telling them where you are going and when you will be back, though better yet, you should always have one of them with you."

He nodded, pleased that someone besides him and Keeva could tell her how it should be.

"But why?"

Tauren sighed. "I know that you were left on your own for so long." The man blinked back the water in his eyes. "But when you were young, when we were a family, we always made sure the others knew where we were. You are part of something bigger now."

She looked up at him then turned her head to face Keeva. "We are a family?"

He swallowed hard. "If you will have us."

She looked back at him, her violet eyes brilliant from crying. "I want to be a family."

Joy flew through him and he lifted her into the air.

At her scream, Keeva came to her rescue, but she was laughing when he set her down and into Keeva's arms.

"Good." Her father strode toward his room. "I need to grab my bag and meet Ickis. We plan to travel at night since lawbreakers are not as likely to see us at night."

He frowned. "I thought lawbreakers were not out at night."

Tauren came back into the living area, slipping his arms into the infragile vine that would hold his bag on his back. "Why would you think that? They move about at night as much as during the day. It all depends on their abilities."

He and Keeva looked at Mya.

She shrugged. "I made an error."

He smirked. "You mean you are not perfect?"

"Almost." At her cheeky grin, he laughed, his heart lighter than he'd ever felt.

"Come daughter. Walk me to Haven's door. There is no portal for me. I must travel as your mother has."

At Tauren's words, he sobered. The man had endured so much. He'd told them how once taken, he'd cut his own Crius chip from his body and destroyed it to keep Yanek from obtaining it. Then to see his beloved sold, be made to appear as a boarox, and know that his own daughter lived nearby but he could never contact her was more than any man should have to live through. Yet Tauren held onto hope, determined to find his beloved.

Haldone admired the man. "I wish you success. I do not envy you your task, but I understand it and would do the same." He kissed Mya on the cheek and let her go. "Keeva and I have something we need to attend to. When you have said goodbye, come back here."

"I will." Mya took her father's hand and they strode out the door together.

"What is it we need to do?" At Keeva's question, he stepped closer, keeping his voice down.

"I need you to go to Mykl's and I will step in there to talk to Lennix."

"Of course. Their beloved must have been traded like Mya's mother." He glanced toward the doorway. "The news may help, but it may give false hope."

"At this point, I think any hope at all will help."

Keeva nodded. "And if they do as Tauren is doing, it will leave the leadership of Haven open again." He paused. "Were you thinking to settle here?"

Surprised, he raised his brow. "Me?" He chuckled. "I have never been the leader type, though I do appreciate your compliment."

"I did not say it was a good idea."

Stung, he stared at the brother of his heart whose mouth twitched. He was being teased, something no one but Sandale had ever done with him. "Good, because I do not think the men of Haven would sit still long enough to listen to you."

Keeva laughed. "I agree completely. We will leave Haven to those better equipped to lead it, but first to give some men hope."

Haldone nodded as Keeva stepped outside. He turned toward the closed door of Lennix's sick room. He just hoped that the news was in time.

Chapter Twelve

Mya raised her arms as Keeva secured the table covering around her at the east end of her caves. "I don't understand why Earth women wear this. It restricts movement. Not very pradical."

"Practical." Keeva repeated the word correctly for her. She was proud at how much she could speak now without him needing to do that. Still, she was nervous about entering Naralina in visible form.

How odd, especially when she'd bemoaned the fact she would have to enter Naralina invisible just days before meeting Keeva. So much had changed.

Haldone grumbled. "I think it impedes my view substantially."

"That is the point." Keeva finished and stood back to view his work. "She must look like an Earth woman so she needs to wear that at least for a little while."

Haldone shook his head. "Toni had something else she wore. It was a short wrap about her hips and a tight covering just over her breasts that went over her shoulders."

"I like Toni."

"I know." Haldone grimaced. "Since we will go to my brother's home first, maybe she can let you use one of her sets."

She smiled. "I'd like that." She walked the width of the tunnel and back. "I'm glad we're using a portal. I wouldn't get three steps in this."

Keeva shared a look with Haldone.

"What? What aren't you telling me?"

Keeva took her hand. "Naralina is full of steps, just like the ones you painted in your vision of it, only there are hundreds more."

"That makes this wrap even more dum."

Haldone chuckled. "After we talk to my brother, Akasha and Toni and get you a different covering, we can look for your grandparents. I think Erin, who is in charge of the Hall of Records, should be our first stop for that."

Keeva smiled encouragingly. "Unless your brother knows them. If I remember correctly, the Ruling Circle sees just about everyone in Naralina."

"As does the Triad and the High Poetess, but her grandparents will be older than most of them." Haldone checked the status of Helios as it shone inside the cave exit. "Mykl and Jerumbala should be here soon to wish us well. Do you have your bag?"

She tried to bend over to pick it up but the wrap was too constraining and she stopped. "Keeva, could you hand that to me?"

"I think I should carry it for you since you will have to focus on walking in that." He gave her half a grin.

He better not be enjoying her predicament or when they arrived at Haldone's home, she was going to wrap him up in the closest hesta.

She smiled. Actually, she'd already done that when they first met.

"It is time." Haldone held his hand out to her.

Grasping it, her heart started to race. She wasn't afraid exactly, except maybe a little. But she was excited, too. Slowly, she walked between her men out into the jungle where Jerumbala and another man, Mykl, just appeared. They closed the portal and strode toward them.

Jerumbala held out his hands to her. "I wish you all the happiness in Eden."

She smiled. The healer acted as if she were leaving for another planet, which she hoped to convince her men to do to see if her grandparents on Earth were still alive. Now that her father had written down the names of all her family, that was a trip she wanted to make. "Thank you. I wish you the same."

Mykl strode to Keeva. "Thank you. You have given Lennix and I a glimmer of hope."

"So, you will go after your beloved?"

"As soon as Lennix is well enough."

Jerumbala joined in. "Which should be within the week. Hope is an amazing cure."

"Hope." She whispered the word reverently.

Haldone over heard her. "What is it, Mya?"

She looked to Keeva. "When I first found Keeva, I didn't know his name, so I called him Hope."

Haldone squeezed her hand to get her attention. "What did you hope for?"

Her eyes grew misty. "I hoped that he would be the key that would get me inside Naralina and find my family." She turned her head to gaze at Keeva. "Not only will that hope be folfulled, but I have my own family now."

Keeva swallowed, his Adam's Apple revealing his emotion. "Yes, you do. Forever."

She stiffened at Keeva's words. They still had not bonded with her. She didn't even know how. If she asked, she was sure Keeva would tell her and Haldone wouldn't hesitate to show her, but they waited for her to initiate it. She wanted to, but a part of her still felt wild and something about "forever" scared her.

What if she'd lived alone forever? What if her father looked for her mother forever? It was such a very long time.

"Haldone, Keeva, Mya, please come visit and let us know how you are doing." Jerumbala stood opposite them.

She smiled. "We will."

Haldone stood two shoulder-widths apart from Keeva.

She was excited that Keeva finally had a Crius chip again since Donte had inserted Sandale's old one into him. He'd said it was appropriate, but that was about all the quiet man said.

Haldone and Keeva reached beneath their arms and opened the portal onto a white patrio with gold edging. Through it were white double doors set apart from the white walstone by ornate gold trim.

The glimpse of Naralina was enough to set her heart racing.

Keeva took her hand. "This is what we have been wanting since the day we met. Are you ready?"

She nodded, swallowing down her excitement.

Once they stepped onto the white stone, Haldone followed. "Thank you, Jerumbala. I will give your message to Wareson and Nassic."

She turned to look behind her at the view of her jungle until it disappeared as the portal closed. Beyond it, spread out below her was the city of Naralina. "By the Crius, it's more boodiful than I imagined."

She stared, taking in the sight of the many leveled city below her with white stone roads and walstone buildings edged in gold and topped with golden spires. It was like a fantasy world in one of the fairy tales her mother used to tell her.

Haldone pulled her against his side. "I do not think I appreciated what this city looked like until today. It must seem exciting in the same way I was excited to be in the jungle."

She nodded, reluctant to take her eyes from so many details.

Keeva tucked her hand around his arm. "I think both have a unique beauty all their own."

She turned around, forcing the men to turn with her. "This is the very top of the cidee. This is where Toni, Sandale and Akasha live?"

Haldone stepped forward. "Yes. My brother and Akasha were voted Ruling Circle members after Naralina rid itself of a corrupt oligarchy." He looked at Keeva and grinned. "I do not think I told you. Your father, Eldus, is on the Ruling Circle as well."

Keeva widened his eyes then nodded. "That was an excellent choice."

Haldone chuckled as he stepped before the door and faced them. "I am sure they know someone is outside here since all portal openings are monitored and the Ruling Circle is alerted to anyone near the member's home. I think Nassic was trying to get similar systems set up for others as well."

The door behind him opened and Mya smiled.

"Brother!" Sandale pulled Haldone into a fierce hug before stepping back and examining him. "You are alive. Toni will not believe it."

She watched as Haldone took it all in, first happy then not so much. She'd figured out that he and Toni didn't always get along. She, on the other hand, had liked Toni and Sandale when they first found her in her cave. It had been Akasha with his blue light that exposed her and Haldone with his intense stare that had bothered her.

"Sandale, who the hell is it? Don't leave them standing on the door—Well hell, if it isn't the prodigal son come home. Come here." Toni, dressed in a short feroon wrap about her hips and another that came from behind to cover her breasts and tie behind her neck, wrapped Haldone in her arms before she noticed her.

"Mya!" Toni pushed Haldone away and gave her a hug. "Woman, I am so glad to see you." She let go and gave Haldon a glare. "He didn't hurt you, did he?"

She was about to say yes, but Keeva shook his head at her. She wasn't supposed to tell Toni about Haldone's lie? Not sure what she was supposed to do because it was wrong to lie, she switched the subject. "This is Keeva. He and Haldone are my filoz."

"No shit." Toni stared at Haldone before walking toward Keeva. "Welcome to our home. I didn't think there was a soul on Eden who could pair up with him. You must have the patience of a saint."

Keeva smiled. "I do not remember studying something called a saint, but now I am anxious to discover what one is. Is it a profession? As it needs patience I am guessing it is a man, so are they only on Earth? Maybe I could learn more from—"

Toni's laughter stopped Keeva's usual word flow. "Oh, I see how this," she gestured with her hand to the three of them, "all makes sense. So, if you are in Haldone's filoz, that means we're family, so I get to hug you too."

Before Keeva could open his mouth, Toni had embraced him as well.

Family? She and Toni were family because Haldone and Sandale were brothers? She cocked her head at Keeva, who was finally being released by Toni.

"I will explain, but perhaps we should do so inside." He looked past her. "We have many curious onlookers out here."

"Yes, please, this way." Sandale held out his arm, and she followed Haldone inside the enormous doorway.

Keeva's hand on her shoulder was reassuring. She already felt unprepared for functioning in the city between its lack of vegetation and the relationships among Haldone's family.

Once inside, the small room they entered sported five doorways. Haldone led the way through the second from the right. They walked into a light blue living area. The walls and floor were still white but the furnishings were as blue as the bonabus vine's flower.

The ceiling was very high and halfway up the wall appeared to be a railing across an opening, so anyone up there could see into the space.

Movement from the opposite doorway caught her attention and Akasha stepped into the room.

She halted, stepping back against Keeva. He seemed bigger in the bright room than he had when she'd first seen him in her cave, the intricate design across his upper chest darker. His gaze rested on her and she suddenly knew why the room was that particular color. It matched his eyes exactly.

"Mya, it is a pleasure to see you in Naralina. Please, relax. No one will hurt you here."

Keeva put both his hands on her shoulders and massaged them. "It is all right. As Toni said, we are all family."

Haldone took her hand and led her to a longseat. She sat and her men joined her on either side, which did make her feel better.

Toni turned to Akasha. "Could you bring us some ambrosia? And maybe something to eat? Don't look for the leftover baka buns. I finished those for lunch."

Akasha's brows rose. "There were ten left."

Toni shrugged. "I was hungry." She took a seat in one of the chairs opposite them. "I'm working on a new physical fitness routine to help some of the women here get into shape. Most can't climb a set of stairs without losing their breath."

Keeva grinned. "Mya can. She can run from here to Haven with no problem."

That was a bit of an exaggeration as she would definitely be tired, but she didn't say anything, still not sure what was acceptable.

Sandale sat on the arm of Toni's chair. "It is good to see you brother. I feared the worst."

Next to her, she sensed Haldone sitting straighter. "We have vanquished Yanek."

Sandale shook his head. "Who is Yanek?"

Her stomach clenched. Haldone had obviously hoped for praise and Sandale didn't even know who Yanek was.

"Yanek is the lawbreaker who saddled you with another mind."

Sandale brows lowered, making him resemble his brother even though his coloring was just the opposite. "I did not remember his name. I am mostly relieved that you came back unscathed. That man, as I understand, has no guilt."

Keeva rubbed his neck. "I would not say unscathed, but we did survive…thanks to Mya."

She smiled at Keeva. He seemed to be making an extra effort to make her appear special. It was not important to be special, just to be loved as he'd taught her.

Akasha came in with the drinks and food. "I think I need to hear the whole story."

Haldone took a cup and handed it to her. "We will be happy to tell you, and I have messages from Haven and additional information that the Ruling Circle will want."

Keeva spoke up. "I will also meet with the Discoverists and inform them of new information regarding the jungle."

Toni exaggerated a yawn. "This all sounds absolutely thrilling. Mya, any chance you'd like to join me in my room for some girl talk?"

The word reverberated in her memory, something her mother had said. "Yes, I'd like that."

"Also, do you think you could let Mya borrow some of your wraps. She does not care for the one we got for her." Haldone said it like he expected Toni to deny him.

"If that would be acceptable to you?" Keeva smiled.

Toni looked at him and then Haldone. "Wow. Just wow."

Mya rose, not wanting Toni to fight with Haldone. "Can we do gulltalk now?"

Toni's attention switched to her. "Girl talk and yes, part of which you need to tell me how you learned to talk at all. Last time I saw you, you couldn't."

Mya nodded, happy to be alone with Toni. Being in a room with so many people at once was unsettling. With Haldone and Keeva in her dome, there was plenty of space, but Toni's home was divided too much for her.

Toni started out of the room then stopped. "Oh, I almost forgot. Jasmine is supposed to be here this morning. When she arrives, just send her up to our room."

At Sandale's nod, Toni led the way upstairs, through a much smaller tunnel than at her caves and into another room, which though smaller than the living area, didn't feel so tight with just the two of them.

Toni immediately hopped on the bed and patted the spot next to her. "Okay, lady, spill."

Mya looked at her cup of ambrosia. "You want me to spill this on the bed?"

"No, not at all." Toni studied her. It wasn't an uncomfortable feeling as she felt Toni's interest in her was kind. "You didn't grow up on Earth, did you?"

She shook her head and joined Toni on the bed. "I grew up in our cave."

"You mean yours and Theron's?"

"No, I mean my family's."

Toni scooted farther back and leaned against the elaborate wood carving against the wall. "You better start at the beginning."

~~*~~

Mya wiped the tears from her eyes. Just when she'd thought

her voice would give out completely, Toni had let her choose two outfits that Toni had actually created. She'd quickly changed into one that was what Toni called short shorts and a halter and put the other in her bag.

Then Toni proceeded to tell her how she and Akasha and Sandale became a yenea, a filoz with a beloved. The way Toni told the story had her laughing so hard her eyes teared up.

Once Toni assured her there wasn't anything wrong with her eyes, she'd enjoyed the entire story. "Can I ask you a question?"

Toni grinned. "Seriously? You should have figured out by now that I'm happy to talk about anything. Shit, I even told you about kitchen sex."

Mya grinned. She hoped Haldone had a kitchen like Toni's. "I want to know how a filoz bonds."

Toni nodded. "I did notice that you didn't call Haldone and Keeva your agapaytos, so I figured you hadn't yet." A chirping like an elseire bird could be heard downstairs. "That's probably Jasmine. They'll send her up."

She shook her head. "Does bonding have to do with pleasure, what you call sex?"

"Oh, my girl, it sure does." She paused. "Those two men must really love you to not have bonded with you."

"What do you mean? I thought they would have bonded with me if they loved me. I think they are wading for me to iniate it, but I don't know what it is." She grabbed a handful of her hair and played with it.

"What I mean is that if you don't know what bonding is then they could have done it with you already and not told you, but they obviously want it to be the special connection it's supposed to be."

"So, what is it?"

"It's very easy. They simply each have to come, I mean release inside you one right after the other. And if what Erin told me, you have to be on Eden for the bond to take effect. She said nothing happened until she came here. Then a day or even a week later, you discover the new bond you have with your men."

"Bond? What do you mean?"

Toni grinned then waved her hand and an opaque cloud of green light appeared in the room.

"You are an Edenist, too? I thought there were no female Edenists cept me."

Her new friend laughed. "No, I'm as human as they come, but when I bonded with my men, I received the ability to create that opaque green light from Akasha and from Sandale, I can speak eloquently and without all my usual swears and slang, which I can tell you has come in handy with all the dignitaries we've had to meet with over Grandall's grand portal." Toni rolled her eyes. "But it's different for every woman and with you being an Edenist, who knows what it will be like."

In a way, knowing the bond was so physical made it even more scary.

"You don't look too excited." Toni studied her.

"The foreder part is hard for me to understand."

Toni laid her hand on hers. "Do you love them?"

"Yes, I do. But what if that is because they are the only men I have had pleasure with. What if I had pleasure with other men and found I loved them, too, or more?"

Toni laughed. "Oh Mya, you remind me of half my girlfriends back on Earth."

She looked away. "How do you know that the men you are with are the men for foreder?"

Toni stilled, cocking her head as if listening. Mya listened, too. The sound of feminine laughter floated up from downstairs.

"Come with me but be quiet."

Mya scooted off the bed. "I can be invisible, too."

"That's right. Oh, this could be fun. Can you make me invisible?"

She squeezed her right hand then took Toni's.

"Am I invisible."

She pointed to the giant reflection over the bed. "As long as I'm touching you, you are invisible."

Toni chuckled. "That is a very cool ability you have. Let's go."

She followed Toni along the skinny tunnel back toward the stairs, but instead of heading down, she continued past them until they arrived at the opening in the wall where they could see into the living area.

Toni put her finger to her lips.

Mya shook her head. She had no idea what that meant.

Toni rolled her eyes and brushed her thumb across her chest.

Ah, she wanted her to be quiet. She nodded then looked down below.

Toni's friend Jasmine was beautiful. Unlike Toni, her skin was a dusky color, closer to Keeva's eye color and her long black hair had pretty waves in it. She was very curvy with breasts much bigger than her own and her butt was bigger as well, but her waist was narrow.

Mya felt a touch of envy at the woman's shape. It didn't help that she had bright green exotic eyes, a petite nose and full lips which at the moment were smiling widely showing pretty teeth.

Everyone was standing, talking in groups when Jasmine put her hand on Keeva's arm and pressed her body against him.

Mya gripped the railing hard with her free hand.

"I'm so grateful you survived." Jasmine seemed to purr the words so her breath brushed against Keeva's shoulder.

He swallowed before pointing to Haldone. "He was the one that kept us all safe with his air boxes."

Jasmine moved away from Keeva and wrapped her arms around Haldone from behind as he spoke to Akasha. "So, you're the hero who saved everyone?"

"Ouch." Toni's exclamation made her tear her gaze from Jasmine, but before she could scowl at Toni for making a noise, the woman dragged her back into the tunnel and twisted her hand away. "Become visible again." Toni's whispered words were angry.

Quickly, she did as she was told, already feeling sorry Toni was mad at her. "What did I do?"

Toni rubbed her hand. "You *are* freakin' strong for your size."

She shook her head, still not understanding what she'd done.

"Mya, you almost broke my hand because you were jealous of Jasmine."

"Jellous?"

"Yeah, jealous because she was all over Keeva and Haldone. She's a cythera from the Pleasure Temple where I used to live. She likes to give and receive pleasure with men who are not bonded. She keeps her eye out for a possible filoz for herself, but in the meantime, she enjoys herself."

Fury tightened her stomach. "Not with my men."

Toni shook her head. "They aren't yours exclusively until you are bonded, if you bond."

Jasmine's laughter floated up to them, making her feel sick. "What is excusiviy?"

"That means that once you are bonded, you don't have sex with anyone else, ever. And the men you bond with won't have sex with anyone but you, forever."

"I like sex with Keeva and Haldone."

"Then why are you afraid to bond with them? You say you are afraid of forever, but would you prefer to live the rest of your life without them forever?"

"No!"

"Would you prefer if they give you pleasure but also give other women pleasure, forever?"

"No!" She didn't like what Toni was saying. "If I bond with them then we will be a family forever?"

Toni smirked. "Plus, you'll have the dubious benefit of calling me sister."

She couldn't imagine there was someone better than Toni to be a sister with, and she definitely didn't want Jasmine or others from the Pleasure Temples having sex with her men. "I'm going to bond."

"Are you sure?" Toni lost her smirk and looked searchingly into her eyes. "Once you do, you are bonded for life."

At Toni's words, her father's reasoning for searching for her mother finally made sense to her. If a lawbreaker took either of her men, she wouldn't stop looking for him.

More laughter filled the silence in the tunnel above stairs.

She may not be as curvy as Jasmine, but she had her men's hearts and they had hers. Impulsively, she gave Toni a hug. "Thank you."

Toni wrapped her arms around her. "Anytime, sis."

She pulled back smiling, then turned on her heel to gather her men. It was time to bond.

"Go get'em, Mya."

She stomped down the stairs determined to show Jasmine who her men belonged to. She stifled the urge to show off her invisibility, her father's concerns forcing her to control herself, but as she stepped into the room, all conversation stopped.

No one said a word. They just stared at her.

Toni tapped her on the shoulder. "Told you a little material goes a long way."

Actually, she said a little hidden is sexy, but since she hadn't understood that word, she hadn't paid it any attention. She leaned back and whispered. "This is sexy?"

"You bet." She brushed by her. "Sandale, you better close that mouth of yours or I'll give you something to fill it with."

Sandale pulled Toni close. "Just tell me which room."

Toni laughed, which at least had Akasha and Jasmine moving, but Haldone and Keeva still stood frozen in place. She strode over to them and took Haldone's hand. "I want to go to your home now and bond."

He didn't move.

Keeva nudged him. "Did you hear what she said?"

Haldone blinked twice then grabbed her hand. "We're leaving." As he strode for the door, Keeva waved.

Just as the door closed behind them she heard Toni starting to explain their sudden departure. She didn't care how they left, just as long as Jasmine remained at Toni's.

Haldone continued across the giant white patrio that also boasted other very large buildings. Though he kept a good pace, it wasn't as fast as she traveled in the jungle, but she could understand why.

The paths in Naralina were wider but they had more people everywhere and there were smells from bakeries and meat providers and drinking establishments. She noticed a public bath house, a bedding storehouse and a place that provided pleasure toys. She wanted to ask what they were, but two men stopped in front of it and they had to weave around them.

As they walked farther down the mountain, it seemed to grow more crowded. Finally, Haldone stopped before a modest door with single gold edging that boasted beautiful round windows with ornate gold sprinkles in them like a sparkler she remembered from her days visiting her Earth grandparents. None of the other buildings they'd passed had round windows. Most had arched or rectangle ones. These were so much nicer.

She didn't have much chance to appreciate them before Haldone pulled her into his home and Keeva shut the door. The inside was one large room like her dome only half the size and with a set of stairs to the left. But her attention was immediately taken by the wall of windows directly across from them.

Releasing the men's hands, she walked to it. Inside the glass were abstract shapes so intricate that her hand itched to try to paint them. Through the glass she could see greenery, a welcome change from all the white and gold they just passed.

Opening the glass door, she stepped outside onto what was

a walled patrio full of bushes and flowers and two large trees with infragile vines. The plant life crowded the space and seemed to go on forever, but it was actually a large reflection, the back wall looking like the wall of windows she'd just walked through.

"Do you like it?" Haldone's voice sounded nervous.

She turned around to face him. "This is bootiful. I was beginning to think no plants could live in Naralina."

His relieved smile showed exactly how much her opinion meant to him.

Keeva came through the door. "Now this feels like home."

"I agree." She reached her hands out to both of them. "I want to bond. Here."

Haldone took her hand. "We want to bond, too."

"Are you absolutely sure?" Keeva took her other hand. "Once we bond, it is forever."

She brought his hand to her lips. "Yes, I'm sure. I want to be a family."

"I never thought I'd say this because I find your body so exciting, but you in those small clothes makes it hard for me to keep my hands from you."

She laughed, thrilled that Haldone liked the clothes Toni had given her. She wiggled her butt causing what Toni called short shorts to fall a bit lower. "The bottoms are a little yoose."

Haldone dropped to his knees. "Then allow me." With his teeth, he tugged on the bottoms, pulling them lower until they dropped to her ankles.

She stepped out of them. "I do like them, but this is mush better."

Keeva dropped her hand and moved behind her. "Allow me

to help you with this as well." He swept her hair over her shoulder before the top loosened and fell forward.

"I agree, that is better." Haldone blew at the juncture of her legs, and she moved them apart. He took the hint and blew again.

Keeva nuzzled the bare side of her neck as he untied the last tie on her top. "You already have me ready." He pushed his hard cock against her butt as he spoke, his hands coming around to capture both her breasts.

She smiled. "Me too."

"Really? I think I better check." Haldone leaned forward and licked at her pleasure point, and she rose on her toes.

Her heart began to race just before Haldone stroked her folds with his fingers, teasing her.

She tilted her pelvis toward him, wanting him to fill her, but then Keeva's fingers found her nipples and rolled them. Spikes of excitement went straight to her sheath making her moan.

As if he didn't want her to forget him, Haldone moved his fingers to her opening and slowly pushed them inside.

Her body felt like liquid gold, and she raised her arms and grasped on to Keeva's shoulders to stay standing. He took that as an invitation to play more and began to pinch her nipples sporadically.

Haldone's tongue once again swiped across her pleasure nub, but this time he swirled it around while moving his fingers in and out of her. Each man knew her body better than she did. She gave them free reign of it.

But her pleasure was so much, her knees started to give way. Keeva took her weight and before she knew what was happening, two vines had wrapped beneath her arms, holding her up.

"Yes. Like this." She grasped on to them, making Keeva's access to her nipples even easier. He didn't disappoint her, as he ducked beneath her arm and took one nipple into his mouth while Haldone began to nip and suck at her pleasure point, his fingers pumping into her.

She lifted her legs on to his shoulders pulling him closer as her pleasure built. Keeva reached his hand behind her and squeezed her butt. She let her head fall back as her men brought her closer to that feeling she loved.

Then Keeva's teeth took her nipple and nipped it as Haldone's teeth scraped across her nub. The tension inside her snapped, and she was swept away in the ecstasy. Her body floated in air as shock after shock of pleasure rolled through her. She gasped for breath, not realizing she'd held it.

Panting, she let her legs fall, thrilled with the experience her men could give her. *Her men!* She lifted her head and opened her eyes as Haldone finally released her only to stand next to Keeva who was looking at her.

They hadn't started the bonding yet.

Haldone looked at her as well, as she hung by the vines, but he scratched his beard as he spoke to Keeva. "Do you think she is ready now?"

Keeva rubbed the back of his neck. "Hmmm, I am not sure."

She could do that, too. Toni had given her some "pointers." Mya lowered her gaze to the men's hard cocks and licked her lips. Without even looking at them, she knew the instant they decided that *they* were ready by the jerk their cocks gave. She'd have to remember to thank Toni.

Keeva walked to her and cupped her face in his hands. "I love you, Mya." His lips touched her and she opened for him, letting him in. The kiss was gentle, loving and so him. Her body lowered so her feet touched the ground and the vines unwrapped only to rewrap.

When Keeva broke the kiss, she had one vine under both arms and across her chest while another was wrapped around her abdomen. She didn't mind as long as they held her up.

Haldone nodded. "Perfect." Then he walked up to her and put one hand behind her head. "I love you, Mya." His lips descended on hers in a loving, passionate kiss. She tangled her tongue with his as he slanted her head to better kiss her. Then he stepped back.

The vines lowered her torso so she was bent over but then the ones at her hips lifted. She hung in the air, her hair and toes touching the ground, her head even with Haldone's cock. Oh, she liked this position.

He took her head in his hands and ran his thumb along her lips.

She licked it, hoping he'd bring his cock closer.

His thumb stilled then he pressed it against her bottom lip, and she sucked it into her mouth. His cock jerked again. She took his thumb between her teeth like he'd taught her with his cock and scraped the underside lightly.

He moaned, which made her feel good. She liked pleasing her men, if they would just start bonding.

Keeva's hands on her butt told her it was about to start and her heart leapt in anticipation. His fingers moved between her legs and found her opening, but he didn't move them inside. Instead, he wet them then moved them to her pleasure spot.

She tried to push her hips back into him, but she couldn't

because she was hanging. Maybe this wasn't such a good posit—Haldone's cock tip touched her lips. Oh yes, she did like this position. Sticking her tongue out, she licked the head.

Keeva removed his fingers, much to her disappointment, but then she felt his cock at her opening. Again, she became frustrated because she had no way to speed up his entrance.

Haldone grasped her shoulders at the same time Keeva grasped her hips and pulled her back toward him, spearing his cock inside her to his hilt. She closed her eyes as her sheathed filled with him, happy to be complete again.

Then Haldone pulled her toward him, his cock sliding into her mouth, but Keeva gliding out of her. The true purpose for her position became clear and her heart jumped with excitement. She grasped Haldone's hips to steady herself.

Again, Keeva pulled her back onto him and then Haldone did the same. Then back and forth she went between both men her excitement building again as they rocked their cocks into her. The movements grew faster and her body tensed as she drew close to her pinnacle.

Then as she glided back over Keeva, he yelled, and he filled her sending her own release slamming through her. No sooner had he finished then he pulled out and Haldone stepped around her and slowly pulled her toward him, filling her to his hilt.

Keeva sat down beneath her, facing her legs.

She thought about asking what he was doing, but before she could, she felt his fingers on her nub. Her sheath immediately tightened and Haldone moaned, though all he did was keep himself deep inside her.

She steadied herself by grasping Keeva's shoulders as he began to stroke her pleasure point. Her whole body tensed, not just her sheath as he continued to wind her up, yet all Haldone did was hold her to him.

The stimulation continued until finally Haldone groaned, his fingers digging into her hips before he pushed her away and back again. At the first movement back toward him her body reached its peak and she yelled as rapture took over and joy spread through her from her center to the very tips of her toes.

Haldone's yell followed as he pushed himself inside a second time and joined her, filling her and taking her with him.

When they both calmed and she could breathe again, she opened her eyes. The vines lifted her up and into Keeva's waiting arms. "Now you deserve some rest and ambrosia." He headed toward the glass door and Haldone stepped before them to open it.

As he brought her to the longseat in the living area, she couldn't help but ask. "Are we bonded now?"

"I will let you explain while I get the drinks." As Haldone walked to the meal area, she admired his butt. He really had a nice one.

Then she looked at Keeva who sat down next to her.

"The bonding does not happen immediately. It can take a few days before we discover what our actual bond to you is. Usually, a woman will become connected with her filoz."

"Like how Toni can produce a green light and have Sandale form her words for her?"

Haldone returned and handed her a drink. "Yes. And how Erin, the beloved of two other Ruling Circle members, can feel Wareson's emotions and Nassic's energy."

She took the cup but didn't drink. "So what will I have?"

The two men looked at each other before Haldone pulled a chair opposite them closer. "It is different for every woman."

"Every Earth woman." Keeva looked at her seriously. "You are the first female Edenist, so we have no idea if the bond will be stronger or weaker. It could take longer or not at all, and we would have to try again."

She took a sip as she contemplated what they said. Their faces far too serious for how happy she felt. She wiggled her brows. "I don't mind trying again."

Haldone laughed. "I knew you were the only woman for me."

"I did not know. I thought she was a male when she found me. She was invisible so I had no idea." Keeva gazed at her with love in his eyes. "I am so glad I was wrong."

She touched his smooth cheek with her hand. "I'm so glad I found you."

Haldone nodded. "My quest for revenge may not have been the noblest of deeds, but that it brought me to you makes it palatable. From the moment I first saw you, you knocked me off my feet."

She grinned. "I think it was the rock I hid you with that did that."

"You hit him?" Keeva eyes were wide with shock.

She nodded. "He was dijing my eyllen and he didn't even ask."

Haldone shook his head. "Yes, I had a lump for days, but I still loved you the moment you appeared in Akasha's blue light."

She looked from one man to the other. "I'm glad I was found. Now I have a family again and unterand so much more. Now I know that I was deepy loved by my parents because I unterand what love is. I love you."

As both men leaned in to kiss her cheeks, her heart filled with contentment, a feeling she hadn't had since she was thirteen years-old before she understood what contentment meant.

And when she was content, she liked to play. Squeezing her right hand, she disappeared and ducked out from both men, running for the stairs. "I owe you pleasure, but you have to fine me first!"

As she took the stairs two at a time, she heard the men knock over a chair. Giggling, she raced through the house, her happiness impossible to contain until a strong arm caught her about the waist and she was tossed on the bed.

Her happiness had made her visible again and she smiled at the men who loved her with all their hearts because she loved them back. Then she stretched her arms wide. "Who's first?"

Epilogue

Haldone smiled as Mya's grandmother squeezed her hand. He'd been smiling a lot in the last couple days and it was all because of her. The joy of watching her reconnect with her family had filled him with happiness, and their warm welcome to not just Keeva but him as well had made him feel like he was normal.

Maybe he was now. He'd be the first to admit he'd changed, and it was all because of Mya. Wanting her had forced him to give up his old ideas and to make an effort with those around him. As Keeva had predicted, he wasn't perfect as much as he'd striven for that in his creations, as an Edenist he was "rough around the edges" as Mya's grandmother had been so nice to point out.

His own parents were thrilled, his mother overjoyed he'd found love and fawning over Keeva for understanding "her boy." Though it was a little embarrassing, it was nice to see he'd may his mother happy, too. His three fathers were a little stunned by Mya's beauty, which just made him want to show her off to his other brothers.

Keeva's parents had been so relieved to find him alive that it had taken them awhile to understand that he'd bonded outside his filoz, but they supported him completely and welcomed he and Mya into the family.

Keeva rose. "I know that Mya and Haldone will be happy to stay longer, but I have a well overdue visit to make."

One of Mya's grandfathers, the one closest to Keeva, patted him on the back. "I understand. We do not mind as we know we will see you again."

"You can depend on that."

Haldone stood. "I will walk with you outside." It was a phrase Keeva had taught him for when he wanted to stay something in private.

To a chorus of farewells, they stepped into the dead-end pathway where Mya's Mind Fathers' parents lived.

He closed the door behind them. "You go to tell your filoz?"

Keeva nodded. "Yes. I have put it off for too long. I need to tell them."

"You do not think they have heard that you are back?"

"I am not sure. My family may have told one of them, but probably only if they crossed paths in the last two days. They live on the west side of Naralina."

He raised his brow. "That is not very close to your family."

"No, but it was close to the Discoverist Center where I spent most of my time." He shrugged. "Besides, two of the four of us lived over there, so it was a good spot."

That made sense. "Good luck. We will wait for you at the house. Do you think you will be back by mealtime?"

Keeva looked at Helios just past its zenith. "Yes. But there is something else on your mind."

He smirked. Keeva was becoming an expert at reading him. "There is." He scratched his beard.

"Come on, tell me. If you don't, I will stand here and ask you eleven questions."

"I know." Still, he paused. Voicing his biggest fear was hard. "What if the bonding did not work?"

"I thought that might be on your mind. If it did not, we will just do it again." Keeva smirked. "You heard Mya. She would not mind."

"I understand that, but what I fear is that the way Edenists bond with Earth women may not work with a female Edenist. Maybe we are supposed to do something different."

Keeva didn't respond at once which just made him more nervous. He wanted Mya bonded to them. He didn't fear another filoz so much as Naralina discovering her true origin.

"You have a valid point. Tomorrow I will go to the library and see if I cannot find anything on this. If not, then we may have to experiment with different attempts. It is how we discover new information every day."

He liked that idea, but it didn't completely ease his biggest fear.

"Haldone, we are a filoz now. If there is something more, you need to share it with me. We work well together when we take our strengths and combine them."

Immediately, he remembered them planning the attack on the lawbreakers, figuring out where Mya had run off to, and most recently, how to break the sad news to her Air Father's parents. At least seeing Mya again had eased their pain somewhat.

He rolled his shoulders then took a breath. "What if there

is no way to bond with a female Edenist? What if bonding only occurs between two different species?"

Keeva shook his head. "Humans and Edenists are not two different species. We are the same species but have evolved differently."

"Fine, so we are the same species, but what if because we are all three Edenists, there is no way to bond?"

Keeva studied him. "What would it matter? What are you afraid of if there is no way to bond? Mya loves us. She would not leave us if that is what worries you."

He shook his head. "No, I do not worry she would leave us… or I should say that I know she would not leave us permanently." He rolled his shoulders again, his body suddenly very tense. "I do not know. I guess being in Naralina I feel as if she could be taken away at any moment because someone has discovered she is an Edenist. My gut tells me that if we are bonded to her, we would be in a better position to protect her."

"I see what you are saying. You have a valid point. Let me think on that."

His whole body eased at Keeva's acceptance of his fear. "Thank you."

Keeva shook his head. "Thank you for pointing it out. It may not be something we need to worry about as it could take up to a week to discover our bond, but if after that time we find the need to try again, I agree we should definitely be looking at this closer."

He gave the brother of his heart a grin. "Good. That alone makes me more confident."

"I am glad." Keeva smiled. "Now I better go. As much as I am not happy to have to tell my filoz I am with you and Mya now, I look forward to it being done."

He nodded. "I understand. Do you want us to go with you?"

"No. This was my decision. I need to face them alone."

Haldone nodded. He knew Keeva was smart, but he tended to forget the man had great inner strength. "I do not know what they will say, but I do know that you belong with me and Mya."

"You are right. I will keep that in mind." Keeva turned and strode to the end of the pathway and headed up the busy main thoroughfare.

He did not envy him his task. Watching the many men and few women bustling by on the cobbled stones made him uncomfortable. Naralina had always been his home, but after spending weeks in the jungle, he found himself missing it. Maybe taking Mya out of the city would keep her safer while they figure out the bond.

He opened the door to the house and Mya's laugher filled the air. But could he take Mya from the only family she had left? No. He closed the door. He had told the truth when he told Keeva days ago that he would do anything for her. If she wanted to stay, they would stay.

He'd been surprised that her grandparents had known about her, but he shouldn't have been. Of course Tauren would be sure they were able to meet their granddaughter. That they hadn't told anyone about her in all the years since was a relief.

But he, Keeva, and Mya only had a year before Akasha and his brother insisted they would need to tell the others in the Ruling Circle, despite Toni's protest. It was thanks to Toni that they had that long. He had a feeling she wanted the three of them to grow closer to weather whatever storm the news of a female Edenist might bring. It made him feel guilty for how he'd been jealous of her time with Sandale when he'd first met her.

"Haldone, come here. Look at this imidge of my father. He had a beard just like yours!"

He strode into the living area to find Mya smiling with the anticipation of him sharing the discovery. He grinned, taken in by her brilliant violet eyes. "Where? Show me." He glanced at the image, but his gaze came back to her. "I knew I liked him."

~~*~~

Mya sat by the window watching the people walk by Haldone's home. Where was Keeva? For someone who had been alone more years than not, she was stunned by her need to have both her men with her all the time.

She understood that what Keeva had gone to do was right. From what she'd learned already, men rarely left a filoz. Haldone's brother had to because his filoz bonded when they thought him dead, so he had no choice. That would have been devastating if Sandale had remembered his old filoz, but since he'd had his mind wiped, he didn't.

Mostly men walked down the wide path but the few women she saw were wrapped as Haldone and Keeva had said. She didn't understand that. Her Air father's mother had tried to explain it, and she pretended to understand, but she didn't. If it was cold on Eden she could understand, but even then, the clear hestas could keep a person warm.

Naralina was everything she'd hoped it would be and a lot that she didn't understand or like. The homes she'd been inside were like Toni's with too many rooms in a small space, and the whole city had too many Edenists.

She did like that there were buildings where she could obtain baka buns or hestas or even furniture and unlike Earth, there was no bartering or exchanging of remuneration. One of her grandfathers explained that rancels were mainly for trading between cities.

Though she'd seen many men since arriving, she still thought Keeva and Haldone were the most handsome. She was glad Toni had shown her that she really did want them forever. Though she was a bit disappointed in the whole bonding thing. She felt no different at all.

The stride of a man down the path caught her attention. She watched until Keeva's face appeared between the walkers. "Keeva's here!" She jumped out of the chair she'd dragged to the round window and ran to the door. Opening it, she waved.

His serious look changed. He grinned as he picked up speed until he was running toward her.

He lifted her in his arms and spun her around. "I missed you."

"I missed you, too." She gave him a kiss to show him how much.

Footsteps approached behind her. "You should probably come inside, naked woman."

Oh, she completely forgot. She grasped Keeva's hand and pulled him inside.

He closed the door behind him. "Something smells good."

She grinned. "Haldone's cooking hinni."

Keeva didn't let go of her hand. "You mean henny."

"I know, I was just testing you."

He chuckled but didn't laugh.

Something was wrong. She brought him into the meal room where Haldone had returned to work on the hennys. Pulling out a chair, she made him sit.

She ignored the lifting of his brow to pour him ambrosia then sat down with him. "What happened?"

He glanced at Haldone, who'd just set the hennys in the roaster box.

Haldone came over and stood behind her. "I am guessing from your silence it did not go well?"

Keeva lifted his hands. "Honestly, I am not sure what to think right now. I feel hurt, but that doesn't make sense."

She reached across the space and took his hand. "What did they do to you."

He focused on her, his usual warm brown eyes very light. "They bonded with one of their chosen ones as soon as I was exiled. It was as if that was all they had waited for, to get me out of the way."

"Did they have something to do with you being exiled?" Haldone's angry voice made it clear he was ready to take on Keeva's old filoz all at once.

Keeva shook his head. "No, not at all. They are far too wrapped up in their own lives to think about the Ruling Circle and what they do."

She tried to think of something that was good about the situation like Keeva often did. He seemed so sad. "That means they weren't mat at you then, right?"

"Mad? No. Surprised I was alive? Yes."

Haldone squeezed her shoulder, and she looked up at him, but he focused on Keeva. "They were surprised because they have no idea how wonderful and exciting the jungle is. They see it as a death sentence, not as a place to learn about, or a place to grow up like Mya, or even a place to feel free and less stifled like me. Their world is too small for you now."

Keeva nodded, his shoulders relaxing. "You are right. They are ignorant of all that is beyond Naralina."

She just had to ask. "Did they ask about me?"

Keeva shook his head and looked at Haldone then smirked. "I did not tell them I was bonded."

"What? Why not?" She thought that was why he went to see his old filoz.

His smirk grew. "I wanted them to feel bad. I know it was wrong, but I guess I was so hurt in that moment that I did not want them to know how happy I was. As far as I was concerned, they did not deserve to know."

She lowered her brow. "You lied."

"No, I simply did not tell them all there was to tell."

She looked up at Haldone, trying not to smile as he crossed his arms. He was thinking exactly what she was thinking. She let go of Keeva's hand and crossed her arms as well. "Yes, you did. Just like Haldone lied to us by not telling us about Lora…"

"Loraleaf." Haldone finished for her.

She nodded. "Yes, Loraleaf."

Keeva looked from her to Haldone then threw his hands up. "You are right. I lied."

Haldone chuckled but she was confused. "But it's not right to lie."

Keeva sighed. "True, it is not, but sometimes we do it out of anger."

"And sometimes we do it to get what we want." Haldone unfolded his arms and laid his hands on her shoulders again.

"And why are we not telling anydone about me being an Edenist? Because we are lying everytine we don't?"

The two men looked at each other. Finally, Haldone spoke. "Because Keeva and I want to protect you."

"From what?"

Keeva reached over and took one of her hands, forcing her to unfold her arms. "Because we have not taught you about society and how it functions. It is very complicated like the jungle, and until we can teach you and give you all the information you need to make a good decision, we need to keep this a secret."

Oh, she understood secrets. "A secred is something that is evendualee told, right?"

Keeva nodded. "Yes. This secret will be told eventually." He glanced above her head at Haldone. "But first we want to be sure we all agree when."

"I understand, but I was never good at keeding secrets. It's harb."

Haldone released her shoulders and moved to the roaster. Pulling out the hennys, he placed them on the table in front of them. "It is hard to keep this to ourselves while in Naralina. It would be easier if we were back in the jungle."

"The jungle?" Keeva turned around as Haldone took a pile of dally greens from the inducer. "You mean like if we were in Mya's caves?"

Her heart raced at the idea. She thought once she'd left, she'd never get to go back.

Haldone shrugged as he sat. "I admit that I would feel more

comfortable with Mya there. We can always come back and visit our families. But living here, the chances of us making a mistake are high."

She piped in. "And there are too many people."

Keeva chuckled as he placed some henny on his plate. "I agree. I also find the minds of the Discoverists are not as open as I thought they were."

Haldone scooped dally greens onto her plate. "I am happy to live wherever Mya wants to live."

Her heart swelled as she bit into the henny. After chewing she looked up to find them both waiting for her answer. She swallowed and grinned. "How about the Samuvian deserd? I always wanted to see it."

At the shocked look on their faces, she laughed. "That was a joke. Did I do it right?"

Keeva chuckled, but Haldone frowned. "Where did you learn about a joke?"

She grinned. "When Toni was here yesterday."

Haldone groaned.

She winked at Keeva who seemed to appreciate her joke. "Toni also explained what pleasure toys are."

Haldone had been taking a swallow of water when it sprayed across the table at her.

She jumped up as the water dripped from her chest. "Hey, why'd you do that?"

Haldone stood, picked up a small towel, and started to wipe her down. "I apologize. I was so surprised it was either spit out what was in my mouth or choke on it." His lips twitched, telling her exactly how *not* sorry he was.

She frowned at him, but he didn't look at her. He was focused on her nipples, his wiping causing them to harden. At his focus, her whole body came to attention.

His voice lowered. "I will be happy to make you some pleasure toys. What else did Toni tell you? Did she tell you about having food with your pleasure?"

She shook her head, her belly tightening at what that could mean.

Keeva pushed back his chair and rose, his cock already hard.

She licked her lips, wanting to taste him even as Haldone's mouth found her breast.

Keeva immediately stepped up to her and sucked her other breast into his mouth.

She closed her eyes before she grasped the heads of both men, her happiness too much to contain. Keeva's hand stroked down her belly and Haldone's down her back before he pinched her butt.

"Ouch." She opened her eyes as she pulled his head back and stared. "What's happening?" All three of them were visible but not.

Keeva jerked his head up as Haldone's eyes widened.

She stared at them, fear racing up her spine.

They stared right back until Keeva's mouth started to twitch and he looked at Haldone. "I do not think you have to worry about the bonding."

Haldone lowered his brow in confusion.

Stepping back, she disconnected from them completely, but they didn't turn visible. "I don't like this."

Keeva moved his arm through her chair. "I have no

substance." He looked at her and smiled kindly. "Mya, try to be visible again."

She squeezed her left hand and immediately could tell she was visible. "It worked." Relief flooded her.

Haldone looked at Keeva. "Are we invisible?"

She shook her head. "I can see you."

"I am not so sure. If this is the result of the bond…we need to check in a reflection." Keeva strode through the room, even through furniture, but when he tried to open the door to the courtyard, he couldn't. Shrugging, he stepped through the wall.

She stood with her mouth open.

"Come Mya, let us see what this is all about. I have a feeling Keeva will figure it out faster than you and me."

She nodded, still uncomfortable with her men being semi-visible and without substance.

Haldone walked through the wall as well, but she opened it and exited the house.

Keeva grinned at her and pointed to the reflection wall. "Look."

She stood in the courtyard by herself but when she looked at them, she could see them.

"Make yourself invisible again." Keeva's voice was excited like he couldn't get the words out fast enough.

She squeezed her right hand and disappeared from the reflection but she could still see herself only it was as if she was an outline. "I don't understand."

Keeva lifted his hand like he usually did when commanding plant life and he became visible again. "Holy Bendis."

He turned toward her but she was invisible. How could

that be? "What does this mean?" She squeezed her left hand and became visible again. "I can tell now when I'm visible."

Keeva walked toward her. "Yes. It is the bonding. Haldone, become visible again."

They both waited and finally Haldone became more than an outline. "That was better than a ride on a logar through the empty streets of Naralina at night!"

Keeva frowned. "Where would you get a logar from?"

Haldone waved him off. "Youthful fun, nothing more. Tell us about our bond."

Keeva squinted one eye at Haldone, but then looked at her and smiled, obviously happy about this new development, though she wasn't so sure.

"Just from what happened right now, I can say this. We all now have the ability to be invisible and even better, when we are, we can see each other and tell we are invisible because it is not simply a refraction of light anymore but something far more sophisticated. Not only can we be invisible, but we have no substance except touching each other."

Haldone wiggled his brows, so we could theoretically take pleasure while invisible in the middle of a crowded thoroughfare and no one would know we were there doing that?"

Keeva shook his head. "Only you would think of that, but yes. I also think it means that we will have no scent and our minds may not be sensed."

Oh, she did see the advantage of that. "But you couldn't open the door."

"No, I could not, but I did not need to because I could walk through it. We will need to experiment some more with this."

Keeva looked down at his feet. "Since we did not sink through the ground, which is Eden, it makes me believe that somehow all our Kindreds were combined to make this."

"Yes. The outline we see is just like what I see when I make my air boxes, or slides or windows." Haldone raised his hand then walked forward, stopping when he bumped into what had to be an air wall. "Good. I was afraid I had lost my ability."

Keeva raised his hand and two vines came down and made a seat for her.

She sat and lifted her feet off the ground swinging back. When she returned, Keeva caught her. "I think this bond will be very helpful to all of us in the jungle."

"I agree." Haldone walked over.

The two men looked at her. "What?"

Haldone held the other vine. "Are you happy with the bond?"

That was a good question. "I think so. I will have to get used to it."

"I am very happy with it because now you cannot disappear on us." Keeva laid his hand over hers on the vine.

Haldone scratched his beard. "So now we can travel through the jungle unseen but without having to hold hands."

She looked up at Haldone. "I like holding hands."

He took her hand in his. "I do too, but now we can do it whenever we want, not because we have to."

She nodded as that did make sense.

Haldone tilted her chin up. "Mostly what I like about the bond is that it means we are tied together forever."

For the first time, that word didn't scare her.

Keeva stood next to Haldone. "It is what I am most happy about also."

She gazed at them, her love for them almost too big to keep inside. "I think I will like forever with you."

They each gave her a soft kiss on her lips. When they stepped back, she rose. "Let's go home."

Keeva nodded. "I am ready."

Haldone stepped to the side of Keeva. "I am too, but first we need to make a stop and tell a man about the dirgon."

Of course, she'd forgotten about that. "Does that mean we are finally going to Loraleaf?"

Haldone cringed but smiled as well. "Yes, if you'd like to see it."

Keeva spoke before she could. "Absolutely! Is it true that it cannot be seen because of a reflection? How do they keep all the walkways so high in the trees? You said there were domesticated animals, are they in the trees or below? How can you walk underneath it and not know it was there?"

Haldone laughed. "You can ask all your questions to the men who built it. They will be more than happy to give you the answers. Now let us open the portal so you can see it."

Mya's heart swelled with happiness. Who knew hitting a man on the head with a rock would bring him back to her or that saving a bleeding man from wild animals would bring her so much joy. No matter what adventure she tackled next, she had no doubt she'd always have them by her side…forever.

As the portal opened Keeva gasped. "Holy Bendis!"

She grasped his hand and then Haldone's. As far as she was concerned, forever started right now.

For free books, updates, sneak peeks, and special prizes, sign up
to receive the latest news from Lexi Post at
http://bit.ly/LexiUpdate

Be on the watch for Beast of Eden (Eden Series: Book 6)
(http://www.lexipostbooks.com/beast-of-eden/)

Read on for an excerpt from Heart of Frankenstein.

Chapter One

He stared at the almost naked woman frozen on the ledge of the mountain. She was breathtaking, especially to him. The women in the far northern regions of Alaska were bundled up so much that he couldn't tell they were women. This woman had shed most of her clothes.

Her face, turned in profile, was white from the cold and her light eyelashes reminded him of dried cotton grass in the late summer. Her long neck revealed no pulse and her golden hair, spread out on one side, appeared as if it had been frozen while blowing in the wind.

He needed to move her, but he couldn't help staring. Her breasts were covered by a thin white top that left her toned arms bare. Her waist was narrow, but her hips flared out in the shape that was the epitome of woman. She had long, tight pink leggings that disappeared beneath her socks, but her boots were thrown amongst her scattered outer clothes.

She looked like a fallen angel. If she was alive, they would make a good match because his past made him closer to Satan than any other angel in man's lexicon of religions.

He looked back along the route he'd come. His tracks were obvious and unless a heavy snowstorm came in, they would remain so. Images of being attacked in Geneva sped across his mind. If anyone found her dead body here, he would be accused of murdering her.

With no choice, he crouched down, his heart heavy that such a beautiful woman in the prime of her life was gone. At least with hypothermia, her mind would have slept before she felt the final breaths of life leave her. Unlike his mate, who was gone before she could take her first breath. The age-old rage that used to fill him barely caused more than a stutter of his heart now.

Unable to resist, he stroked his bare finger over her cheek. At its softness, he drew back as if stung. Her cheek should be hard.

Hesitantly, he set his finger beneath her nose. Was that breath? He couldn't be sure. If it was, it was so shallow that she would die soon. Taking her delicate wrist in his hand, he felt for the pulse he couldn't see in her neck.

Nothing. Disappointment and sorrow rifled through him. Was he so enamored of her looks that he wished her alive? Doubting his own senses, he lay two fingers along the side of her neck. At first, he couldn't concentrate, her skin so soft it distracted him.

Finally, he forced his mind to cooperate. Thump————thump————. Elation swept through him almost toppling him over. He had only felt so once before. Now, on the heels of his euphoria came panic.

He *had* to save her. His mind raced as memories sped by of a search party he'd participated in years ago, shortly after he'd settled on his mountain. He had found the young male and thought him dead as well, but a rescue crew had taken over. He'd asked numerous questions, fascinated by the human body and how his own was different.

Taking off his coat of bearskin fur that he donned when traveling anywhere he might be seen, he laid it on the ground next to her. Carefully, he moved her light form onto it and wrapped her tight. It was critical in this late stage that she not wake and try to move on her own or it could kill her.

Lifting her in his arms, he was thankful for the extra strong limbs he'd been given and carefully strode down the mountain to his home. It was a simple one room cabin set against the mountain, hiding the cave he'd originally lived in when first arriving in the region.

Having moved about the arctic for almost three hundred years, he was always careful to keep his presence a secret until he could determine where the closest inhabitant was and who or what they were.

After entering his home, he laid the angel on her back on his handmade bed. Wrapped in his grizzly bear coat, she looked small. He thought back to the young man that he'd found. The rescuers had used warm rubber containers at the man's neck, on his hands, under his arms, and between his legs.

Quickly, he grabbed the smooth rock that he used to hold the door open when carrying supplies inside and set it in the coals of the wood stove. Striding outside, he grabbed up five smaller ones from his porch that he used for chasing away wolves and added them to the fire.

The marten skins he had drying wouldn't be large enough to wrap around the rocks, so he unbuttoned his shirt, pulled it off, and ripped it. The material was flannel and its texture was perfect for her soft skin.

Retrieving the rocks from the fire with his bare hands, he wrapped them in the material and carefully positioned them against her in the important areas. He placed the largest rock between her thighs then wrapped the coat around her again. He took the quilt hanging on his wall and laid that over her as well before standing back.

What if he was too late? What if she'd been there too long? What if she was already dead, slipping away while he prepared the rocks?

Then you'd be no worse off than you were before.

But that wasn't true. Before he didn't know of her. Now, her path had crossed with his. Only twice before had he gazed upon such femininity with awe. The first time was while still in Germany when he'd watched Felix and Agatha, the people he learned to speak from while living in a shed attached to their house. They never knew he was there until the day he tried to befriend their blind father.

He fisted his hands and tore his gaze from the face of his angel. The ensuing attack upon his person when he was found inside with their father was only the second betrayal of his miserable existence. It was less the stick Felix raised than the fact Felix raised anything against him that hurt, though it was less painful than his first betrayal, but a true harbinger of the exile to come.

Turning back to the woman, he focused on the memories of what else the rescuers had done. He glanced at the wood stove. It might be too cool in his cabin. Immediately, he walked to the wood pile set against the wall and added two more split logs. They caught as they landed on the red coals, filling the stove with yellow flames.

He returned to his bed and knelt down. Once again, he positioned his index finger beneath her nose. His stomach loosened as a faint breath stirred the tiny hairs below his knuckle. She lived.

To help the body warm from the inside out, we use warm sugar water until we can get the victim to a hospital. The words of the rescuers ran through his head, his memory sharp, and in *this* case, he was grateful for that.

He rose and moved to his long counter to pour fresh water into a small pot. He didn't have sugar but he had birch syrup he'd boiled down himself. Pouring a liberal amount of his late season harvest into the water, he set it on the wood stove to warm.

If he hadn't seen the sun reflecting off something near her, he would have never spotted her. She must have been lost, which meant someone would be looking for her. He'd had no choice but to leave her clothes where they lay. He would need to go back and retrieve them for her.

Though he understood he couldn't keep her, nor that she would want to stay, he wanted to be sure she lived long enough to make that decision. If she died while under his care, he would be hunted down…again.

Pulling the pot from the stove, he poured a small amount of the sweet water into a tin cup. Dipping his finger in, he guessed at its warmth before picking up his spoon from the counter and moving toward the bed. Kneeling on one knee once more, he dipped the spoon into the sweet water and lifted it to her mouth.

Carefully, he dripped a little on her chapped lips, but it rolled to the side and down her jaw. Emptying the spooned water into the cup again, he used it to part her lips, but they closed again.

He hesitated to touch her face. The action seemed too intimate. Moving her body to warm her was like any other body, but her face, so smooth and unblemished, was what made her different just as her brain and heart made her who she was. Who was she?

Angela Ellis luxuriated in the warmth, a hot tub one of her favorite guilty pleasures. Letting her head fall back, she looked up but there was only fog. Where was she? Moving her gaze toward the ground, she couldn't see it. She closed her eyes again. She must be in heaven.

She chuckled. With a job that took her around the world, it wasn't a surprise she couldn't remember where she was for a moment, and really, how much did it matter? She was warm and happy and alone. Life couldn't get any better than this...except on her next adventure vacation.

She lifted her head as excitement thrummed through her. That was coming up soon. A month-long cruise along what she referred to as the people-less frontier. She loved the idea that there were billions of people on Earth, yet there were still places devoid of human life— except for visitors like herself.

She moved her arms through the bubbling water. Or was she already on her vacation? She tried to think. Images of a dark bar with round outside windows flowed through her mind. More followed, standing in formation in a life jacket for a muster drill, eating fresh caught salmon, staying up to see the lights of the Aurora Borealis. She let her head fall back again. She must be in the hot tub on the outer deck, the ecological ship's only nod toward the cruise industry. They must be traveling through fog.

No wonder she was a little disoriented. She wouldn't even be able to tell which way was up if not for the hot water. The fog didn't seem to move. Why was everything so fuzzy? Did she drink too much last night?

He steeled himself and gently forced his angel's lower jaw down, effectively opening her mouth and dribbling a little of water into it before releasing her. He watched, but she didn't swallow. Not wanting her to choke, he turned her head toward the wall and lowered her chin so the water could leak out.

She was in too deep a sleep. What if she never woke? The thought sent a chill through him far greater than simple cold temperatures. There had to be something else he could do.

A conversation he'd overheard at the outpost came to mind. A woman had been joking with her husband about sharing body heat with his hunting partner. The man had fallen through the ice and needed to get warm.

He could do that for his angel. Standing, he quickly removed all his clothes. Since his sensitivity to temperatures had lessened over the centuries, he had no idea if his body would give off heat, but he had to try.

He folded the quilt down, and careful not to dislodge the heated rocks, moved her toward the middle of the bed. He opened the coat and lay next to her, quickly pulling the quilt over them. Gently, he lifted her head onto his arm and wrapped his other across her stomach.

Her body felt cold even to him. Would she ever warm? Moving his leg against her to make contact all along the side of her body, he carefully covered her legs with his other one, bending it at the knee to avoid putting any weight on her.

She smelled like the Arctic air and a faint hint of mint, her hair beneath his nose already softening. Her curvy body yielded to his hard one. He let his warm breath pass by her nose, hoping she'd bring that heat into her lungs.

As he lay with her, a new sense of how fragile she was penetrated his brain. She wasn't like most of the women he came into contact with. Though she was a nice size, her face was not weathered by the harsh elements of Alaska and her skin was far too pale to have been hit by the northern sun for years.

She was even more beautiful than he'd originally thought. She was precious, like an angel. Fate had brought her to him. With her, saving her, he might finally find peace. Despite his newfound hope, or maybe because of it, his body came alive with the sensations of touching her.

Though she retained a layer of clothing, he'd shed all of his. His cock, nestled against her hip began to grow firmer. The skin on his arm where it touched hers, prickled with pleasure. And he couldn't resist stroking his nose over her cheek.

His body wanted to mate, but he never could. He wasn't a man. He was something else, something reprehensible, something other than human. The only hope he had for his existence was peace. But it didn't keep him from yearning for what could never be.

Though he was regulated to finding snippets of comfort in the mundane, with her in his arms he found a sense of happiness. Even if just for a fleeting moment in his timeline, he would treasure it.

He held her a little tighter, enjoying the feel of his hard cock pressed against her and the silkiness of her hair upon his arm. As desire built inside him, he embraced it for the oddity it was, reveled in its sensations.

The heat in the room finally began to cool as the wood he'd added burned down. Despite the unmet ache in his loins, he was loathe to move from her side. Not only did he enjoy having her in his arms, but he didn't want to undo what he may have accomplished by sharing his body heat.

He remained where he was, ignoring the movement of the sun that now hid behind an adjacent mountain, covering the cabin in a half-shadow. Instead, he watched his angel breathe, confirming she still lived.

Then her lips parted, and she took a deeper breath.

He froze, afraid she would wake immediately. When her eyelids didn't open, he carefully extracted himself from around her. Wrapping the fur coat about her, his concern increased that she might look upon him and be horrified. With his heart racing in near panic, he quickly replaced the quilt and grabbed up his clothes.

He dressed in his jeans and boots faster than a wolf snatching up its prey. With his flannel shirt now in shreds around the rocks keeping the woman warm, he needed to cover his torso before she woke. He didn't want her to fear him.

Moving to the chest at the end of his bed, he pulled out another shirt. It was wool, which would be far too hot once he added more wood to the stove. Digging beneath it, he grasped a white linen shirt he hadn't worn in decades. Donning it, he buttoned it high enough to hide the horizontal scar across his chest, yet it still remained open at the collar.

Stepping before the triangular piece of mirror he'd found in the Savik dump, he checked to be sure the leather choker with Inuit symbols on it still covered his harshest scar. The one on his forehead was concealed by his hair, but the one under his right eye was visible. He once tried an eye-patch for that, but with his height, it seemed to cause more fear.

Confirming the leather around his neck was still in place, he strode to the wood stove and added two more logs, watching as they were engulfed in flames. He returned the pot to the stove top and waited for it to steam before pouring it into his tin cup again and walking back to his bed, back to Angel. That's what he would call her. Men and women liked names, and in the Arctic wilderness, they took on names that meant something.

Once again, he sat next to her and carefully opened her lips. Spooning in a small amount of the sweet water, he waited, anxious to see some sign of life in her. Excitement hit him as her throat worked to swallow the warm liquid. Since she didn't wake or choke, he repeated the procedure, this time letting more from the spoon drip onto her tongue.

She groaned, and he pulled his hands away, but she didn't wake.

He quickly gave Angel more sugar water. This time her tongue darted out and licked at her lips. His gut tightened with yearning. The need for companionship spiked hard through his chest. He had little time to recover before her lashes fluttered. He held his breath, anxious to see the color of her eyes.

"Oh." Her lids, which didn't appear to open, squinched together. She tried to lift her hand, but it was caught beneath the blankets and fur coat.

"Don't." He whispered the word because his normal voice was very deep and scratchy. He didn't want to alarm her, but he couldn't allow her to move. "Don't try to move yet. You could stop your heart."

Her sudden intake of breath was the only sign that she'd heard him. That, and she ceased her struggles, much to his relief.

"Am I in a hospital?" Her voice, though soft, flowed over him, loosening his tense muscles.

"No. You're in my cabin. I discovered you on the mountain."

Her eyelashes fluttered again followed by a moan of pain before she closed them tight. "My eyes. Burn."

She must have become blinded by the snow. She'd had no eye protection. He should have realized that. "Don't try to open them. You're snow-blind."

Her head turned toward his voice. "Blind?" The one word was choked out.

The fear in her voice caused sympathy to rise in his chest. "It's not permanent, but it could last a couple of days. If you'll allow it, I can bandage your eyes so they can heal."

Her tongue darted out to lick her chapped lips again. "Please."

At her request, he rose. Striding toward the corner of the room that held the wood stove and cabinets, as well as a sink with cold running water, his mind quickly inventoried what he might use. He didn't wish to use the tape he had as her skin was already sore from the cold. He could wrap her eyes with a scarf, but he needed something hard beneath it to protect her eyes from light.

Jar lids could work if large enough. Quickly, he chose two from the cabinet and went back to his chest for the scarf. As he approached the bed, he purposefully shuffled his feet so she wouldn't be startled by his voice. Laying everything next to her, he pulled his only chair from the table at the center of the cabin and set it next to the bed.

"I'm going to wrap your head and protect your eyes. Don't lift your head or move. It's very important you remain still. Your muscles don't have the proper blood flow yet, and the strain could cause your heart to fail."

Her brows lowered. "Are you a doctor?"

"No, but I have lived in the coldest regions of the Earth for most of my life. I understand what has happened to you." He sat on the chair and lifted the jar lids.

Her tongue darted out to wet her lips again. "I guess that's the next best thing."

He didn't respond, too focused on soothing her. Her eyes would simply take time to heal. As gently as he could, he laid a lid over each eye socket, resting the edges on her eyebrows and cheek bones. Slowly, he lifted her head with one hand while he maneuvered the scarf beneath it. The silky strands of her golden hair made it hard to concentrate.

Finally, he had the scarf where he wanted it and he tied it around her head to keep the lids in place. "Now if you open your eyes, it shouldn't hurt, but I would suggest keeping them closed for at least a couple of days."

"Thank you." Her soft voice came out in a throaty whisper.

"You're welcome." He stared at her. How long before her body warmed enough to cause her excruciating pain? He had nothing he could give her to take it away, but sleep might help. Rising, he headed back to his counter.

"Where are you going?" Her panic in her voice stopped him cold.

"I'm just across the room. I'll make you warm tea to help your body heal though it may not be the most pleasant."

"Tea? I think a shot of whiskey would be more beneficial."

He quickly pulled out his small herb box. Mixing valerian with hops, he poured it into the pot of birch syrup water still simmering on the wood stove. Then he retrieved the cup and emptied the cooled water into the sink. "Alcohol will hurt you in your condition."

"It sounds like you know a lot—" she coughed.

He was beside her in an instant. "Don't." Laying his finger against her throat, he stroked it, ignoring the pleasant feel of her skin. "Coughing will hurt your heart."

She swallowed against his finger. "Got it." Her tongue came out again to lick her lips.

He tore his gaze away and pushed back the chair, uncomfortable with the desire pushing through him. He stepped to the stove and poured the liquid into his cup, small pieces of crushed herb floated within it.

As he returned to the chair, her lips lifted in a small smile. "I guess I'm lucky you found me. Do you have a name?"

"I have the tea, but don't lift your head. Allow me to do it for you." He tested the liquid with his finger. With his sensitivity to temperatures less than hers, he hoped he had it right.

"Okay, but when will I be able to move again?"

He lifted her head with his hand. "Tomorrow. Until then, you should try to sleep." He pressed the lip of the cup to her lips, and she didn't flinch, which was a good sign. Very slowly he tilted it. He pulled it back to allow her to swallow.

"That tastes weird. Is that herbal tea?"

He nodded before remembering she couldn't see him. "Yes. It will help you sleep so you can heal, but you need to finish it all."

She lifted her lip at that pronouncement, but as he tipped the cup again, she drank. When she'd finished it, he set it aside.

"Okay, I was a good girl and took all my medicine. Now can you tell me your name?"

He walked away and rinsed out the cup. Over his shoulder, he answered. "You need to sleep now.

"I'll sleep if you tell me your name."

He took a deep breath. "I don't have one."

ALSO BY LEXI POST

Sci-fi Romance

Cruise into Eden

(The Eden Series: Book 1)

Unexpected Eden

(The Eden Series: Book 2)

Eden Discovered

(The Eden Series: Book 3)

Eden Revealed

(The Eden Series: Book 4)

Avenging Eden

(The Eden Series: Book 5)

Beast of Eden

(The Eden Series: Book 6) *Coming Soon*

Paranormal Romance

Masque

Passion's Poison

Passion of Sleepy Hollow

Heart of Frankenstein

Pleasures of Christmas Past

(A Christmas Carol Series: Book 1)

Desires of Christmas Present

(A Christmas Carol Series: Book 2)

Temptations of Christmas Future

(A Christmas Carol Series: Book 3)

One of a Kind Christmas
(A Christmas Carol Series: Book 4) *Coming 2018*
On Highland Time
(Time Weavers Inc. Series: Book 1)

Contemporary Cowboy Romance

Cowboys Never Fold
(Poker Flat Series: Book 1)
Cowboy's Match
(Poker Flat Series: Book 2)
Cowboy's Best Shot
(Poker Flat Series: Book 3)
Cowboy's Break
(a Poker Novella)
Christmas with Angel
(Poker Flat Series Book: 2.5/Last Chance Series: Book 1)
Trace's Trouble
(Last Chance Series: Book 2)
Fletcher's Flame
(Last Chance: Book 3)
Logan's Luck
(Last Chance Series: Book 4)
Dillon's Dare
(Last Chance Series: Book 5) *Coming Summer 2018*
Aloha Cowboy
(Island Cowboy Series: Book 1) *Coming Summer 2018*

Military Romance

When Love Chimes
(Broken Valor Series: Book 1)
Poisoned Honor
(Broken Valor Series: Book 2)

Eden – English Dictionary

agapayto – wife, but more, woman has a connection with every man in the filoz

amobe – invisible to the eye flat blob like creature that cleans places by eating dirt, including skin, hair, fur and dried stains

ambrosia – mango, coconut tasting drink with a trace of spice in the aftertaste

baka bun – Similar to a jelly donut only filled with citrusy fruit jams like lemon and orange that energize

Bedia – endearment meaning "beloved"

beloved – less formal name for agapayto (wife), a woman can refuse to be a beloved

Bendis – the large moon with pink light often called the second moon

blood sign – marking of lawbreaker band – a circle of blood with an x over it.

boarox – as big as a bison with no hair and black splotches on its legs, large droopy upper lip that covers mouth full of white shark teeth

bonabus vine – a leafy vine with small flowers like bluebells that gives off a calming scent

bonding – the sexual act that connects a beloved with her filoz if she is on Eden breast binding – bra

brother of his heart – best friend who he will share a beloved with

burning ceremony – celebration of an Edenist's life with everything the deceased liked from food to songs to favorite free time activities. Then the dead is placed on a pyre and burned. People take turns watching the fire so the man is never alone as his spirit rejoins Eden

caball – bird with blue feathers

chosen one – like fiancée, but the Edenists choose with no agreement from the woman

cold box – refrigerator

connar bolder – hardest rock known to Eden

Criuson Law – law set up by the original settlers of Eden

crossover – the first time the chosen one goes through the portal to Eden

cyndistone – teal, granite-like stone

Cythera or Cys for short - women of the Pleasure Temples

daemond – honey bee

dally greens – similar to brussel sprouts but with an overtone of onion

decods– like leagues (3 miles are a decod)

Depoteese – Director

Dickinson Law – laws instituted after the Fullamush when the men fought over women

dirgon – Half direwolf and half dragon

direlot – ferocious and cunning animal most closely resembles a wolf but has two heads and two tails

Discoverist Oasis – located on the 8th level of Naralina, it houses animals in their natural habitat much like a zoo

Discoverists – scientists but not only in the scientific field who generally do their work at the Discoverist Center

Eden day – 22 hours

Eden month – 40 days

elseire – Bird with purple wings when in flight but folded up looks green

eyllen – energy rock source

feroon– big beast with tusks, furry and as large as an elephant but no trunk, fairly docile

filoz [filous] – group of men (2-5) who are close like a family

fithee– long brown snake-like creature that burrows into mountainsides with both ends.

Fiya – endearment closest to sweetheart

Fullamush – the great war that almost destroyed the planet but the women and Emily Dickinson brought peace (story in Unexpected Eden)

grapet – purple vegetable that havling pigs like (used as bait)

grendal – like a wild boar but larger, has tusks and squeals, travels in herds

Haven – new walled settlement founded by Nassic and Wareson who escaped Naralina and gathered other "lawbreakers" who were falsely accused to form a society

havling pig – Smaller pig-like animal that wanders alone

head puffs – pillows

heat top – stove

Helios – Sun

henny – chicken like bird

Hermday – Wednesday

hestas – blankets made of see through material that is very thin, but quite warm

High Hall – center (highest) building in the Ruling Circle complex

Holy Bendis – expression of surprise, frustration, anger, etc.

Holy Crius – expression of surprise, frustration, anger, etc.

idonee – nightingale

inducer – microwave

infragile vine – unbreakable a day after it's cut from its live piece

ithio – idiot

jump-off ledge – in Loraleaf where men pick up the vines left on a hook to swing across or down.

jansen tree – a short tree with straight branches that has leaves and roots that are good for tea and healing

kafez – coffee but stronger

keepers – guards

kerasi – mild sleep inducing fruit (cherry flavored) red

Khityki – kitten

Kif – Capital of Eden

Kindred – a broad group that every Edenist is born into but doesn't know his specific abilities until his transition. A family will have multiple kindreds within it.

Latzeran Sea – large body of water known for its depth

lawbreakers – what the Edenists call criminals – those exiled from cities

layfeenya – dolphin like creatures with much bigger tails

liquidator – bartender

living area – living room

logar –horse with a horn

longseat – couch

Loraleaf – an older settlement in the trees founded by Jahl, Khaos and Sandale as an alternative to the city of Naralina which contains men who followed them from the city

magee tree – large tree grows to over 100 feet high with a trunk over 20 feet in diameter and lives hundreds of years

meal room – kitchen

ondile – like a carrot only white

Naralina – white and gold walled city that men of Haven and Loraleaf hail from

pander bush – bush with large dark green leaves

patrio – patio

pecone rolls – cinnamon pastry with tiny nuts

pegwa squash – like acorn squash only purple inside

racide – poisonous plant with large orange flowers

rainbox – shower

rancels – exchange token backed by the city's largest export most commonly used between cities

rhoade – like chicken with chickpea, a mild curry, mild garlic, coriander maybe, a strong flavored potato and a tinge of hotness, maybe a tiny amount of red pepper

rhybat – small rodent with super large ears - afraid of its own shadow

Ruling Circle of Naralina – the oligarchy government of 5 for the city of Naralina

sable worm silk – thread

salis bush – looks like a small weeping willow

Samuvian desert – large cactus filled desert

savinstone – gold

Scrat – swear, like "shit"

Selene – moon with silver light

sherry flower – light pink flower with strong scent that grows on a thin stem (very fragile)

shilla – lube

shiner – lantern powered by eyllen

siris webbing – silky soft webbing made by large, amber-colored, furry caterpillari often used for head puffs - pillows

sitki – barn

Stass! – whoa!

table cover – table cloth

Talia – tigran Theron befriended while living in his cave

tigran – sabretooth sized cat with chameleon abilities, loves to be petted

tyree – dairy product like cheese with less salt and each type with a different spice.

Valex pit – mythological pit for refuse, evil deeds, and ignorance

villain's mark – blood sign

vulture – swans

waterhole – swimming pond or stream

walstone – white stone they built walls of Naralina with

yenea – filoz with a beloved

About Lexi Post

Lexi Post is a New York Times and USA Today best-selling author of romance inspired by the classics. She spent years in higher education taking and teaching courses about the classical literature she loved. From Edgar Allan Poe's short story *The Masque of the Red Death* to Leo Tolstoy's *War and Peace*, she's read, studied, and taught wonderful classics.

But Lexi's first love is romance novels. In an effort to marry her two first loves, she started writing romance inspired by the classics and found she loved it. From hot paranormals to sizzling cowboys to hunks from out of this world, Lexi provides a sensuous experience with a "whole lotta story."

Lexi is living her own happily ever after with her husband and her cat in Florida. She makes her own ice cream every weekend, loves bright colors, and you will never see her without a hat.

www.lexipostbooks.com

www.ingramcontent.com/pod-product-compliance
Lightning Source LLC
Chambersburg PA
CBHW071724190726
48292CB00003B/599